AMERICA'S REIGNING WHODUNIT QUEEN CHARLOTTE MacLEOD

Don't miss any of the MacLeod excitement! Charlotte MacLeod's two mystery series—starring campus criminologist Professor Peter Shandy and private detective/art investigator Max Bittersohn—are available in these Avon editions:

The Peter Shandy Mysteries

Rest You Merry
The Luck Runs Out
Wrack and Rune
Something the Cat Dragged In
The Curse of the Giant Hogweed

The Max Bittersohn Mysteries

The Family Vault
The Withdrawing Room
The Palace Guard
The Bilbao Looking Glass
The Convivial Codfish
The Plain Old Man (coming soon!)

Wrack And Rune

CHARLOTTE MACLEOD

AVON
PUBLISHERS OF BARD, CAMELOT, DISCUS AND FLARE BOOKS

AVON BOOKS
A division of
The Hearst Corporation
1790 Broadway
New York, New York 10019

Copyright © 1982 by Charlotte MacLeod
Published by arrangement with Doubleday & Company, Inc.
Library of Congress Catalog Card Number: 81-43256
ISBN: 0-380-61911-3

First Avon Printing, January, 1983

AVON TRADEMARK REG. U. S. PAT. OFF. AND
IN OTHER COUNTRIES, MARCA REGISTRADA,
HECHO EN U.S.A.

Printed in the U.S.A.

WFH   10   9   8   7   6   5

For Nancy and Charles Copeland

CHAPTER 1

Cronkite Swope, demon reporter of the *Balaclava County Weekly Fane and Pennon,* made some more scribbles on his wad of yellow copy paper, then fixed his eyes on his interviewee with that combination of compassionate interest and no-holds-barred determination expected of a rising young journalist. "And to what, Miss Horsefall," he demanded in suave but relentless tones, "do you attribute your longevity?"

Miss Hilda Horsefall sent a stream of tobacco juice a neat five inches to the right of Cronkite's snappy new red and green jogging shoe. "Hell, you birds been askin' me that same dern-fool question ever since I turned a hundred. Can't you think o' nothin' more interestin'? I got bread dough riz an' a floor to scrub an' no time to set here gassin' with little squirts like you."

As Cronkite was at least a head and a half taller than she, the diminutive was clearly intended to put him in his place, which it did. "If you mean how come I lived so long, it's because I never had no dratted fool of a husband to aggravate me into kickin' the bucket. Clean livin' an' high thinkin' an' a slug o' my own homemade damson gin at suppertime's as good an answer as any if you got to write somethin'. It's them vitamins in the gin, see? Blasts open the arteries an' keeps the blood circulatin'. Wouldn't hurt you to try some, sonny. You look kind o' peaked to me. Trouble with you young'uns nowadays, settin' around on your backsides pesterin' folks that's got work to do so's you can dish out tripe for the papers 'stead o' doin' a decent hand's turn yourselves now and then."

Roger Mudd probably had days like this, too. Doggedly, Cronkite pressed for the story behind the story. "You appear to enjoy remarkably robust health, Miss Horse-fall, for a lady who's about to celebrate her hundred and fifth birthday. Have you ever been bedridden?"

"That's a fine question to ask a respectable maiden fe-male, ain't it? No, I ain't never been bedridden."

Nevertheless, Miss Horsefall's marsh-hawk eyes grew dreamy with recollection. "O' course there was a few times in Canny Lumpkin's buckboard an' once on a sleigh ride in February. An' let me tell you it ain't all it's cracked up to be at ten below with a gale whistlin' under your petticoats. Canny dern near friz his fly buttons that night, I can tell you. Though if you print a word of it, I'll snatch you bald-headed. Not that I care much now an' I don't s'pose Canny would give a hoot. He's been pushin' up daisies this past forty year an' more. Ayup, that was down by the runestone that night. Canny always had funny notions about that runestone. Canute, his real name was."

"What runestone was this?" Cronkite demanded. "I never heard of any in these parts."

"Prob'ly a dern sight more things you never heard of, neither," said Miss Horsefall. "Though I s'pose I can't blame you for not knowin' about the runestone. I ain't thought of it myself since the Lord knows when. Buried six foot deep under poison ivy an' squirrel briers by now, like as not, an' there it'll stay for all the work that gets done around this farm. Ain't much like what it was when my father was alive, I can tell you. He kept things hummin'. Oh my, yes. Not but what he had seven grown sons an' two hired hands.

"Now there's only Henny an' that poor fool of a Spurge Lumpkin that ain't worth the powder to blow him to hell an' gone. Don't nobody want to do farm work no more. If it wasn't for Professor Ames bringin' them kids over from the college to lend a hand with the plantin' an' har-vestin', we might as well fold up an' quit. Now they're all gone for the summer an' here we are, piddlin' along from one day to the next. I'll be spendin' my next birthday in the poorhouse, like as not."

Balaclava County's poorhouse had been torn down some forty-five years ago. In its place was now a block of pleasant little modern apartments for senior citizens. Cronkite thought perhaps he wouldn't try to explain that fact to Miss Horsefall.

"I'd like to get a peek at that runestone," he said. "Darn shame, letting old landmarks get lost like that. The stone may have important historical interest."

"Canny always thought so," Miss Horsefall replied. "Not but what he was kind o' fuzzy-headed some ways. Fun in a buggy, though. You take these here snippers, sonny, an' let's see if we can hack a path to the stone. It's just down over the ridge a piece. I wouldn't mind gettin' a gander at it myself once more for old times' sake."

She handed Cronkite a pair of enormous hedge clippers and walked briskly down the veranda steps, scorning the handrail, which looked to be a good deal more rickety than she was.

"Come around to the side o' the house. You see the tops o' them big old oak trees there behind the swale? Used to be a loggin' road cut through when I was a girl. All grown over now, I s'pose. Can't get Henny to take no interest in keepin' the place up like it ought to be run."

"Henny is your nephew Henry Horsefall, isn't he?" asked Cronkite, who was still making a valiant effort not to let this interview get totally out of hand. "He's about eighty-five, right?"

"Wrong both ways, sonny. First place he ain't Henry, he's Hengist. Always been Horsefalls named Hengist back since the Lord knows when, though don't ask me why, for I can't tell you. Anyways, Henny was named for my own Uncle Hengist, who was named for his great-uncle that fought with General Herkimer at Oriskany an' got a musket ball where it didn't do him no good which is why he was a great-uncle instead of a great-grandfather in case you was plannin' to write it down. In the second place Henny ain't but eighty-two an' I don't see why he can't do a respectable day's work like a proper man. Henny's always been kind o' puny. Takes after his mother's side o' the fam'ly. She was a Swope from over Lumpkinton way. None o' them Swopes ever did amount to a hill o' beans. I s'pose he's out there now gassin' with Professor Ames instead o' gettin' on with the cultivatin'."

"I saw your nephew and Professor Ames riding the cultivator together as I came by."

Cronkite didn't add that the sight of those two old men side by side in the midst of all that well-tilled acreage had given him an odd sort of lump in his throat. He hadn't been aware Henny's mother was a Swope. That must mean he himself was somehow connected to the man who'd been named for the man who'd fought with General Herkimer. There had been Swopes around Lumpkinton almost as long as there'd been Horsefalls at Lumpkin Corners. Far from taking umbrage at this slur on his paternal ancestry, Cronkite began to feel a proprietary interest in Miss Hilda and her nephew.

"Are the Swopes related in any way to the Ameses?" he asked hopefully.

It would indeed be something to boast a family connection with the renowned Professor Timothy Ames of Balaclava Agricultural College. To be sure, the Balaclava Busters had wiped up the ring with the Lolloping Lumberjacks of Lumpkin Corners at the Balaclava County Draft Horse Competition two months back, but Cronkite liked to think of himself as a cosmopolite who could rise above petty regional animosities even if he did still harbor a smoldering resentment at the shafting the Lumberjacks had got in the Junior Plowmen's Event. Everybody knew the winner, Hjalmar Olafssen, had been personally coached by Thorkjeld Svenson, college president and Grand Master of the Straight Furrow.

It was strange, now that he thought about it, how many Scandinavian names kept popping up here in this out-of-the-way corner of Massachusetts, generally considered to be Wasp country despite its enclaves of Irish, Italians, French, Armenians, Chinese, and a good many others. Balaclava County was different. Everybody had always known Balaclava County was different, though nobody had ever quite been able to figure out why. There were people in Suffolk, Norfolk, and Middlesex counties who thought you needed a tourist visa to go there and some in Plymouth and Bristol counties who wouldn't have made the trip if you gave them the place, just on general principles.

That runestone—Cronkite thought of the many legends about the Norsemen, of the controversies that had raged about whether the Vikings had actually sailed these stern and rockbound coasts long before Felicia D. Hemans did such an effective public relations job for the Pilgrims. Was it possible—Cronkite had forgotten his question about being related to the Ameses, which in any case Miss Horsefall wasn't answering. He was gazing at that distant oak grove like stout Cortez doing his thing on the peak in Darien, although Cronkite himself was lithe, lissome, and at the moment ready to brave any amount of poison ivy for a look at that alleged runestone. There might be a feature story in it, and even a Cronkite Swope by-line.

Still, he was a considerate and well-brought-up young man. "Are you sure you feel up to showing me the way, Miss Horsefall?" he inquired solicitously.

"Why the hell shouldn't I?" she replied, and set off at a pace that could hardly be called brisk but would still have got her a creditable place or show at the Senior Citizens' Sunday Saunter.

"Do me good. Work up an appetite. Never meant to end my days settin' an' rockin'. See, now we're under the dip o' the hill, we can't see the house. Couldn't be seen from it, neither, if there was anybody home to look. That's how come me an' Canny—land o' Goshen, what's that all-fired caterwaulin'?"

Unearthly sounds echoed over the ridge. Somebody or something was in terrible trouble back in the barnyard. It was a fair way from here, but a legman for even a country weekly knows how to leg it. Leaving Miss Horsefall to follow as best she might, Cronkite Swope took to his new jogging shoes and covered the distance in one minute seventeen and a quarter seconds. It was the best time he'd ever made, but it wasn't good enough. By the time Cronkite got to the barnyard, Spurge Lumpkin was horribly, suddenly, gruesomely dead.

There wasn't a thing Cronkite could do now but reel over to the tansy patch and get rid of the lunch he no longer wanted. He was still heaving when Henny Horsefall and Professor Ames drove in on the tractor, dragging the cultivator behind them.

"For God's sake, don't look," he gasped. "It's—it's—"

The two old men shoved him aside and examined the evidence.

"Mighty Jehu!" Henny Horsefall whispered. "What happened? Must o' been one o' them flyin' saucers with a death ray."

For a wonder, Timothy Ames had his hearing aid switched on. "Death ray, hell," he snorted, making the long hairs sprouting from his nostrils vibrate like antennae. "What was Spurge doing messing around with quicklime?"

"Quicklime?" cried Henny. "I wouldn't have none o' that stuff on my place. Get it wet an' it can burn the hell out of—Christ A'mighty, Tim, you think Spurge—" He shook his head and couldn't say any more.

"What was Spurge supposed to be doing?" Ames asked.

"I told 'im to get out the hose an' wash the spreader. We was limin' the back field last Monday an' it come on to rain just about the time we got finished. You know how lime cakes in a spreader if you leave it set. Spurge was s'posed to clean it out soon as we got back to the barn, but he left it layin' there all gaumed up till I laid into him about it yesterday afternoon. So he promised faithful he'd tend to the spreader today. Spurge is a good worker, but you got to keep after 'im every minute. His memory's about as long as—Godfrey, Tim, this couldn't of happened. We was usin' plain, ordinary ground limestone, same as always. 'Twouldn't o' done nothin' 'cept cake up if it got wet. Even if he sprayed the hose on it an' it splashed up in 'is face like—like it must o' done—it couldn't o' hurt."

"Maybe it couldn't, but it sure as hell did," said Ames. "Do you suppose if he saw the lime beginning to seethe and smoke, he could have been fool enough to bend over it without shutting off the hose first?"

"Spurge was fool enough to do anything. An' he was a curious sort o' bugger. Always stickin' his nose right up to—yep, that's what he must o' done. Kep' squirtin' to see the bubbles an' got it smack in the—"

Henny couldn't say "face." There wasn't any face left, to speak of.

"Quicklime?" Even in the last extreme of nausea, Cronkite Swope couldn't let pass a chance to ask a question. "Wasn't that the stuff they used to bury criminals in after they were hanged?"

He wished immediately he'd forgone this one. Spurge must have felt as if he'd thrust his face into a lighted blowtorch. Cronkite had nothing left to be sick with, but he tried.

"That's right," Professor Ames replied. "Very hygienic. Nothing left for the rats to gnaw on. Quicklime, because of its property of generating intense heat immediately after it gets wet, is useful in a number of ways. Back in the early days of telegraphy, for instance, they used it to set poles in frozen ground. They'd bust a barrel of lime where the pole was supposed to go, sluice a few buckets of water over it, come back in the morning and there'd be a circle of thawed earth under the lime deep enough to set the pole in. Of course, the men had to be damned careful how they threw the water. I had an uncle who used to be a lineman up in Aroostook County. Face carved up like a pirate's from quicklime burns, and a black patch over one eye. No workmen's compensation in those days, either. Your phone working, Henny?"

"Damn well better be. I paid the bill. Leastways I think I did."

"Come back to the house with me, then. We'll have to call for help."

"Nothin's goin' to help that poor bugger now."

"I know, but we can't leave him like this and nobody'd better touch him till the police have seen what happened. I still don't understand how—God Almighty, here comes your Aunt Hilda."

"Go head 'er off, young fella," Henny told Cronkite. "The Ladies' Aid's plannin' a big wingding for 'er birthday. They'll raise Old Scratch if I let 'er die o' shock an' ruin the party. Hustle 'er back to the house an' call over to the police station. Better see if you can get hold o' Doc Fensterwald, too, just so's we can say we tried."

Glad of an excuse to get away, Cronkite obeyed. The two old men covered Spurge as decently as they could with a tarpaulin, then followed. By the time they got to the house, Miss Hilda had the gin bottle out and the coffeepot on.

Timothy Ames did not like using the telephone because of his deafness, but after the police and the doctor had been duly notified and Henny had got Miss Hilda back to kneading her bread dough and ladling damson gin into Cronkite to settle his stomach, Tim made a call of his own.

CHAPTER 2

"And what is so rare as a day in June?"* inquired Helen Shandy, assistant librarian for the Buggins Collection.

"A drink on the house in a Scotch saloon,"† replied Peter Shandy, professor of Agrology and co-developer with Timothy Ames of *Brassica napobrassica balaclaviensis,* that super rutabaga which has brought fame to the college and wealth to its propagators. "I grant you the point, my own. Now, if ever, come perfect days, with Commencement finished and summer sessions as yet uncommenced. Do you realize I have three whole weeks to goof off in?"

"Big deal! Do you realize I have three whole weeks in which to catalog the Buggins Collection while nobody's hanging around the library pestering me to look up hog statistics?"

"Must you? I'd rather thought we might spend our days in wanton play among the asphodels."

"Don't you get enough wantoning as it is?"

"No."

Shandy made a grab for his wife but she eluded him and went on setting petunias. "Unhand me, you ruffian. I want the place looking nice for when Iduna and Daniel get back from their honeymoon.‡ I'm planning to give a tea."

"Hadn't you better make it a potlatch? Iduna and Daniel like their grub, you know."

* James Russell Lowell.

† Fred Allen.

‡ *The Luck Runs Out* (Doubleday Crime Club, October 1979).

"Speaking of potlatches, did I tell you we're invited to the Ameses' tomorrow night for dinner?"

"You did not. Who's cooking?"

"Laurie. She's decided to go in for the housewifely virtues."

"Egad and a rousing forsooth. What are we having, fried penguin?"

Professor Ames's only son, Roy, had recently married the former Laurie Jilles, a fellow biologist on an Antarctic expedition. Both had got teaching fellowships at Balaclava and moved in with Tim, to the relief of his neighbors around the Crescent, especially the Shandys, who lived directly opposite. The elderly widower had been far too preoccupied with his work on soils and fertilizers to bother with trivia like clean shirts, balanced meals, and keeping the lawn mowed.

The day Roy brought Laurie home, Tim had wiped the mud off his trifocals, taken a close look at the perky brunette, switched on his hearing aid, heard her warm young voice say, "Hello, Daddy Ames," and decided she'd do. As Laurie herself was not the type to do things by halves, she'd adored the hirsute gnome on sight. Since Roy was understandably fond of both his wife and his parent, the arrangement couldn't have been a happier one.

For a wedding present Tim had handed Laurie his checkbook, waved a hand around the fine old house his late wife had so dismally neglected, and said, "Fix it up to suit yourself." Roy and Laurie were spending a glorious summer obeying their father's wish. They'd picked out a living room carpet in a wavelike design of blues and greens. They'd bought white leather furniture that loomed up like a field of midget icebergs from the sea of blue-green shag to remind them of those halcyon days when love had bloomed on the Ross Sea. They'd selected wallpaper with a design of diatoms and coelacänths. They'd done over Tim's bedroom and study in earth tones of umber, ocher, and terracotta to make him feel truly at home. Their own bedroom had a frieze of Emperor penguins and a pinup poster of Jacques Cousteau.

The kids had also got a car which they were paying for out of their own meager stipends because they didn't

want to take unfair advantage of Tim's generosity. The
clunker once driven by Jemima Ames and later, briefly,
by the infamous Lorene McSpee had flunked its last
sticker test and been reduced to a foot or two of squashed
recyclement. Now President Svenson had undisputed
possession of the crummiest car in Balaclava County.

"I do think it's sweet that Laurie and Roy are taking
such marvelous care of Tim," Helen remarked as she
reached for another petunia.

"Tim's taking pretty damn good care of them if you
ask me," Peter grunted, forking in a handful of 5-10-5.
"Where are they all off to today?"

"Laurie wanted to look at more wallpapers. She and
Roy dropped Tim off at some old farmer's over in Lumpkin Corners and they're going to pick him up on the way
back. I wonder if he took his soil auger with him? Darling, do you remember back in May when we had that
gaggle of visiting congressmen up at College? Tim came
wandering by with that huge drill in his hand, almost as
tall as himself, and one of the congressmen asked him
what he used it for."

"And Tim said, 'Constipation.' That's what is known
as a Great Moment in History, my love. Would we happen to have any cold beer in the house?"

"Yes, but you're not getting any till we finish planting
this border. You'll just get besotted and pass out in the
hammock. Take a slurp of water from the hose if you're
thirsty."

"What am I, a petunia? Strong men need strong drink.
Is that the telephone I hear?"

"If it is, I'll answer it. I don't trust you alone with the
fridge." Helen brushed peat moss off the knees of her
gardening pants and went into the charming litle brick
house of which she had been chatelaine for six intermit-
tently halcyon months. The telephone was indeed ring-
ing and the voice on the wire was Tim's. He was, she realized at once, in a dreadful taking.

"Pete, get out here!"

"It isn't Pete," she screamed. "What's the matter, Tim?
Where are you?"

All she received for an answer was, "Get Pete!" She

could still hear him yelling the same words over as she laid down the phone and rushed to the front door.

"Peter, come quickly. It's Tim and he's frantic."

"What about?"

"He won't tell me. He just keeps howling for you."

Shandy was in the house and at the telephone in three bounds. "Tim," he bellowed over the tumult, "what's wrong?"

Helen stood by, watching her husband's face slowly lose color as he listened. "Okay, Tim," he shouted at last, "I'm on my way," and hung up.

"What is it, Peter? Roy hasn't had an accident with their new car?"

"No, nothing like that. Tim's out at Henny Horsefall's. Henny's hired man just got burned to death by quick-lime."

"Quicklime? That's ghastly! But how?"

"That's what Tim wants me out there for. Henny claims there was no quicklime on the place and hadn't been since God knows when. No damn reason why there should have been. Helen, I've got to go right this minute. There's no telling when Roy and Laurie will show up. Henny's over eighty and he has nobody else left on the place but an aunt who's going to be a hundred and five next week."

"Then maybe I ought to go with you. I could help take care of the old lady or something."

"I expect the neighbors will rally around. You stay here and finish the petunias. We're late getting them in as it is. I'll give you a ring as soon as I see how the land lies."

He gave her a quick kiss and ran down the hill toward Charlie Ross's Garage, where they kept the car, since they had no driveway and to park around the Crescent was not the done thing. Helen stook looking after him, her fair-skinned face tender and her bluebell-colored eyes a little moist. Peter wasn't a big man and he could have stood to lose a pound or two around the waist, but he could move like Paavo Nurmi in an emergency. How intelligent she'd been to marry him.

And how remarkably sweet of him to have married her. There was a lot to be said for monogamy, she thought, getting back to her petunias. Peter had begun developing a new strain just because Helen had remarked how elegant it would be to have flowers along the front walk that were exactly the same rosy old-brick shade as the house. These were not yet a perfect match, but they were going to be lovely all the same.

When Peter had got precisely the tone he was after, he intended to market the seed as Helen's Fancy and rake in another pot, no doubt. Then perhaps they'd blow themselves to a trip. The Galápagos Islands would be fun, or Vermillion, South Dakota, or some other exotic and romantic spot. Unless Peter got himself embroiled in another mess such as wifely intuition told Helen he was heading toward at the moment.

Now that Shandy had revealed an unexpected talent for detection, somebody was always after him to unravel an insoluble mystery that usually turned out to be nothing of the sort. But Timothy Ames was not one to panic over trivia, and Tim had been definitely panicking. Quicklime, ugh! "And all the while the burning lime eats flesh and bone away." What blasphemy, on a day like this.

Helen's joy in planting the petunias that were to be named for her was gone. A cloud passed over the sun. She felt it only right and proper that the glorious light should be veiled.

Some fifteen minutes later, over in Lumpkin Corners, her husband was thanking God he'd made Helen stay behind. This was no sight for a woman's eyes, or a man's either.

Shandy didn't see any way Spurge's death could be due to an honest mistake. Henny Horsefall, despite his years, was as bright as he'd ever been and at least one of his eyes was in good working order. Henny hadn't got around to throwing out the big, heavy paper bags from which he and Spurge had originally filled the spreader. They were stamped "ground limestone," and Shandy and Tim had tested the residue, proving conclusively that the bags had contained only the harmless white powder they'd been supposed to hold. Traces of plain limestone were still caked on the bottom of the spreader. It was obvious the quicklime had been dumped in on top of the

clogged openings, but why? How could one human being
do this to another?

"Maybe they didn't mean to kill 'im," Henny Horsefall
replied to the question Shandy must have asked aloud.
"Wouldn't nobody 'cept a dern fool like Spurge stick their
face down inside to see why 'twas bubblin', would they?"

"You might if you didn't have your specs on," said his
aunt, who had refused to be shooed back to the house. "I
would of myself, like as not."

"You wouldn't of been hosin' down the spreader, Aunt
Hilda."

"Only because I've got one pair o' hands instead o' six.
The way you let everything slide around here, maybe
you let the lime go bad afore you got around to usin' it."

"That wouldn't happen, Miss Horsefall," said Shandy.
"Quicklime is an entirely different thing from what your
nephew was using. The only way it could have got into
the spreader, as far as I can see, is for it to have been put
there between the time the spreader was last used and
the time Spurge Lumpkin started washing it out. From
the violence of the reaction, I'd say the lime hadn't been
exposed to the air very long. Can you remember what
day you last used the spreader, Mr. Horsefall?"

"Thursday, I think it was. Four, five days ago anyway.
I told Spurge to clean it time and again, but he forgot."

"Might o' known he would," sniffed the aunt. "Why
didn't you keep after 'im like you should of? If I've told
you once I've told you a million times—"

"Well, don't tell me again," her nephew snapped back.
"I'm in no shape to listen. Neither's Spurge, poor bastard."

"I s'pose we'll have to lay out for the funeral." Miss
Hilda was determined to get the last word one way or
another. "Not that we can afford it. Times is hard, in
case you don't know."

"You seen 'em a dern sight harder an' so have I,"
grunted Henny. "You go to bed with a full belly every
night, don't you?"

"Nice way to talk in front o' strangers an' learned
men, I must say. Couldn't you at least o' said 'stomach'?
Won't nobody around here get nothin' this night if I don't
bestir myself in the kitchen." She grumbled herself off

toward the house and nobody tried to prevent her leaving.

"As to the funeral," said Shandy, "I shouldn't be surprised if the college could finance it out of the Agricultural Laborers' Assistance Fund. Eh, Tim?"

"Huh?"

Professor Ames looked blank for a moment, as well he might, since his colleague had invented the Agricultural Laborers' Assistance Fund as of that moment. Then he nodded. "Sure, Pete. Why the hell not? We'll get Harry Goulson over here from Balaclava Junction. Let him handle the doings and send the bill to me. I'll put the arm on Svenson."

"I ain't takin' no charity," Horsefall protested.

"What charity? Spurge would be as much entitled as any farmhand in Balaclava County, far as I know. It comes out of the endowment, doesn't it, Pete?"

It would come out of the pockets of Ames and Shandy, but neither was averse to stretching the facts a bit in a worthy cause and both had enough furrow mud on their own boots to realize what state the Horsefalls' finances must be in. It was a miracle Henny had managed to keep the farm operating as long as he had. It would take another miracle, no doubt, to find a replacement for the dim-witted but willing Spurge. Lumpkin had most likely been working for his board and keep and a plug of chewing tobacco now and then; and chances were that was about all Henny and Miss Hilda could afford to pay.

That problem would have to be faced when the more immediate one was taken care of. "Who around here has it in for you, Mr. Horsefall?" Shandy asked.

The old farmer shrugged. "Don't ask me who, but some bugger's been pesterin' the daylights out o' me for the past three months. First it was kid stuff. Trash thrown around the dooryard an' whatnot. Then it was limbs broke off the apple trees. I suspicioned at first it might be that young hellion Billy Lewis, an' threatened 'im with a pantload o' rock salt from my old shotgun if he didn't cut it out. He knowed I meant business, too, 'cause I done the same to his father thirty-two years ago."

Henny hitched up his suspenders and scratched his left armpit. "But Billy swore up, down, an' sideways he never, an' I believe 'im. The Lewises might be hellions buy they ain't liars an' never have been. Anyways then it begun to get mean. Chicken wire tore away an' dogs let loose in the hen yard. Killed all our best layers. Then a while later it was ground glass in the pig swill. Lucky for me I seen it glistenin' when I went to slop the hogs an' managed to head 'em off with a sackful o' grain till me an' Spurge could get the feedin' trough cleaned out. Last week I set out a hundred tomato plants I been nussin' along since March an' bejesus if I didn't come out two days later an' find every dern one of 'em dusted over with snuff."

"Great balls of fire!" exclaimed Shandy.

"What's so awful about that?" said Cronkite Swope. "I thought nicotine was supposed to be an insecticide or something."

"Tobacco is a member of the Solanum family," Shandy explained, "the same as tomato plants, and it's subject to a fungus that can be communicable. I don't know whether dusting snuff over a planting of tender young tomato plants would spread a disease that could wipe out the entire crop, but it shows a damned nasty experimental bent on somebody's part. And you're quite sure it's none of the Lewis family, Mr. Horsefall?"

"They wouldn't do nothin' like that. No call to. Hell, we been neighbors for three, four generations now. Kids actin' up is one thing. This is somethin' else."

"It certainly is," said the professor, thinking of what Spurge's body had looked like by the time he got there. "You have no idea whatsoever who else might have done these things?"

"Cripes, if I had do you think I'd be standin' here jawin' instead o' loadin' up the old over-an'-under an' goin' gunnin' for the bugger? I sure as hell wouldn't be usin' no rock salt this time, neither."

"I understand how you feel, Mr. Horsefall."

"The hell you do. Spurge an' me, we worked these fields—" The old man choked up.

Tim took his friend by the arm. "Come on, Henny. You'd better go back to the house and have yourself a snort of Aunt Hilda's headache medicine. The police will be along soon and they'll want to talk with you."

"Talk? Too damn much talk already, an' not enough action."

Nevertheless Hengist Horsefall allowed Professor Ames to lead him into the farmhouse. Young Cronkite Swope hung around looking hopeful.

"You going to detect something, Professor Shandy?"

"How in Sam Hill do I know? I detect you're standing there with your tongue hanging out for a story that will get your by-line splashed all over the front pages of the *Berkshire Eagle,* if that's any use to you. Who's that coming? Not the doctor, surely?"

A massive heap of blue denim and orange whiskers was waddling toward them from across the road, waving the sort of straw hat that used to be worn alike by man and beast in rural areas.

"What's goin' on?" the slightly bogus-looking hayseed bellowed when he got more or less within earshot. "I ain't seen so much commotion around here since the day Spurge got his shirttail caught in the cream separator. What's he been up to now?"

"Why should you assume he's been up to anything?" Shandy asked.

The newcomer spat into the dust and plunked his cow's-breakfast hat back atop his ginger bush. "Just that he most gen'ally has. Spurge is the kack-handedest critter around a place I ever did see. Beats me how Henny's been able to stand him all these years."

"Mr. Horsefall acted real upset to me," said Cronkite Swope.

"You mean really upset," Shandy snapped. "An adjective is modified by an adverb. If you don't know what an adverb is, I suggest you look it up. Since you're so obviously eager to rise in your chosen profession, young man, it behooves you to learn the rudiments of your craft."

Cronkite took the rebuke with good-humored disdain. "Oh, nobody bothers much about grammar and stuff these days. It's all common usage."

"You are perhaps not familiar with Mark Twain's observation that God must have hated the common man since He made him so common? In fact it is we who degrade ourselves by allowing our standards to be debased without a struggle."

The stranger emitted something that might have been a derisive hoot and Shandy turned on him. "As for you, sir, the rube getup would be more convincing if you didn't happen to have today's *Wall Street Journal* sticking out of your pocket. Would you care to enlighten us as to your identity?"

"Not particularly." The man spat again. "Man's got a right to know what's goin' on in the world, ain't he? Since you're so free with information nobody wants, who the hell are you?"

Cronkite might be weak on his adverbs, but he clearly held strong views on lèse majesté. "This is Professor Shandy from the college," he informed the offender in a voice of icy rebuke. "And this is Fergy, Professor Shandy. He runs Fergy's Bargain Barn down the road a piece—I mean a short way. You must have passed it on your way here."

Shandy did recall having averted his eyes in pain from what he'd at first taken to be a junkyard and then realized was some sort of open-air emporium. He'd been glad he hadn't brought Helen along, since any place that advertised itself by means of a battered mannequin got up in a long skirt, bonnet, and shawl and had a lot of rusty hot-water boilers and bedsprings strewn about would have been sure to bring on that irresistible urge of hers to run in for a minute and see what they had.

Fergy nodded, animosity forgotten in the presence of greatness. "Thass right. I seen you burnin' up the road as if Smokey Bear was on your tail. Nice car you got. Wouldn't want to jazz 'er up with a genuine 1937 Pierce-Arrow radiator ornament?"

"No, I—er—think we'll pass on the Pierce-Arrow. My wife has simple tastes."

Fergy eyed Shandy's unassuming figure up and down. "Stands to reason," he grunted. "Well, can't blame a man for tryin', as my old man said to the doctor when he got his first look at me. No doubt Spurge's folks felt the same about him. Say, you said Henny was upset, Cronk. What happened to Spurge, anyhow?"

"He got splashed with quicklime cleanin' out the spreader. God knows how, but he got it smack in the face."

"Gorry! That could kill a man."

"It did."

"I want to know!"

When a Yankee says, "I want to know," he is not asking for information. He means, "I am expressing a suitable degree of amazement at the news you have already
imparted." Cronkite Swope knew that perfectly well, of
course, but being a reporter, he continued to report, pol-
ishing up his journalese as he went along.

"Little did Spurgeon Lumpkin reckon the morning of
June 18—say, I wonder if Spurge was descended from
that Canute Lumpkin Miss Horsefall used to—I mean
the one she said used to be interested in the runestone?"

"What runestone?" Shandy asked.

"The one over behind that swale where the big oaks
are. Miss Horsefall was just taking me to see if we could
find it when we heard this God-awful screaming and—I
guess you know the rest of it. Spurge must have been
just about the last of the Lumpkins, mustn't he? Any
more of them left around here, Fergy?"

"There's my hated rival Nutie the Cutie."

Fergy appeared to think this a great joke. So did Cronkite Swope. After a moment's cogitation, Shandy realized
whom Fergy meant. Helen had not long ago coerced him
into visiting an overwhelmingly precious little antique
shop called Nute's Nook over in Lumpkin Center, on the
flimsy pretext that they needed a new conch shell for the
whatnot. She'd surprised her husband beyond words by
walking out after a few minutes without so much as asking the price of anything. Afterward in the car she'd
spoken her mind.

"What an odious man! Pretending to be a nice, innocent little homosexual and all the time giving me that
old come-back-without-your-husband look. I'll bet you a
first edition of Havelock Ellis that if you hadn't been
with me, I'd have wound up in a wrestling match on his
bogus Queen Anne sofa. Don't you dare ever try to get
me back into that place."

"Fear not, my love" he'd assured her, finding Nute's
brand of duplicity a queer one in every sense of the word
but doubting not that Helen knew whereof she spoke.

"You mean that chap who runs the antique shop is

also a Lumpkin?" he said to Fergy. "Then he and Spurge
would have been related in some way?"

"First cousins, not that either one of 'em ever done
much bragging about the connection."

"How do you know? Are you acquainted with this
Nute?"

"Oh sure. I was just kiddin' about that rival stuff. Us
dealers always trade among ourselves. We have to. See,
what folks come to me for is junk. If I happen to get hold
of a real good piece and put it out for sale at what it's
worth, my customers think I'm tryin' to be funny. So I
take it to Nute. He pays me a fair price, then turns
around and sells it for maybe double that, which I could
never do in a million years. Same with him. If he picks
up stuff that ain't good enough for his shop, he peddles it
to me cheap and I make a buck or two on the resale. One
hand washes the other, see? I can't say me an' Nute's
any great pals, but we see each other maybe once or
twice a week when I'm around."

"Nute's real name is Canute, I suppose," Cronkite ventured.

"Danged if it ain't. How'd you know that, Cronk?"

"We members of the press do not divulge our sources
of information."

Cronkite had been itching to pull that line ever since
he'd opened Lesson One of the Great Journalists' Correspondence Course. It was a pity the circumstances were
not such as to get him charged with contempt of court for
saying it, but at least it was practice.

"Funny you should o' mentioned that runestone just
now," Fergy rambled on, oblivious of the fact that journalistic history had just been made in Balaclava County.
"Poor Spurge was shootin' off his mouth about it a couple
o' nights back. He'd wander down to see me most evenin's, see. Nothing' much doin' here on the farm after supper. Miss Hilda an' Henny go to bed with the chickens. I
used to have Spurge help me unload the truck, shift
things around, odd jobs like that. You know how it is,
you buy out a house after some old codger dies, you got
to take everything from the garbage pail to the Aunty
Macassars. Sometimes you get a few good pieces among
the junk, mostly you don't. Anyways, me and Spurge

would maybe do a little work around the place, then I'd
give him a beer or two or three. What the hell, he'd
earned it. No sense in givin' him money. He'd just lose it
or throw it away on the first gewgaw that caught his
eye. So we'd set an' have our beer. He was company, in a
way."

"So he mentioned the runestone," Shandy prompted.
"What did he say?"

"To tell you the truth, I can't remember. Most likely
wasn't listenin' in the first place. I never did, much. Just
gave 'im his beer and let 'im talk and he was happy. How
in blazes did he ever get hold of quicklime?"

"You don't happen to have any around your place?"

"Not so's you'd notice it, Professor. I get kids comin'
with their parents an' that stuff's dangerous if they ever
got into it. Besides, it's heavy to lug and who'd be likely
to buy it from me? I don't know offhand who'd be apt to
sell it around here, but all's I can figure out is that
Henny must o' picked up the wrong bag when he went
for supplies. Henny ain't the man he used to be, not by a
long chalk. Now me, I'm twice the man I used to be." He
slapped his beer belly and grinned.

"You haven't any idea whatever what Spurge might
have told you about that runestone?" Shandy insisted.

"Oh, I s'pose it might o' been some foolishness about
buried treasure. See, them Vikings was like King Tut
an' the rest o' the heathens. When somebody died, they'd
bury him with his bow an' arrow or whatever he had so's
he could fight his way into Valhaller. If he was captain o'
the boat, say, or first mate or chief engineer or somebody
important, they might throw in some dishes or a string o'
beads or somethin' that the relatives didn't particularly
want. Some o' them graves they dug up over in Norway
an' England an' places had real nice stuff in 'em but,
hell, you know as well as I do them Vikings never got as
far as Balaclava County. Them so-called runestones ain't
nothin' but some kind o' freak geological formation. You
bein' an educated man, Professor, you'd know the name,
I daresay. Anyway there's these so-called runestones
scattered from hell to breakfast all over New England.
Every once in a blue moon somebody gets het up about
one of 'em and starts diggin'. Find a few Indian bones or

somethin' and there's a big stir, but it dies down soon enough."

"Has anybody dug under this one?" asked Cronkite Swope.

"Not to my knowledge, Cronk."

"But why not? I should have thought they would, just for the heck of it."

"S'posed to be bad luck or somethin', ain't it? Like when they opened King Tut's tomb and everybody died o' measles or somethin' an' people claimed the spooks got 'em? Anyways, there's an awful mess of poison ivy there in the summertime an' it's friz over in the winter an' it's all moonshine to start with. Well, I better be moseyin' back in case somebody wants to buy somethin' for a change. Tell Henny I'll be over to my place if he wants any help. All he has to do is holler. Cripes, who'd o' thought that damn fool Spurge wouldn't even have had sense enough to haul his head out o' the spreader!"

CHAPTER 3

Shaking his orange fuzz, the human haystack walked back the way he'd come. Shandy gazed after Fergy's tattered rear elevation with narrowed eyes.

"Does that man make any sort of living with that junk business of his?"

"Enough to buy himself a new pair of coveralls, you mean?" Nobody could accuse Cronkite Swope of being slow on the uptake. "I'd say he does a lot better for himself than you might think. Fergy just has a notion he can skin the suckers easier—I mean more easily—if he puts on that hick-from-the-sticks routine, and I shouldn't be surprised if he's right. He doesn't kill himself working and he goes to Florida every winter in his trailer. Claims he eats out every night down there for three months in a row. Of course, he can't very well stay here because there's no heat in that barn of his except a wood stove, and I expect the eating out is a hamburger plate and six or eight beers in some greasy-spoon joint, but it does sound kind of classy and glamorous," Cronkite finished wistfully.

Shandy grunted. "Fair amount of traffic along this road, is there?"

"Oh yes, quite a lot. It's a shortcut to the state line. Folks around here are apt to go up to New Hampshire a lot. Something to do with the state liquor tax, or so I've heard."

"M'yes, we've all heard rumors, haven't we, Mr. Swope? Has this Fergy chap a wife?"

"Off and on as you might say. Though why any woman would look at him twice is more than I can imagine."

Cronkite smiled a secret, inscrutable smile, thinking

of the dash he himself was going to cut in his brand-new
three-piece light beige polyester suit when he covered
the Miss Balaclava Beauty Pageant a fortnight hence.
He thought also of Miss Lumpkin Corners, whom he
planned to photograph with the paper's official Polaroid
camera for conspicuous display on the front page of the
Fane and Pennon, unless Miss Balaclava Junction or
Miss West Hoddersville proved more complaisant with
regard to attending the Grand Annual Pea-shucking and
Salmon Bake in his company after the votes were in and
the calories no longer had to be counted.

Cronkite, be it said, was no roué. He simply hadn't yet
made up his mind which of the ladies he was in love with
should become the official recipient of his plighted troth.
Furthermore, he had a sneaking hunch that somewhere
might be blooming a still fairer rose who wouldn't mind
being plucked by a rising young journalist.

He could have been right, at that, for Cronkite was a
comely youth who operated on the same alternating current of breezy self-confidence and boyish gaucherie that
had, though he didn't know it, made the late Canute
Lumpkin so irresistible to Miss Hilda Horsefall some
eighty years before. He would no doubt have charmed
Helen Shandy insofar as a happily married woman ad-
mits of being charmed by anybody other than her own
spouse.

Peter Shandy, however, saw Cronkite only as a source
of possibly useful information and a bit of a pest because
the lad was so obviously waiting for him to rare back
and haul off a miracle and Shandy as yet had nothing to
haul with. He was glad when the local GP and the local
constabulary arrived together, having both been at the
scene of a traffic accident when summoned by radio.
Some thrifty folk returning from New Hampshire had
been sampling their purchases en route.

The doctor found, as Shandy had expected, that
Spurge Lumpkin had died of quicklime burns to the face
causing blockage of the air passages and either suffoca-
tion or heart failure, whichever came first, not that it
mattered because both sure as hell would have and he
hoped he wouldn't have another day like this in a hurry.
The police chief decided, too precipitately in Shandy's

judgment, that death should be labeled misadventure due either to Henny's using the wrong kind of lime or else a prank that had got out of hand because the victim didn't know enough to stay away from the dern stuff once it started to bubble and therefore brought it on himself, poor bugger.

"I fail to see the force of your argument," Shandy protested. "Mr. Horsefall tells me he's been subjected to a series of these so-called pranks during the past three months, and each has been worse than the one before."

"Cripes, you know how these old codgers are," snorted the chief. "Henny's got hardening of the arteries and softening of the brain, like as not. Wind blows a limb or two off his apple trees, he gets riled at the kids next door for smashing up his orchard. He forgets to shut up the hen run, a dog or a coon gets in and kills a few hens, so he comes yelling to me about vandalism. What am I supposed to do, send a posse out here to guard the place night and day? I'm shorthanded as it is. Can't get Town Meeting to vote me the price of new mufflers for my cruisers, let alone salaries for extra men. You didn't happen to be a witness, did you?"

"No. As far as I know, Lumpkin was alone when he got burned. As Swope here has already told you, he and Miss Horsefall were over behind the swale when they heard Lumpkin screaming with pain. Swope came running, but Lumpkin was past help by the time he got here. My friend and colleague Professor Ames happened to be out on the cultivator with Mr. Horsefall. When they found out about Spurge, they sent immediately for you. Then Ames phoned my house in Balaclava Junction and asked me to come over. My name is Peter Shandy, by the way."

"Oh yeah. Fred Ottermole told me about you."

Shandy could imagine what he'd told. Ottermole and Shandy didn't get along. Ottermole, who was Balaclava Junction's police chief, thought Shandy tried to make a fool of him. Shandy thought nature had already taken care of the matter. The Lumpkinton chief was clearly on Ottermole's side.

"Well, Professor Shandy, I don't see there's anything you can do here except maybe try to talk some sense into

Henny Horsefall and that old aunt of his. Pair of 'em ought to be in an old folks' home by rights. I don't know why the family haven't done something about it already. Suppose I'll have to step in myself one of these days, though I can't say I relish the prospect."

"Naturally you wouldn't," Shandy replied. "Once Horsefall has to call it quits, I expect this will become just another parcel of prime farmland fallen into the hands of the developers. That's the worst kind of crime that ever happens around here, don't you think?"

The police chief, who was a smallish, middle-aged man, took off his uniform cap and wiped the crown of his bald head. "I better get a move on. Care to give me a hand with the remains, since you came to help out? Can't leave him head down in the spreader. Guess I don't have to tell you to watch what you touch."

Cronkite Swope, anxious to demonstrate that he was no poltroon despite his unruly stomach, helped Shandy roll what was left of Spurge Lumpkin onto a plank, cover him with a horse blanket, and carry him into the barn while the chief did the heavy looking on.

"That's it, you two, lay the plank right over them sawhorses. Now, Professor, you can tell Henny I'm sending Jack Struth over for the body, if you don't mind."

"I believe he's already made arrangements with Harry Goulson," Shandy answered.

"The college is taking care of the funeral out of the Agricultural Laborers' Assistance Fund," Cronkite added. "Isn't that right, Professor Shandy?"

Shandy couldn't remember what he'd said, so he felt it safest to nod. "Unless Lumpkin's next of kin prefer to handle that matter themselves. I understand there's a cousin over in Lumpkin Center."

The chief shrugged. "Yep, runs the antique shop. You won't hear no objections out of little Nutie if it's a case of getting something for nothing. How much is this fund good for, Professor?"

"Not enough to sue for damages, if that's what you mean. It's merely a—er—small private bequest. I expect it will cover the cost of the coffin and Goulson's fee, though he's generous about donating his services in needy cases. There must be a Lumpkin family plot around here Spurge could be buried in, isn't there?"

"Three or four of 'em, I expect. Ask over at Town Hall. I got to get back on over to the station." He climbed into the cruiser.

"Say, Chief," Cronkite interrupted as he was about to start, "do you know anything about that runestone over in the oak grove?"

"Runestone?" The lawman stalled his engine and said a bucolic word. "What's a—oh, I know. Seems to me somebody asked me that same question not long ago. Wasn't there an article about runestones in *Yankee Magazine* some time back? Why don't you go ask Janet over at the library?"

"You don't remember who else besides me was asking?"

"Can't say as I do." A sputter came over the car's police radio. The chief managed to get his engine started again and tore off in a cloud of blue smoke. Town Meeting had better vote him a ring job, too.

"I must go see if I can get hold of Goulson," Shandy observed. "Are you coming to the house, Swope, or do you have to rush off and tear out the front page?"

As the *Fane and Pennon* didn't go to press for another two days, Cronkite did not really have to rush anywhere. He was greatly tempted to spend another while basking in the reflected glory of Professors Ames and Shandy. Then he realized he was still in possession of Miss Horsefall's hedge clippers, and a brilliant thought surged through his mind. A good reporter was a good investigator. It said so in Lesson Three of the Great Journalists' Correspondence Course.

"I'll see you later, Professor," he replied. "Right now there's something I have to see about."

"Good hunting, then."

Shandy ambled off, thinking of the police chief's sudden attack of uninterest and wondering which of the man's relatives was trying to get hold of the Horsefalls' ancestral acres. He found Tim and Henny seated at the kitchen table drinking coffee out of crazed white ironstone mugs that had their glazes worn away around the rims from the lips of many a long-gone farmhand,

Spurge Lumpkin among them, poor devil. Miss Horsefall
was at the black iron stove dropping bits of raw bread
dough into hot fat and frying them up into golden puffs
the men were eating with home-churned butter and
home-canned strawberry preserves. Shandy needed little
urging to sit down and dig in.

The boiled coffee was delicious, the fried doughboys
sublime. Old folks' home, his left eyeball! Miss Horsefall
was good for another quarter-century or so, from the look
of her. Henny was still somewhat green around the gills,
but that wasn't anything to write home about. Any farmer who was half human would naturally be shaken up by
the death of his hired hand, especially when it happened
as suddenly and horribly as Spurge Lumpkin's. Shandy
decided perhaps he'd better not eat any more of Miss Hilda's fried doughboys.

"Tell me, Mr. Horsefall," he asked, "who's been trying
to buy up your land lately?"

Henny let the knife fall back into the butter dish.
"How'd you know that?"

"See, Henny," said Tim with his mouth full, "I told
you Pete would know what this is all about."

"As the moment I'm only taking what you might call
an educated guess," Shandy demurred. "The most logical
explanation I can think of for these so-called practical
jokes your chief of police is trying to brush off so lightly
is that somebody wants to get you angry enough or
scared enough to sell out. Have you been approached
about your land since the vandalism began?"

"I sure as hell have," said Horsefall grimly. "That
dratted Loretta Fescue for one, she's been pesterin' the
livin' daylights out o' me. I bet she's brought six different
customers around here, all with ready cash bulgin' out o'
their pockets, or so she claims. Keeps givin' me an' Aunt
Hilda a big song an' dance about how much better off
we'd be in a nice retirement home out in California with
the earthquakes an' the volcanoes an' the mud slides an'
them painted hussies traipsin' around with one piece o'
rag tied over their tits an' another—"

"Henny," snapped his aunt, and just in time, for the
nephew was starting to get a contemplative gleam in his
one reliable eye. "I'll have none o' that filthy talk in my

kitchen, thank you kindly. Anyways, all you ever done
was talk. If you'd had anything but wind in your britches
you'd o' married Effie Evers when you had the chance
an' riz six or eight good, strapping' sons that would o'—"

"Gone off an' went to work in the soap factory same as
Bill Lewis's done. Effie snored in 'er sleep like a goddamn billy goat. I wasn't goin' to listen to that the rest o'
my life."

"How'd you know Effie snored?"

Henny leered. "How the gol-dern blazes do you think I
know? Furthermore, her feet was always colder'n a dead
mackerel." He picked up the butter knife again and began slathering another piece of fried bread.

Shandy rather hated to interrupt this interesting vein
of reminiscence, but he did want to return to Helen
sometime or other. "Er—getting back to this Loretta Fescue. I gather she's a real estate agent. May I take it that
she's related in some way to your local police chief, the
chap who was just here?"

"Godfrey mighty, Tim, he's as good as them TV programs," cried Henny with his mouth full. "She sure as
hell is, Professor. His own sister, if you want to know.
Married Jim Fescue that drunk hisself to death, as who
wouldn't bein' married to a human gramophone like Loretta? Cripes, she's a nagger. Worse'n Aunt Hilda an'
that's goin' some, I can tell you. She'd argue the left hind
leg off'n a deaf mule."

"Is Mrs. Fescue dependent on her real estate business
for a living?"

"Is, was, an' always will be for all the help she's ever
had," snorted Aunt Hilda. "Loretta had to work from the
day she married that good-for-nothin' Jim Fescue, which
she should o' known better in the first place. Henny can
run Loretta down all he's o' mind to but he can't say she
ain't a worker. She put them two girls o' theirs through
college all on 'er ownsome after Jim died. She'd o' done
the same for the son if she could o' got 'im to go, but he's
no dern good an' never was. Spittin' image of 'is father
an' he'll wind up the same way, you mark my words.
Workin' for Gunder Gaffson last I heard. Diggin' ditches,
I wouldn't doubt. That's about all he's fit for."

"Would that be the Gaffson Development Corporation, Miss Horsefall?"

"I shouldn't be surprised. Seems to me Gunder's callin' hisself by some fancy name these days. Settin' up to be somethin' special when everybody knows the Gaffsons ain't lived around here more'n fifty, sixty years. Dern foreigners. Furthermore, I know for a certain fact Gunder's father come steerage class with nothin' to 'is name but the clothes he stood up in. Gaffson Development Corporation, my foot!"

"I don't really think you can fault a man for trying to rise in the world, Miss Horsefall, provided his methods are honest. I gather the son is doing pretty well for himself."

"So they say."

"And Gunder Gaffson is one of the interested customers Mrs. Fescue has brought here recently, right?"

"I'll be hornswoggled if he ain't!" Henny was by now regarding Peter Shandy with a sort of frightened reverence.

"Has Gaffson been more persistent than any of the others, would you say?"

"He sure ain't hung back none. Keeps uppin' the price he's willin' to pay. Even offered to move me an' Aunt Hilda into one o' them condyminiums he's buildin' over to Little Lumpkin. Three rooms you couldn't swing a cat in an' neighbors yammerin' on both sides o' the wall. I told 'im where he could put 'is condyminium. Loretta didn't look none too pleased at that."

"I don't suppose she would."

Shandy made a mental note to check out both Loretta Fescue and Gunder Gaffson. A hard-driving widow after a big commission, with a no-good son perhaps willing to do a spot of dirty work for his boss rather than get sacked for incompetence, wasn't the world's unlikeliest suspect. Having the chief of police for a brother might be more of a help than a hindrance. Instead of putting a stop to his sister's shenanigans as he ought to, the chief might be willing to look the other way either out of fraternal affection, because he didn't want to get stuck with supporting her and his nephew, or because he intended to cut himself in for a share of the profits.

But what about the rest of those half-dozen or so who'd come looking at the farm with armloads of dollars to swap for the deed? Shandy asked for names. Henny couldn't remember any offhand, and neither could Miss Hilda. Was that because Gaffson had scared them off by upping the ante? Was he the only genuinely interested prospect? Or was he simply the only one honest enough or unsubtle enough to make a plain showing of his hand?

CHAPTER 4

Shandy knew better than to jump to any conclusions about Loretta Fescue and her clients. There was an even more obvious and uncomfortable possibility.

"Mr. Horsefall," he asked, "would you mind telling me who stands to inherit this property in the event of anything's—er—happening to you and Miss Horsefall?"

"At my age only one thing's likely to happen," the aunt took it upon herself to answer. "I'll be kickin' the bucket pretty soon an' I don't expect Henny's goin' to last long without me to look after 'im. Don't think we ain't talked about who's to get the place. The one thing we're agreed on is that we don't want to split up the property. There's Henny's two great-nephews, Eddie an' Ralph, would both give their eyeteeth for the farm though they ain't neither of 'em come straight out an' said so because they're both likable cusses an' don't want to hurt our feelin's. Trouble is, we can't decide between 'em."

"Then why couldn't you leave it to them as joint heritors?" Shandy suggested.

"We thought o' that, too. Eddie an' Ralph would pull fine in double harness an' so would their kids, but them two she-devils they're married to can't set in the same room with each other for five minutes without gettin' into a hair tangle. They'd have this old place tore apart before we was cold in our graves."

"So in short, you haven't made a will in anybody's favor."

"Not yet we haven't."

"What would happen if you should both die before you got around to doing so?"

Miss Hilda snorted. "Whatever happened, we wouldn't

neither one of us give a damn by then, would we? I s'pose what would happen would be that every Horsefall from here to hell an' back would flock around clawin' at each other's throats to see who could get the biggest piece. They been at us for years now, hintin' that they wouldn't mind havin' this an' they wouldn't mind havin' that an' didn't we think it would be a good idea to sell off now an' divide the money up among the fam'ly to save payin' inheritance taxes. I tell 'em I think it's a dern poor idea an' they'll get what we're o' mind to leave 'em when Henny an' me get through with it an' not before."

"Then there's no one relative who has a stronger claim than any of the rest?"

"Not so's you'd notice it. It'll be every man for himself an' the devil take the hindmost. I still think we better make out a will in favor o' Ralph, Henny."

"An' I say the farm should go to Eddie," her nephew shot back, though he was too dispirited over losing Spurge to put much enthusiasm into his reply.

"As of now, though, both Eddie and Ralph are aware that you have not made a choice between them. Is that correct?" Shandy persisted.

"Well, they don't know we have," Henny replied with true Yankee caution.

"And either of them would prefer the land to the money?"

"Damn right they would. They're both Horsefalls. Real Horsefalls, I mean."

Shandy knew exactly what he meant. They were farmers like their great-uncle, the kind who'd hang on to their acres until the last gun was fired and the smoke cleared away. Loretta Fescue and her ilk could dangle all the money in the world before their eyes and they wouldn't budge an inch. But if they didn't have the land to cling to, that was something else again.

"Are Eddie and Ralph both farming now?" he asked.

"Makin' a fist at it. Can't get hold o' no decent land these days. Dern developers drivin' prices up so's an honest farmer can't afford a piece big enough to do much with. Eddie's over to Hoddersville. Runs a variety store to make ends meet. Ralph's got a few acres here in Upper Lumpkin an' works at the soap factory part time. Cussed shame."

Indeed it was. Peddling cat food or punching a time clock was no work for a true farmer. Neither Eddie nor Ralph lived all that far from the ancestral acres, it appeared. Suppose one of them got desperate enough to pull a few tricks in the hope of convincing Henny and Hilda they needed somebody younger and stronger on the place? Suppose he even thought of a way to remove the faithful though slack-witted hired man? He'd know Spurge was supposed to clean the spreader, most likely, if Henny had been nagging about it all week. Maybe he hadn't intended to kill Spurge, just to lay him up with burns long enough to get a foot in the door. Eddie and Ralph would have to go down on the list.

"You know, Henny," Miss Hilda said in a less belligerent tone than usual, "I'm not sure but what we ought to leave the farm to the pair of 'em regardless an' let their wives fight it out as they're o' mind to. We don't want to stir up the same kind o' hornets' nest Canny got 'is fam'ly stung with."

"Canny who, Miss Horsefall?" Shandy asked.

"Canute Lumpkin, Spurge's great-uncle. Don't ask me the legal ins an' outs of it, but the gist is, Canny muddled 'is estate somehow so's none o' the Lumpkins could claim what they was s'posed to get after he died. Canny was never much of a business head, though I will say he had 'is good points in some ways."

Cronkite Swope would have understood why Miss Hilda cast a glance out the window toward the distant oak grove.

"So the upshot of it was that they went at it hammer an' tongs, first one of 'em haulin' another into court, then that one goin' after the next, an' nobody ever makin' a cent out of it but the lawyers. So finally they quit suin' each other an' set around chewin' their fingernails tryin' to think o' somethin' else. Folks begun jokin' that the only Lumpkin who'd collect on Canny's estate would be the last one left alive. An' then, by the Lord Harry, if they didn't start droppin' off one after another. First Hannah that went to school with me, then her brother Floyd an' his son Malcolm, an' I can't rightly recollect how it went after them but it was funerals from one week to the next, seemed like, till the fam'ly plot could hardly hold 'em all."

"What did these Lumpkins die of?"

"One thing or another. An' don't think there wasn't talk."

"Never known a time when there wasn't," Henny grunted.

His aunt shook a finger like a knobby twig at him. "Scoff an' jeer all you're o' mind to. Just remember them scoffers an' jeerers that got et by the bears."

"I got worse things on my mind than gettin' et by bears. Any more coffee in that there pot?"

"No there ain't, an' I wouldn't give it to you if there was. Stuffin' your face an' spoilin' your supper when you ought to be out stirrin' your stumps for once in your life. Just 'cause poor Spurge—"

"Getting back to Spurge," said Shandy in near-desperation, "what happened to the Lumpkin inheritance?"

"Well, like I was tryin' to explain when this good-for-nothin' nephew o' mine that I never asked for an' wouldn't o' took as a gift if I'd o' had any say in the matter come buttin' in where he wasn't wanted, the Lumpkins kept dyin' off an' dyin' off till there was only Spurge an' his cousin Nute left. So then Nute waltzed hisself up to the courthouse an' tried to get Spurge declared mentally incompetent an' hisself made legal guardian so's he could scoop the pot, see?

"But me an' Henny, we spiked 'is guns. I will say for Henny he stood up like a man that day in court. Spurge Lumpkin earns 'is bed an' board as competent as the next man an' a dern sight more honest than some, 'e says, givin' Nute a look that would o' froze the tail off a brass monkey.

"So then I got up an' spoke my piece. Men's incompetent by nature, I says, an' there ain't none of 'em fit to tie their own bootlaces, let alone be guardian for anybody else far's I ever seen, an' the Lord knows I seen enough of 'em in my time. The judge's wife was in court an' she begun snickerin' into 'er handkerchief tryin' to make out she was havin' a sneezin' fit but she didn't fool me none.

"So the judge give 'er a look an' says was me an' Henny willin' to keep Spurge on as our hired hand. An' Henny told 'im Spurge would have a roof over 'is head as long as we had one ourselves. So the judge says, 'Petition denied,' an' we went an' had a sody at the ice cream parlor."

"Did Nute Lumpkin go with you?" Shandy asked.

"That pantywaist?" Henny sneered. "What in tarnation would we want him for? Anyways, he stomped off madder'n a wet hornet. He knew there was nothin' he could do. I'd o' mopped up the road with 'im."

Shandy surveyed the loam-caked octogenarian and thought Henny was probably right. "How long ago did this hearing take place?"

"Right after Spurge's brother Charlie an' his wife an' two sons was all killed in an automobile accident on their way back from New Hampshire. 'Long about November, seems to me."

"Of this past year?"

" 'Twas Thanksgivin' time," said Miss Hilda. "We was havin' Eddie an' his family for dinner an' I'd bought the brandy for my mincemeat before we went into court an' afterwards you an' Spurge snuck it out o' the bag an' drunk it up on me to celebrate. We used to have the Eddies an' the Ralphs together, but I got so sick o' them two wives o' theirs wranglin' that now we have the Ralphs on the even years an' the Eddies on the odd. So 'twas just you an' me an' Spurge an' Eddie an' Jolene an' their seven an' young Eddie's wife an' the baby. Didn't hardly seem worth layin' the table for them few, but I done it an' nobody couldn't claim they went away hungry, neither."

"So to make a long story short," Shandy replied, hoping it would, "these—er—persecutions started as soon as the snow was off the ground after Nute Lumpkin lost the hearing."

"What's this about snow?" asked Timothy Ames, who as usual had missed a good part of the conversation.

"Snow makes it easy to track a trespasser," Shandy explained. "We had snow last Thanksgiving Eve, as I recall, and the ground was never bare again until late March of this year. If you'd been able to see footprints, you'd have had no doubt about how your apple trees got broken down or who put the dog in your hen yard, would you, Mr. Horsefall?"

"Dern right I wouldn't," said Henny. "So you're sayin' that cussed Nute Lumpkin bided 'is time an' done me dirty soon as he could do it without gettin' caught 'cause he had it in for me an' Aunt Hilda over losin' the case about Spurge."

"M'yes, that could have been his motive, but I'm afraid I can think of a better one. You see, Mr. Horsefall, if we accept the possibility of Mr. Nute Lumpkin's being your phantom trickster, we pretty much rule out the possibility that Spurge's death was an accident. Nute must have known his cousin well enough to know how Spurge would react to anything out of the ordinary. There's also the fact that your neighbor Fergy was away during the winter but must have returned sometime during the period when the tricks started."

"I think 'twas about the time we found the ground glass in the pig swill."

"Yes, that would make sense. The broken apple trees and the business with the dog and the hens would require no particular advance information, you see. The really nasty stuff would require more precise timing. Now, we know from Fergy himself that Spurge was in the habit of dropping over there and talking to him most evenings. What would you suppose Spurge talked about?"

"Why, the farm, I s'pose. What we done in the daytime, what we had for supper, any little thing like that. Spurge didn't know much about anythin' else."

"So he'd no doubt have mentioned to Fergy that you'd been spreading lime and he was supposed to wash out the spreader."

"I guess likely."

"And Fergy has dealings with Nute over the antiques he picks up, and Fergy also appears to be the chatty type. It wouldn't be hard for Nute to keep himself informed about what happens over here and take advantage of any opportunity that presented itself to kill or maim the one man who stood between him and the Lumpkin inheritance. If he'd happened to kill Mr. Horsefall instead it wouldn't matter from his point of view, because he could then get custody of Spurge as he'd tried to do earlier and carry on with his original plans. I'm not saying Nute was your phantom trickster, but I think I'd better run over there and find out how much he knows about quicklime."

CHAPTER 5

Shandy asked to use the Horsefalls' phone and told Helen he didn't know when he'd be home. "I'm about to pay a call on your chum at the antique shop," he told her after he'd given her a rundown of events to date.

"Then stay away from that sofa. Nutie the Cutie may be ambidextrous. Peter, are you sure there's no way I could be of use over there? That frail old woman—"

"That frail old woman is out in the kitchen at this moment plucking a chicken and blasting out her arteries with a slug of bathtub gin."

"My stars and garters!"

"You may well say so. Did you finish the petunias?"

"How can you talk of petunias at a time like this?"

"Never mind how, just be sure you water them in well. If we let them wilt, Mirelle Feldster will start telling everybody our marriage is on the fritz. Arrivederci."

"If you say so." Sounding doubtful, Helen hung up.

Peter went back to the kitchen. "Tim, I'm going to pay a visit or two. Do you want to come with me or stay here?"

"I'll keep Henny and Miss Hilda company for a while longer, I think. You planning to swing back this way before you go home?"

"If you'd like me to. It may be an hour or so."

"No hurry. Come on, Henny, we might as well finish cleaning out that spreader. The lime ought to have simmered down a little by now and we don't want it hanging around for a reminder. Thanks for the coffee, Miss Hilda."

The two old men walked out with Shandy. As he got into his car and turned out into the road, he could see them back there in the barnyard like a painting by Millet. A mighty rage toward all the sons of bitches who tried to grab land from hardworking farmers rose within him. If somebody was out to put the screws on Henny Horsefall, then somebody was going to feel the personal vengeance of Peter Shandy. He floored the accelerator and zoomed toward Nute's Nook, wondering how many different crimes he was going to have to solve before he arrived at the true reason for Spurge Lumpkin's death.

Seeing an expensive new car draw up in front of the shop, Nute came to the door all smiles, settling the cuffs of his lilac-striped shirt under the cuffs of his purple suede jacket. He reminded Shandy of a chipmunk that had fallen into a paint bucket. When the driver got out in corduroys and flannel shirt with the marks of petunia-planting imperfectly erased, the chipmunk face changed momentarily to a weasel's. Then Nute got back his professional smirk and went through a pretty routine of searching his memory.

"Dear me, I know I've—ah yes. You were here last week with a petite blond lady. A charmer, if I may say so."

"The lady is my wife and I do not care to have her charms commented on by strangers, so I'd rather you didn't say so," Shandy replied. "Mr. Lumpkin, are you aware that your cousin Spurge has been killed?"

"Spurge dead?" The artificial smile became all too real before Canute Lumpkin managed to smooth his features into a more decorous expression. "Then I'm—"

"The king of the cats. Precisely how much do you stand to inherit, Mr. Lumpkin?"

"Please don't keep calling me Mr. Lumpkin. It's such a dreary name. And surely you can't expect me to be thinking of anything so crass as money when I've just lost my last, lone relative."

"You appeared to have money rather firmly in mind a few months ago when you were trying to railroad Spurge into the loony bin."

"I see you've been talking to the Horsefalls. By the way, may I have the pleasure of knowing who is taking such an interest in my personal affairs? It's not that I don't appreciate your concern, you understand. It's merely that one does like to know."

Posturing fop! Suppressing a natural urge to kick Nutie the Cutie where he most needed to be kicked, Shandy acceded to what was, after all, a reasonable request. Nutie was delighted.

"Professor Shandy! I had no idea I was being so signally honored. Why signally, I wonder? Should one be waving flags or working a heliograph? Do come in and sit down, Professor. Please forgive the disorder. I've just this minute finished with a customer in from New York who positively raided the place. One does enjoy dealing with people who have a sincere appreciation of the rare and the beautiful. And the wherewithal to indulge their tastes," he added with an insinuating glance out the window at Shandy's car. "By the way, I noticed your wife taking a particular interest in my Bow tea set the other day. Quite a rarity, as I'm sure you realize."

"We already have a tea set, thanks."

Shandy had no idea whether they did or not, but wouldn't have touched anything from Nute's Nook with a ten-foot pole. "Since you've had such a successful run of business, no doubt you'll want to get in touch with Harry Goulson about paying the costs for your dear departed cousin's funeral."

He'd never seen anybody bridle before. It was interesting to watch Canute Lumpkin definitely and distinctly bridle.

"Really, Professor, I don't see where I have the smallest responsibility in the matter. As you know, I did try to assume legal guardianship of my cousin, not, as the Horsefalls may have tried to make you believe, out of any pecuniary motive, but from a genuine concern for Spurge's welfare. However, the judge saw fit to deny my petition. Therefore it would be inappropriate and probably illegal for me to go barging in and upset whatever plans the Horsefalls have made. Miss Hilda would adore to get me pinched for contempt of court."

He spread his beautifully manicured hands and showed his dimple. "I'll send a wreath or something, of course. Lilies, do you think? Consider the lilies of the field and all that? Though one could hardly say my cousin Spurge toiled not, could one? Old Horsefall worked him like, as one might expect, a horse. That was why I thought I should take steps to relieve the poor chap from what virtually amounted to slave labor. But since everybody chose to misunderstand my motives—"

"Who could possibly misunderstand your motives, Mr. Lumpkin? As to the value of the property you stand to inherit, no doubt it's a matter of public record and I can easily look it up. What I'm most curious about is why you haven't asked me what happened to your cousin. Perhaps you already know?"

"How could I? You've only this minute come galloping in here like that Ghent to Aix fellow—oh dear, he was carrying good news, wasn't he? Now I shall be accused of another breach of taste. How ghastly! Very well, then, what happened to my cousin?"

Shandy told him, not sparing the details, and he said, "How ghastly!" again. "There, you see how right I was about Spurge's incompetence? It appears to me, Professor Shandy, that I have ample grounds to sue the Horsefalls for negligence."

"It appears to me that you have a fat chance of winning, Mr. Lumpkin. Furthermore the Horsefalls couldn't afford to pay damages if you did by some wild chance succeed in winning your case."

"Why couldn't they? There's the property," Lumpkin replied a shade too quickly.

"Indeed there is. I see you've already been giving it some thought. How embarrassed will you be if the incident that resulted in your cousin's death proves to have been perpetrated by some person or persons or your personal acquaintance desiring to get hold of that property?"

"Why should I be embarrassed at all? It's entirely possible I do know the perpetrators, as you so learnedly refer to them, him, her, or it. One does know everybody in a place like this. And naturally I've heard about all the goings-on at the Horsefalls', with Henny cavorting around with a shotgun full of rock salt and Miss Hilda stirring her cauldron and thinking up juicy new anathemas. I adore local gossip. Far more fun than watching the soaps, and there's not the bother of being interrupted by somebody wanting to pick up a nice bargain in Spode just as Linda is about to confess to Michael that she's having an affair with Claude, though I expect it would be Claudia these days.

"But to be appallingly frank with you, Professor, I don't quite get the drift of this entire conversation. You wouldn't by any chance be threatening me, would you? Because if you were I might be able to sue you as well as the Horsefalls, and perhaps the lawyer would give me a wholesale rate."

Canute smiled ever so sweetly to show he was only joking, thus making it quite clear he'd strike like a cobra if he ever saw an opening. Shandy wondered how many people Nute had already dragged into court on one pretext or another, and how much he'd got out of his lawsuits.

"What a pity you don't have a case, Mr. Lumpkin," he replied with the mildness he usually reserved for his more dangerous moments in the classroom. "I shouldn't dream of threatening you. And with Miss Horsefall's hundred and fifth birthday celebration coming up so soon, I don't suppose your slapping her with a lawsuit would be good public relations, would it? In any event you won't want to be bothered now that you're coming into the Lumpkin estate."

"When I see a chance of picking up some extra money I always want to be bothered, Professor. Appalling of me I know, but there it is. Mercenary to the core. Are you quite, quite sure you wouldn't care to surprise your lovely wife with my adorable Bow tea set? One might offer a reasonable discount to so distinguished a customer. For the public relations value, you know."

Shandy thought he'd better get out of there before Canute Lumpkin acquired visible grounds to sue him for assault and battery. "I shan't take advantage of your good nature, Mr. Lumpkin. Permit me again to offer you my condolences. Or congratulations, as the case may be."

"I do so appreciate your thoughtfulness, Professor Shandy. Allow me." With a self-satisfied smirk, Canute Lumpkin held open the shop door. "Oh, about those flowers. Do you think a simple bouquet of field flowers would be more appropriate? Daisies and buttercups, perhaps?"

"How about pigweed?"

Shandy got back into his car and headed for the Horsefalls'. He'd come out an extremely poor second in that interview, and was perhaps fortunate to have come out at all. Nute was cute all right. Clever as a rat, putting on an act designed to make one think he couldn't possibly be so rotten as he made himself appear, when in fact he was no doubt a lot worse.

Canute Lumpkin was the sort to run a dirty-tricks campaign with enthusiasm and panache. He had his pipeline to the Horsefall farm via Fergy's friendship with Spurge. He had a grudge against the old pair for wrecking his plan to get custody of his cousin and the Lumpkin inheritance. He was wily enough to have started with minor nuisances that would brand Henny an old crank for lodging complaints with the police, and gradually step them up to the point where he could do real damage without much interference.

In his "I'm only concerned for my cousin's welfare" role, he'd have an excuse to ask Fergy details of Spurge's work on the farm. Fergy might easily have mentioned that Henny had been after Spurge to wash out the spreader, and Nute could have guessed how his cousin would react to the novelty of bubbling quicklime. If he got killed, fine. If he didn't, Nute would have a lovely reason to sue the Horsefalls for custody and damages. Since they had nothing but their property to pay him off with, he'd wind up with the Horsefall farm in his pudgy pink hands. After that, he'd no doubt be more than willing to bargain with Loretta Fescue and her eager client. A few years from now, these rich acres would be covered with blacktop and supermarkets, like as not. If there could be a worse crime than murder in Shandy's book, that would have to be it.

CHAPTER 6

It was just about five o'clock now, too late to drop in at
Town Hall. Too bad. Shandy would have liked to get
some specific information about the Lumpkin estate.
Chances were, though, that the Horsefalls would have
some idea of what Nute now stood to inherit. Anyway he
had to go back there and collect Tim, unless Roy and
Laurie had already done so.

As he headed out from Lumpkin Center, Shandy happened to spot a curlicued sign outside a modestly built
but considerably gussied-up frame house that said: "Loretta Fescue, Realtor." He stopped and rang the bell but
nobody answered. He scowled at a plastic gnome that
was supposed to be pushing a toy wheelbarrow full of
salmon-pink geraniums and got back into the car.

At the Horsefall place, Tim, Henny, and Miss Hilda
were all sitting out on the porch in rush-seated rockers,
looking down in the mouth. His coming was obviously a
welcome diversion.

"Hi, Pete," Tim called before Shandy was out of the
car. "Glad you came. Laurie phoned a while back to see
if I needed a lift. I said I'd go home with you."

"Land's sakes, don't leave yet awhile," Miss Hilda
fussed. "That's the trouble with you young things, always jumpin' around like peas on a hot griddle. Let Professor Shandy catch 'is breath, can't you? I'll fix us a bite
o' supper soon as I get my legs back under me. Havin'
that Goulson man come an' cart poor Spurge away was
kind of a facer, I have to admit."

Henny shook his head. "I know, Aunt Hilda. Couldn't
hardly believe it happened till then. Cripes, when I think

of—here, Professor, haul up a chair an' set. We'll be ea-
tin' pretty soon, I guess maybe."

"Please don't bother fixing anything for me," said
Shandy. "My wife will be expecting me."

"How long you been married?" Miss Hilda wanted to
know.

"Since January twenty-first."

"You mean this past January? Took your time about
it, didn't you?"

"Not really. I didn't meet her till the week after
Christmas."

"Mph. Widow lookin' for a meal ticket, was she?"

"No. Neither of us had been married before and my
wife is quite capable of earning her own living. She has a
doctorate in library science."

"Then what in tarnation did she want to bother 'erself
with a husband for?"

"She—er—claims to be rather fond of me."

"Well, I s'pose there's still a few that's old-fashioned
enough to want 'Mrs.' on their tombstones. Lord a' mercy, what's that?"

"It's Spurge's ghost, riz from the dead to git revenge
on them as kilt 'im!" cried Henny in terror.

Henny's mistake was a natural enough one. The tattered, bleeding figure rushing toward them over the
swale would have been enough to scare anybody. It was
brandishing what looked at first to be a broadsword but
proved on closer inspection to be a pair of oversized
hedge clippers. Cronkite Swope was returning from his
journalistic investigation.

"I found it." he was yelling. "I found the runestone!"

Miss Horsefall sniffed. "You look more like as if you'd
lost a fight with a barrel o' bobcats. O' course you found
it. I told you where 'twas, didn't I? Couldn't you o' got
there without ruinin' your Sunday britches into the bargain?"

"The briers down there are fierce." Cronkite dabbed at
a welling scratch on his chin with the sleeve of what had
started out to be a natty pink-and-green-striped shirt.
"I've probably got myself a beautiful case of poison ivy,
too, but what the heck? Look, Professor Shandy, I made
a rubbing."

"By George, so you did." Shandy bent over the scribbled sheets of copy paper that Cronkite was piecing together on the porch floor. "I'm afraid I don't know the first thing about runes, but those marks are certainly—er—interesting." He did not in fact find them so, but it did seem heartless not to give the young fellow some sort of kudos for his enterprise.

"And I found this!" Cronkite thrust a fragment of discolored metal under his nose.

Shandy backed off and fumbled for his reading glasses. "What is it?"

"Might be off a Willys-Knight we used to have back around 1927," Henny ventured.

"It looks a bit ancient for that. Would you mind if I scrape it with my jackknife, Mr. Swope? I'll be careful, I assure you."

"Sure, Professor, go ahead. I tried to wipe it on my shirttail, but the metal's so corroded I couldn't get anything off but some of the surface mud. The thing was sort of half buried next to the stone, see, as though it might have been thrown up by a frost heave when the ground started to thaw. If you hold it up to eye level and squint across the surface you can see a pattern, as if it might have been engraved or decorated somehow."

"M'yes, I believe I can," said Shandy, obediently performing the scrutiny. "The convex side is irregular in a—er—regular sort of way, at any rate."

Intrigued now, he scratched gingerly at the pitted, greenish patina. "Wouldn't you say that might be bronze, Tim?"

"Could be," Professor Ames replied after doing a good deal of prodding with a thick, heavily ridged fingernail. "What do you think, Henny."

"Copper, mebbe? Kind o' hard for copper. Yep, could be bronze. Or brass. More likely brass, if it's off'n a car. Did we have acetylene lamps on that old Pope-Toledo, Aunt Hilda?"

"Doesn't look like anything off a car to me," said Shandy. "It's more like a—it reminds me of something, but I can't think what."

"Well, if you want to know what I think"—it was clear they were going to hear what Cronkite Swope thought whether they wanted to or not, so nobody tried to stop him—"I think it's a piece broken off one of those old Viking helmets. See how it curves around and comes up to a sort of dome shape. And this crescent-shaped hole in the edge could be where the horn came out. You know how they'd have cow horns and antlers and stuff sticking out of their helmets to make them look fiercer."

"So we've been led to believe, at any rate." Shandy hefted the fragment with more respect. Was it possible Cronkite could be right? "I tell you what, young man. The best person for you to show these things to is President Svenson at the college. He's something of an authority on ancient Norse culture."

"I thought he was an authority on plowin'," said Henny Horsefall.

"He is. That and a—er—great many other things."

"A real Renaissance man, would you say?" cried young Swope, his bright green eyes snapping with the thrill of it all.

"I'd place him—er—a good deal further back in history than that."

Shandy could easily picture Thorkjeld Svenson in a horned helmet, slashing away at the Jutes and the Saxons for the sheer hell of it. Authentic or not, Cronkite's find might serve a useful purpose by taking Svenson's mind off his daughter Birgit's marriage to Hjalmar Olafssen. The presidential mansion was going to be awfully quiet without Birgit.

"When can I see President Svenson?" demanded Cronkite.

"Almost anytime, I expect. He's at home, I know. Ride back with Professor Ames and myself if you like. My wife will give you dinner and we'll—er—strike while the bronze is hot, as it were. Then if the president wants to come over here and look at the runestone, as I suspect he will, it will still be light enough to see by. If the Horsefalls don't mind our coming, that is."

"Glad to have you," grunted Henny.

"Be somethin' to break up the evenin' anyway," Miss Hilda agreed grudgingly. "Lord a' mercy, how many times have I gone to get supper an' set a place at the ta-

ble forgettin' the one I meant it for wasn't never comin'
no more. Time I went myself, maybe."

Cronkite was a young man of tact and feeling. He put
his lacerated right arm around Miss Horsefall's bony
shoulders and gave her a little squeeze.

"Hey, cut that out. You've got to stick around till after
your birthday party anyway. We're planning to run your
picture on the front page."

"Then I s'pose that means I'll have to put my hair up
in kid curlers the night before. Pesky things. I hate
sleepin' on 'em."

Yet Miss Horsefall was looking less woebegone as she
went to prepare the evening meal for herself and the one
old man she had left to feed.

CHAPTER 7

"Well, what does it say?" Shandy prodded. "Harald Blue-tooth was here?"

"Shut up," replied Thorkjeld Svenson with that suave courtesy for which he was ever noted. He jabbed a fore-finger the size of a bedpost at one of the more carefully worked out patches in Cronkite's scribbling. "Looks like Orm."

"Orm what? Is Orm a word?"

"Name. Damn good name. What's wrong with Orm?"

"Something must have gone wrong with him if that's Orm's tombstone," Cronkite pointed out reasonably.

"Might not be a grave. Might be any damn thing. Wish Uncle Sven were here."

"Where is he, President?"

"How the hell do I know? Am I my uncle's keeper? Down at the Senior Citizens' Drop-in Center pinching some widow's backside, most likely."

"Thorkjeld, you may not speak with disrespect of your learned great-uncle."

Sieglinde Svenson had entered the room, queenly in a thin summer dress of some soft blue material, though slightly wan about the eyelids from the strain of marry-ing off the fifth of her seven daughters and coping with relatives who had thronged from all parts of the north-ern hemisphere to make sure Birgit and Hjalmar got well and duly hitched.

"What's disrespectful about pinching widows? How many men his age would be up to it? Proud of the old letch."

"Uncle Sven is not a letch." Sieglinde had high moral standards and did not care to have such words bandied about in her presence. "He lived in happy monogamy with your Great-aunt Ylva until her untimely passing at the age of eighty-nine. Naturally he is lonely without her and seeks other feminine companionship. You would do the same."

"Hell, you'll outlive me by forty years," cried Thorkjeld in panic.

His wife shook her noble blond head. "I shall not. Life without you would be unendurably serene. What is this paper you have here, and who is this attractive but bedraggled young man? I trust he does not want to marry our lovely Gudrun or our sweet little Frideswiede."

"He damn well better hadn't," growled the bereft father. "Look at him. Doesn't even have a whole shirt to his back."

"This is Cronkite Swope, a reporter fom the *Weekly Fane and Pennon*," said Shandy.

"And I have lots of shirts," Cronkite protested, stung to the quick. "I tore this one slashing through the brambles to get at the runestone and haven't had time to go home and change. And I don't even know Gudrun or Frideswiede. Though I'd sure like to if they take after their mother," he added gallantly.

Cronkite did have a way with words. Sieglinde awarded him a smile, Thorkjeld a menacing snarl.

"Urrgh! Where's this runestone?"

"In Mr. Hengist Horsefall's oak grove over in Lumpkin Corners. I never knew it was there until Miss Hilda Horsefall, his aunt, told me about it while I was interviewing her this afternoon. I'm sorry this is such a poor rubbing. All I had with me were a pencil and some copy paper."

"Why did you not go better prepared?" Sieglinde asked him.

"Well, gee, Mrs. Svenson, I didn't know I was going till I went. They sent me over to write a little story about Miss Hilda's hundred and fifth birthday party but then the hired man fell into the quicklime so I thought I'd better go find that runestone quick and I ought to be down at the paper only I wanted to make sure it really is a runestone first."

"I see. Your explanation makes more sense to me than

anything else I have heard during the past month. Then, Thorkjeld, this is a genuine runestone?"

"Got runes on it anyway. Have to see for myself. Show Uncle Sven."

President Svenson was still knitting his craglike brows over Cronkite's scribblings. "This doodad here. Might be curse."

"Curse?" Cronkite almost fell down the front steps in his joy. "You mean like 'curst be he that moves my bones'?"

"Arrgh."

"And what about the helmet?" Cronkite proffered his fragment of bronze. "Don't you think this could be part of a helmet? See the hole where the horn came out?"

"Urrgh!" Svenson replied with more enthusiasm. He clapped the metal against his massive skull. One turbulent lock of iron-gray hair stuck out through the hole like an eagle's wing. "How do I look?"

"God," cried Timothy Ames, who hadn't uttered a word until now. "It couldn't be anything else."

"Yesus, wait till Uncle Sven sees this! Swope, maybe in ten years I let you meet Gudrun."

"Thank you," said Cronkite. "I'll be looking forward to it. Right now, though, I've got to write my story. Keep the helmet to show your uncle if you want to. I'll be around to get his opinion first thing tomorrow morning. Nice to have met you, Mrs. Svenson. Thank your wife again for the wonderful dinner, Professor Shandy."

Before Swope had quite finished his polite adieux, he was gunning the motorbike he'd ridden over from Lumpkin Corners.

"I have a feeling we've unleashed a monster," Shandy mused.

Nobody paid any attention to him. Tim didn't hear and Thorkjeld was busy kissing Sieglinde in the old Norse manner, which is to say *molto con brio*, as a prelude to rounding up Uncle Sven and going to see the runestone.

They found the aged relative heading for the college barns with a purposeful expression on his face and a buxom widow trotting eagerly beside him. The widow was much the taller, but Sven had the longer mustache. Though his chin was bare of beard, the hair sprouting

from his upper lip trailed a good six inches below his
mouth, or would have were it not at the moment blowing
out beyond his ears to mingle with the silver locks that
flowed down to his debonair blue and white polka-dotted
collar.

It seemed too bad, Shandy thought, to spoil his plans
for the evening, but Uncle Sven didn't appear to mind.
He was as excited as Thorkjeld over the fragment of helmet and pronounced it without hesitation as having
come from Uppsala circa A.D. 900. He also said, in Swedish so as not to hurt her feelings, that one could always
find a willing woman but a runestone in this benighted
wilderness was a treat he hadn't expected and what were
they waiting for?

Thorkjeld, fired with enthusiasm, clamored to drive
the party over to the Horsefalls'. Shandy said him a loud
and final nay. He'd do the driving himself. He was simply not up to riding with a berserker tonight.

On the way over, Uncle Sven studied the rubbing,
which Cronkite and Helen had patched together at din-
nertime with cellophane tape. He agreed with Thorkjeld
about Orm and thought the next word was "Tokesson,"
which would mean, obviously, "Orm, son of Toke." He
granted the curse but reserved judgment on the rest of
the inscription. At least they were now sure this was not
one of those geological freaks that had aroused false
hopes in the area before.

Helen had predicted Peter wouldn't find the Horsefalls
mourning alone on his return trip, and as usual she
proved right. A fair number of relatives and neighbors
had gathered, bringing cakes, cookies, condolences, and
curiosity. Miss Hilda had changed into what had no
doubt been her best summer dress for the past thirty
years or more: a lilac print, set off by a handsome amethyst brooch that must date from an earlier, more pros-
perous era. At sight of her, Uncle Sven's mustache ends
began to curl upward.

She shoved forward two fiftyish men who might have
been twins. "This here's Eddie, Professor, and this is
Ralph. They're the great-nephews we was tellin' you
about."

Both were tallish and spare, with the stooped shoul-

ders, the weather-beaten faces, and the resigned but res-
olute "What's Ma Nature and the government going to
soak us with next?" expressions that betoken small farmers everywhere. Shandy felt favorably disposed toward
both by instinct, though he knew he shouldn't. Both had
large families, iron-jawed wives, and a general aura of
not being quite able to make ends meet. Already he
could detect murmurs about which of them would get to
move in with the old folks and run the farm, and he recognized one of Ralph's sons as having been a prime trou-
blemaker at the college's Grand Illumination two years
ago, before he himself had taken over that disreputable
role.*

Ralph Junior was fifteen or so, big for his age, and, it
would seem, already angry enough with an unfair world
to do the sorts of damage Henny Horsefall had been
plagued with. He probably owned a bike and didn't live
far away. He must know his folks were in the running to
get the farm; perhaps he'd decided to hurry matters
along by scaring old Henny into feeling the need of protection. Or perhaps somebody else, such as that grim-
looking aunt of his, knew the boy's record as a public
nuisance and was operating on the principle of "Give a
dog a bad name and hang him." Shandy began to feel
overburdened with likely suspects.

"Sorry, President," he muttered. "I might have known
there'd be a mob here as soon as word about the hired
man got around. We'd better not mention the runestone
for the moment. It might start a stampede."

"Then what in hell did you lug us over here for?"
Svenson growled back.

"Don't worry, we'll get to it one way or another. Would
you mind pretending for the moment that you're here as
emissary from the college's Agricultural Laborers' Assistance Fund?"

"We don't have one."

"Yes we do. Tim and I founded it this afternoon."

"Oh."

Svenson didn't need to be told any more. He went
properly and sedately to pay his respects to Miss Hilda

* *Rest You Merry* (Doubleday Crime Club, 1978).

and her nephew, thus elevating them in the local social
scale beyond their wildest dreams. It was a hitherto unheard-of honor for President Thorkjeld Svenson, renowned academician and holder of the Balaclava County
Senior Plowmen's Trophy since God knew when, to appear in person at an informal gathering in Lumpkin Corners.

"And I've brought my Uncle Sven to meet you, Miss
Horsefall. He's here from Stockholm for my daughter's
wedding. Uncle Sven was a hundred and two last November."

"He sure as hell don't act it," was the consensus of the
assemblage. Uncle Sven, though knowing only about forty words of English and not able to pronounce most of
them, was already the life and soul of the party. His
mustache now pointed almost straight up. His round little cheeks glistened like two Rome Beauty apples. His
sea-blue eyes glistened as he ran a connoisseur's eye over
Miss Hilda and her amethyst brooch.

The lady herself must be wishing she'd put up her hair
in kid curlers last night. She kept patting it to make
sure no wisps were flying out from under her hairnet
and fussing about not having had no chance to get red-
ded up for company.

"Ay tank you look svell," Uncle Sven was assuring her
as he steered a forkful of chocolate cake past his mustache. "Ve take valk, hah?"

"Yes, why don't you two go off by yourselves and have
a nice, quiet little visit?" suggested great-niece-in-law
Jolene, perhaps already seeing herself as mistress of the
Horsefall homestead. "You need a breather, Aunt Hilda.
I'll be glad to hold the fort for you here."

"Maybe you'd like to go wash some dishes, Jolene,
since you put on such a performance about claiming the
honor last time," suggested Marie. "I don't mind pouring
the coffee."

"Then quit jawin' an' pour me some," said Henny with
unaccustomed authority. "After that you can go bile up
another pot an' put the kettle on for tea. Here comes the
minister an' his wife. Jolene, you clean up them plates
an' cut some more cake. Step lively, both o' you."

Astonished by this turning of the worm, Jolene and

Marie stepped. Miss Hilda blinked in amazement, greeted the minister and his wife first to show who was still queen of the castle around here, then took Sven Svenson's arm. Shandy saw his opportunity.

"I think President Svenson and I will—er—stroll along behind our two senior citizens," he remarked to Jolene, who happened to be nearest. "As a precautionary measure, you know."

He didn't say what the precaution would be against. Jolene, intent on serving cake to the minister's wife, merely gave him an absentminded nod. The procession was off. Uncle Sven set a beeline course for the barn. Thorkjeld addressed him sternly in Swedish to the effect that Miss Hilda was no pushover and he'd better do some preliminary spadework. Sven protested that at a combined age of two hundred and seven, he and Miss Hilda had no time to waste on preliminary spadework. Thorkjeld reminded him they were here to look at a runestone and he capitulated.

"What are you two gassin' about?" demanded Miss Hilda.

"Uncle Sven wants to see that runestone young Swope found. He knows all about runestones."

"H'mph. I bet I could tell 'im a few things." She squeezed Sven's arm and he cast another wistful glance toward the barn.

"Would it be too far for you to walk to the stone?" asked Shandy, trying to keep the expedition to its avowed purpose.

"Hell no," she replied, "though I'd sooner go in a buggy for old times' sake."

"I wish we could oblige you, but if the path is as bad as Swope described, I doubt whether any vehicle except a bulldozer or a tank could get through."

"Wouldn't o' had no trouble if Henny'd o' kept that loggin' road open like I told 'im to."

"What road is this, Miss Horsefall?"

"Cuts in from the Balaclava Road just down past the old Lumpkin place, or used to. I ain't been that way in a month o' Sundays, myself."

"And the runestone would have been easier to reach by that road?"

"Easy as pie. Used to be a turnaround an' you could drive right up to the stone."

"We might try getting through with your nephew's tractor."

"Can't have no fun on a tractor."

Miss Hilda's argument was unassailable. They compromised by Shandy's driving the tractor on ahead to beat down a wider path over the route Swope had hacked out while Thorkjeld walked behind, carrying Uncle Sven under one arm and Miss Hilda under the other when the going got too rough for their century-old legs.

The distance was not great, less than half a mile from the house, but it was solid brier patch most of the way and Cronkite Swope took an honored place in Shandy's list of unsung heroes. Cronkite had even managed to clear a tiny space in front of the stone itself. Uncle Sven had room to kneel and use Thorkjeld's pet magnifying glass to examine the inscription.

The stone itself was nothing to get excited about as far as Shandy could see. It was merely a slab of granite perhaps four feet high and two feet wide at the base, such as the Great Glacier had strewn so lavishly over the area, to the dismay of early colonists who had to drag the stones off the fields they'd cut and burned clear and were trying to turn into farmland. Plenty of stones like this one had been piled into stone walls to keep out wandering pigs and shoot at Redcoats from behind.

Shandy didn't think much of the runes, either. To him they were only half-obliterated gouges in the granite. Uncle Sven, however, got so rapt in study that he forgot to retain his firm grasp on Miss Hilda, who flounced off in a fit of pique and seated herself on the tractor. He also lost his feeble grip on the English language, so that Thorkjeld had to act as translator as soon as there was anything to translate.

"Well, what's it say?" demanded Miss Hilda, considerably out of sorts at having been ditched for a slab of granite.

"Give him time," grunted President Svenson. "The inscription is badly defaced."

"H'mph. He ain't in none too great shape hisself."

This was pure spite. Thorkjeld didn't bother to relay

the remark to his uncle, being wise in the ways of women and knowing Miss Holda didn't really mean it anyway.

Sven Svenson went on peering and muttering, often using his sensitive scholar's fingers to trace a mark that was too dim to make out by eye. At last he began to chuckle. He rocked back on his heels and read off the inscription to Thorkjeld, who laughed a good deal louder, then translated for the others.

" 'Orm Tokesson found no good drink and only ill-tempered women. This place is cursed."

"Must o' been before my time," said Miss Hilda blandly.

"You mean it's real?" Shandy gasped. "Good Lord! Now what do we do?"

"Damned if I know. Get a bunch of archaeologists out here from Harvard or somewhere, I suppose. Let 'em do whatever the hell they do."

"I must say I find this hard to credit. Why should a Viking expend all that time and effort hacking a complaint about booze and women into solid granite?"

"You don't understand the soul of the Norsemen, Shandy. They were great poets."

"This is great poetry?"

"Well, Orm might have spread himself more if the stone hadn't been so damned hard. Yesus, what if you'd been cooped up in a longship for weeks, maybe months on end, with the ale running out and the meat going bad and not a goddamn thing to do but row or get seasick. Finally you reach land and go ashore all set for a rip-roaring drunk in sympathetic company and there isn't any. Can't you feel the agony behind those simple, poignant words? The dryness in the mouth, the—" Thorkjeld Svenson's eye happened to light on Miss Hilda's prim lilac print and he broke off what for him had been a long oration.

"Poor Orm," he finished sadly, with head bowed in tribute to one he clearly regarded as a fallen comrade.

"M'yes," Shandy conceded. "I hadn't thought of the matter in that light. Besides, I daresay if your—er—profession involved a lot of hewing and slashing anyway, you wouldn't regard a few hours' worth of granite chipping as more than quiet recreation. Has your uncle any idea when this might have been done?"

"The runes are in the later Danish period. Maybe around the time of Sven Forkbeard or Canute the Great."

Shandy felt sweaty up his spine. "Canute?"

"Sure. Even a clod like you must have heard about King Canute."

"I thought he was king of England."

"He was. Also Norway and Denmark. Damn good king, too. Conquered England and married Ethelred the Unready's widow, Emma. Emma didn't find old Canute unready, I'll bet."

"When did he live?"

"End of the tenth, beginning of the eleventh century. Why Canute?"

"Canute happens to have been a popular name among the Lumpkin family, which, as you know, settled this area. Spurge Lumpkin, the Horsefalls' hired hand who was killed this afternoon, had a cousin named Canute who's now the only surviving direct descendant. Canute was also the name of their grandfather, or whatever he was. That Canute left the Lumpkin family estate in such a muddle that in effect it became a tontine."

"Last one alive gets the loot, eh?"

"Precisely. A time-honored Viking custom, I believe."

"Arr!"

Thorkjeld looked rather pleased and proceeded to explain the situation to his great-uncle, who nodded. Apparently they both liked to think old Norse customs were still being observed in Balaclava County. Shandy failed to share their gratification.

"I don't see what's so great about shoving a man's face in quicklime."

"Right. Degenerate. Not in tradition. Brain 'em with a battle-ax. Chop 'em up with a broadsword. Slit 'em down the front while they're still alive and spread open the ribs so you can watch the lung flap."

"Shut up, will you, President?"

"Called it the blood eagle," Thorkjeld went on unheeding. "Crude sense of humor. Almost as bad as the stuff you see on kids' television programs. Interesting thing about Canute. After he married Emma he integrated. Sent his Danish wives home. Some of his Danish troops, too. What were they going to do back in Denmark? Sit around twiddling their battle-axes? Go a-viking to keep their hands in, more likely. Why the hell not?"

"Vy te hell not?" agreed Uncle Sven, who appeared to have followed Thorkjeld's train of thought with no difficulty. "Hah, tootsie?"

"I'd o' went a-viking after that dern Canute if I was 'is lawful wedded Danish wife an' he tried to banish me for some female named Emma, queen or no queen," Miss Hilda replied.

"Hah. You good Norsk voman."

"As a matter of fact, that may not be too far off the mark," said Shandy. "Her nephew's name is Hengist, as in Hengist and Horsa. They were Saxons, of course, but weren't they also sea rovers, and wasn't Hengist also a king in England back around the fifth century A.D.? His progeny would have been absorbed into the local culture by the time Canute came along, but they'd all be—er——brothers under the battle-ax, as it were. Would it be unreasonable to suppose there might be a Hengist in Orm's crew?"

"Hell no," said Thorkjeld. "Lot of conquering back and forth. Lot of other stuff, too. Integrated all over the place. Still at it," he added with a warning glance at Uncle Sven, who was edging up to Miss Hilda again. "What do you say, Uncle Sven? Had enough for tonight?"

"Don't answer that!" cried Shandy. "Come on, President, we'd better get Miss Horsefall back to the house. Her company will be wondering what's become of her. I suppose it's all right to leave the runestone as it is?"

"Been standin' there already for the Lord knows how long an' nobody ain't done nothin' to it yet," said Miss Hilda. "Just don't say nothin' about it back at the house or them kids of Eddie's an' Ralph's will be down here rippin' their clothes off their backs like that young feller from the paper done. Clothes is too derned expensive these days. So's everythin' else."

"Te bast tings in life bane free," Uncle Sven reminded her. "Ve valk alone next time. Hah, tootsie?"

CHAPTER 8

They pried Uncle Sven away from Miss Hilda at last, and got him back to Valhalla. Shandy delivered Tim to Laurie and Roy, refused to arbitrate a dispute over wallpaper samples, and sought the more soothing company of his own beloved spouse.

"Well, what did I miss?" was Helen's greeting.

"A gaggle of the Horsefalls' relatives, a saunter through six miles of squirrel briers, and a lecture from Thorkjeld on Viking customs."

"Sounds too jolly for words. Peter, you're at it again, aren't you?"

"Peace, woman. Why don't you just go get me my pipe and slippers like a good little lady librarian?"

"Why not your violin and hypodermic? You don't smoke and Jane Austen is sleeping on your slippers."

Jane Austen was a tiger kitten the Shandys had recently wheedled out of their neighbors the Enderbles. Peter had wanted to call the infant feline Sir Ruthven Murgatroyd, but the name had proved biologically unviable, so Helen had got her own way and Jane was now busy rearranging the household to suit herself, as even the youngest of cats knows so well how to do.

"Why isn't Jane Austen sleeping in the cat's pajamas?" the alleged head of the house demanded.

"You're overwrought, poor dear," said his wife. "How about some hot tea or a nip of bourbon and branch or something?"

"Nothing, thanks. I had cake and coffee thrust upon me at the Horsefalls' by a great-niece-in-law named Jolene who has a jaw like a Norwegian icebreaker. Aren't you going to ask me about the runes?"

"Certainly, dear. What about the runes? Peter, you don't mean to tell me they actually are? I can't bear it! What do they say?"

"I don't believe it myself, but Thorkjeld's Uncle Sven translated them anyway." He repeated what Sven had said, and added Thorkjeld's footnotes.

Regrettably, Helen giggled. "Poor Orm indeed! But, Peter, if Dr. Svenson is right, this will rock the socks off every archaeologist from here to Helsinki. What's going to happen now?"

"Thorkjeld's attending to the sock-rocking department, Harry Goulson's handling the obsequies, and God only knows what young Cronkite Swope is up to but I fear the worst. We can only be thankful the *Fane and Pennon* doesn't come out till day after tomorrow. That gives us tomorrow to batten down the hatches and man the battlements, anyway."

"Knock wood when you say that. I'll bet every one of that crowd who were at the Horsefalls' is out spreading the word already."

"Not about the runestone. We entered into a conspiracy of secrecy. At least, I hope we did. Anyway, the chief topic of interest appears to be how and whether Miss Horsefall and her nephew are going to manage staying on their property. Nobody is naïve enough to think they're going to find another hired man to take Spurge Lumpkin's place. Farm help is scarcer than hens' teeth to begin with, and those who are willing to do the work have this fanciful notion about getting paid, which more or less lets the Horsefalls out before they start."

"Then what's going to happen to the farm?"

"There are various schools of thought on that point. Would you happen to know anything about a woman named Loretta Fescue?"

"The real estate agent? Yes, Grace Porble was telling me about her a couple of days ago. Grace has been dropping over to help me shelve the Buggins Collection, bless her. We sneak out for a cup of tea at the faculty dining room every so often because the dust in those old books really gets to you after a while."

"Spare me the preamble and get on with the story, my

love. What has Grace Porble to say about Loretta Fescue?"

"Oh, that she's pushy. An aunt of Grace's was left a widow not too long ago and Grace said this Mrs. Fescue was on her doorstep pressuring her to sell the house before the funeral notice was even in the paper. And the aunt didn't want to sell at all. She has seven cats and a trained goldfish."

"It must be not only trained but damned lucky if it's managed to keep away from seven cats."

"Peter, how am I supposed to tell if you keep interrupting? If you want to talk about goldfish, say so. I thought you were interested in Loretta Fescue."

"I waive the goldfish. Resume your narrative."

"It was partly on account of the animals that Grace's aunt didn't want to sell, was what I was getting at. Anyway, she didn't need to because her husband had left her reasonably well provided for and she could always rent rooms. But this Mrs. Fescue kept badgering her and badgering her, and telling all sorts of terrible lies about how the town wouldn't let her take in boarders on account of the zoning regulations and she'd have a terrible time if she did because they'd use up all the hot water and shine their shoes on the bedspreads. And the aunt knew it wasn't true because her neighbors on both sides are widows, too, and they both have boarders and they're lovely people and everything works out just fine."

"Bully for them."

Helen gave him a look. "Then what did Mrs. Fescue do but barge right ahead and put Grace's name in for one of those senior citizens' apartments over in West Lumpkin which she didn't want at all. That started rumors she was planning to get rid of her house after all, and her neighbors got huffy because she hadn't had the courtesy to tell them first, and these were people she'd known forever, Peter! And then other people started wanting to know when she was going to hold her yard sale and wouldn't she like to sell them this or that? And here was this poor old soul who only wanted to be left alone to cry over her husband and comb her cats and feed her goldfish, having to cope with all this ghastly nonsense."

"Good Lord! What happened?"

"Well, Grace says her aunt got so fed up and disheartened that at one point she was ready to sell just to be out of the mess. Then she found out they wouldn't let her keep her seven cats in the senior citizens' apartment. So finally she had to get really nasty with this Mrs. Fescue. And then what did Mrs. Fescue do but turn huffy and begin spreading it around town that the aunt had led her to believe all this garbage, which was a flat-out lie, and Mrs. Fescue had only been trying to do the widow a good turn and maybe the poor old soul wasn't quite, you know, and perhaps the relatives should step in and do something."

"Did they?"

"They certainly did. Grace got her husband to have a little talk with Mrs. Fescue, and you know what Dr. Porble can be like when he loses his temper. He laid Mrs. Fescue out in lavender and threatened to sue her for slander and harassment and a few other things, anc it was just a terrible mess all around. She backed off, finally, but Grace says her aunt is by no means the first person who's had a go-round with Mrs. Fescue and some of them haven't been able to shake her off. Don't tell me we've fallen into her toils?"

"Perish the thought, but she's been hounding the Horsefalls for the past couple of months. I'd have had the minimal pleasure of seeing her in action this evening at the farm if I hadn't been down at the runestone with the president at the time. I gathered from the conversation later that she'd dropped in ostensibly to pay a condolence call. In fact, she managed to work off a spot of propaganda among the relatives about selling the property before the old folks kick off in order to avoid taxes and give everyone a fair shake."

"Was anybody listening?"

"Some of them, no doubt. Two were rather vehemently opposed."

Shandy told his wife about Eddie and Ralph. "Moreover, their families seemed to share their feelings about the old homestead."

"Perhaps they're each hoping to scoop the pot."

"I think it's more than that. Henny claims those two

are the only real Horsefalls in the tribe. With some people, family land is a sort of religion, you know."

"Yes, darling. You've never quite gotten over your father's having to sell the old Shandy place, have you?"

What happened after that is irrelevant to this narrative. Suffice it to say that both Shandys awoke the following morning happy in the knowledge they hadn't frittered away their whole evening in idle chatter.

After breakfast Helen betook herself to the Buggins Collection. Shandy dangled a spool on a string for Jane Austen to bat at, brooding as he did so about where to begin detecting what, or more probably whom. Even as he dangled, his problem was solved by the arrival of Mrs. Lomax, the dea ex machina who maintained order in faculty households and sometimes among the faculty themselves.

Mrs. Lomax had been Shandy's housekeeper for thirteen years before he married Helen. While the employer-employee relationship had always been punctiliously maintained, there was the case of long acquaintance between them. Moreover, Mrs. Lomax was a reliable informant. She either worked for, was related to, or belonged to some organization or other with half the population of Balaclava County, one or the other of whom was able to satisfy her lively curiosity about the other half. This morning she was as eager for Shandy's news as he was for hers, and lost no time getting to the point.

"Understand you were out to the Horsefalls' yesterday, Professor, when their hired man had that crazy accident."

"Strictly speaking, no. Professor Ames was, and he phoned me to come over."

"What for? Did he think Spurge had been done away with?"

Aha! So the rumors were flying already, as might have been expected. Shandy hedged. "Well—er—they're all elderly people, you know, and I suppose they got a bit flustered."

"Humph. Take more than a dead man to fluster old Hilda. Though she's always preferred 'em live and kicking, or so I've been told. Not that I'm one for idle talk, as you know."

Shandy certainly did know. There was nothing idle about Mrs. Lomax. She went to her gossip as energetically as she pursued the spring cobwebs in the ceiling corners. "One for the lads, was she?" he said by way of encouragement, steering Jane Austen away from the broom closet because after all Mrs. Lomax was being paid to work, not to chat, and a fool and his money were soon parted, as she herself would have been the first to remind him.

"Only reason Hilda never got married was that she was cute enough not to put herself in a position where she had to, according to what they say. Why, even my own grandfather—" Mrs. Lomax caught herself just in time. "But that's neither here nor there. I daresay there was never anything in it anyway and I wouldn't repeat it if there was. It's a poor bird that fouls its own nest, as my mother used to say. Did Mrs. Shandy buy that new mop? Scat, Jane. I can't have you swinging on my apron strings when I've got a floor to scrub."

"I expect she did if you told her to," said Shandy, plucking the infant feline off Mrs. Lomax's skirt and tickling its whiskers. "So Miss Horsefall is not quite the—er—sweet little old lady one might be led to expect?"

"About as sweet as a barrel of vinegar pickles." Mrs. Lomax had found the mop and was plying it with vigor. "Mind standing out of my way, Professor? I suppose when a person lives to a hundred and five you've got to make allowances, but I can tell you if Hilda Horsefall wasn't so old there wouldn't be many laying themselves out to make a big fuss over her. She's got a tongue on her, that one. Why, her great-niece-in-law Jolene—I don't know if you happen to have met my sister's husband's cousin Jolene that married one of the Horsefall boys?"

"As a matter of fact I met her last night. She was at the farm—er—helping out."

"Yes, that's Jolene, always ready to do a hand's turn for anybody though she hasn't had an easy life of it herself, by any manner or means. Not that Eddie isn't a worker, I'll say that for him, but it's been hard scratching with the kids and all, though the oldest is married with a child of his own. Premature," Mrs. Lomas added belligerently.

Shandy nodded. Premature babies were common in Balaclava County. Sometimes they weighed in at eleven pounds or better.

"Anyway, as I started to say, you can't imagine what Jolene's had to put up with from that old Aunt Hilda of her husband's. Eddie's fond of the old besom, which is no more than he ought to be, I suppose, since she's his own flesh and blood. I always did say families ought to stick together no matter what. By the way, is it true the Feldsters' daughter wants a divorce?"

"I'm afraid I can't tell you that," said Shandy, who'd often wondered why the young woman's father didn't. "So Jolene has a rough time of it with her in-laws, does she?"

"Oh, not her in-laws. Eddie's mother thinks the sun rises and sets in Jolene. She has her own little place in the senior citizens' housing project over at West Lumpkin now, and works in the school cafeteria two days a week. It's awful for old folks when there's so much going out and nothing coming in. Let 'em keep busy as long as they can, I always say. Anyway, Jolene takes her grocery shopping in the car and has her over to supper faithful every Friday night and they go to Eastern Star together, which is more than a lot of women's own daughters would do. Jane, if you jump into that scrub pail you're going to be one mighty sorry little kitten. The father's dead these fifteen years and more. Worked himself into the grave, and never a nickel's worth of help did he get from Henny and Hilda, I can tell you."

"I doubt if they'd have had a nickel to give," said Shandy.

"That's as may be, but they've got that big place all to themselves and you'd think they might have done something. But anyway, as I was saying about Jolene, she's as decent a woman as they make 'em, but do you think that old Hilda would give her the time of day? Jolene says she can't so much as pick up a dishrag to help in the kitchen out there but what Aunt Hilda's right at her elbow telling her she's holding it the wrong way around.

It's got so she downright hates to go there, though of course she wouldn't admit it on account of Eddie and the kids."

"I understand she and Eddie's cousin Ralph's wife don't hit it off any too well."

Mrs. Lomax looked surprised. "First I've heard of it. They were thick enough last week at the First Parish Church Strawberry Festival. Marie's cousin Bertha that married Charlie Swope was running it—just stand away from the sink a minute if you don't mind, Professor—so Marie and Jolene thought they'd show up and surprise Bertha and let their families get their own suppers for once. I went myself, of course, because Bertha was Mr. Lomax's cousin as well and I wouldn't want it said around that I was slighting the Lomaxes even though some mightn't blame me, all things considered."

Shandy did not want to hear the considerations. "Would Charlie and Bertha be the parents of Cronkite Swope, the reporter for the *Fane and Pennon?*"

"If that don't beat all!" cried Mrs. Lomax. "For thirteen years I've never once heard you take any interest in the community and now it turns out you know the whole place like the back of your hand. Yes, that's who they are, though it was a terrible disappointment to them when Cronk wouldn't go into the soap factory with his brothers. Huntley's going to be foreman of the rendering department, they say, and Brinkley's in charge of the sesses."

"Is he, by George? I thought they only had sesses in crossword puzzles. Well, there's a black sheep in every family, though I must say I found Cronkite a personable young chap. He happened to be the one who found Lumpkin's body, you know."

"No! My own late husband's cousin's son, and Bertha didn't so much as bother to ring me up and tell me." Mrs. Lomax's mouth settled into a thin line and her eyes began to glitter as she disentangled Jane Austen from the wet mop.

"It's—er—quite possible Mrs. Swope didn't know," Shandy replied, appalled by having been the inadvertent cause of a family feud. "Young Swope stayed at the Horsefalls' for some time, then I brought him back here for dinner, then he had to go to the paper to write up his story. He probably never got to talk to his parents at all, and naturally he'd be depending on the—er—power of the press to keep his relatives informed. Business before pleasure, as you yourself have often remarked. Getting back to Mrs. Eddie and Mrs. Ralph, I'm relieved to hear they are in fact on amicable terms, even though I'd been led to believe the contrary."

"By that old Hilda Horsefall, I expect," sniffed Mrs. Lomax, reluctant to let go of a good mad now that she'd worked herself up to it. "The way she keeps at 'em, like as not they do bicker a little when they're over to the farm. They can't very well take it out on her when she's the one who invited them, can they? Jolene was brought up to have manners, which is more than you can say for some, and so was Bertha even though she did marry a Swope."

"What's wrong with the Swopes?"

"Well, they're funny," said Mrs. Lomax. "Look at Cronk, giving up a good chance—"

"To succeed among the sesses," Shandy finished for her. "I see what you mean. Miss Horsefall does seem to bring out the combative spirit in people. I hear she and her nephew had a battle with Canute Lumpkin the antique dealer a while back. He took them to court to get custody of his cousin, didn't he?"

"To get custody of the money, you mean. Nutie the Cutie never did give a rap for anybody's carcass but his own. You met him?"

"Oh yes. Mrs. Shandy and I stopped in there one afternoon. She—er—didn't buy anything."

"No flies on Mrs. Shandy." This from the housekeeper was the supreme accolade. "Didn't stay long either, I'll bet. Jane, if you don't behave yourself I'm going to shut you in the broom closet."

Shandy rescued the kitten, who looked up at him with the eyes of a tiny angel, started climbing his shoulder, and got her little pointed tail across his upper lip like a mustache. He eased her around to the back of his neck and remarked, "I'd say there were no flies on—er—Nutie, either."

"Cute as a fox and twice as big a stinker if you don't

mind me saying so. He must be over there snickering and rubbing those fat hands of his together right this minute. Been scheming and contriving for that inheritance all these years, and didn't it fall straight into his lap without him having to lift a finger."

"M'yes," said Shandy. "Well, I mustn't take up any more of your time, Mrs. Lomax. I expect Mrs. Shandy will be home at noontime to find out if you want any more mops or whatever. Jane, why don't you go take a catnap? Mrs. Lomax and I both have work to do."

CHAPTER 9

Shandy stepped across the Crescent, found Tim running his fingers aimlessly through a pot of humus like a miser fondling his gold, and suggested they drop out to the Horsefalls'. As they'd expected, Henny was attempting to get through the chores alone and not making much headway, so they lent a hand.

"Cripes," said Tim half an hour later, taking a swipe at his moist brow, "this is a damn sight harder work than it was fifty years ago. How the hell do you keep going all day, Henny?"

"Have to." The octogenarian heaved his manure fork with a lifetime's expertise. "If I ever laid down to rest myself, I'd never get up again. Eddie an' Ralph said they'd be over later, but what good's later? Farm chores always has to be done now."

"Or sooner," Shandy grunted.

Though considerably the youngest of the lot, he wasn't finding the job any cinch, either. Still, it was good to be out in a barn again. Maybe Helen was right about his never having got over losing the family place. He could buy a farm of his own now, but what was the point? He wasn't a farmer anymore, and Helen hadn't the faintest conception of what it meant to be a farmer's wife. If they were twenty years younger with kids coming along—but they weren't. And they had a damn good life as it was and what was the sense in bitching over what might have been? He swung his own pitchfork, noting with some satisfaction that at least he hadn't quite lost the knack.

"Well, that much is done," said Tim at last. "How about the hens?"

"Fergy was over an' fed 'em for us 'bout seven o'clock.
Picked up the eggs, too. I was kind o' scared to let 'im,
he's such a hulk of a man, but he stepped around them
roosts spry as a cat. Says he gets plenty o' practice
threadin' his way betwixt an' between them tables full o'
junk he's got over there. He had to go somewheres in the
truck, so he's going to stop an' pick up some groceries for
Aunt Hilda on the way back. Wouldn't take a cent o'
money to buy 'em with, neither. 'Hell,' he says, 'I ain't
got no woman to bake a pie nor nothin' an' what's a
neighbor for?' Fergy was always good to Spurge. He's
goin' to shut up shop tomorrow so's he can come to the
funeral."

"Decent of him," said Shandy.

"Yep, it's at times like this you know who your friends
are. And who they ain't. Oh, dyin' Jesus! Here she comes
now."

Shandy would have known whom Henny was referring
to even if the lettering on the side of the purple Dodge
that was stopping in the barnyard hadn't read "Loretta
Fescue, Realtor," and even if the large woman who got
out of it weren't wearing a purple dress, a purple hat,
and bright purple flat-heeled buckskin oxfords. The man
she had with her was also large and purple, at least in
the face. Intuition whispered that this was Gunder Gaffson the developer, and intuition did not err.

He and Tim lurked in the barn as Henny went out to
meet them, pitchfork in hand, just as a militant colonist
might have confronted a marauding Redcoat. Mrs. Fescue was not afraid of pitchforks. She advanced toward
Henny, all smiles and sympathy.

"We thought we'd drop by and express our condolences."

"You already expressed 'em," was his polite reply.
"Last night. Wasn't no call for you to come again."

"Oh, but we wanted to. You see, Mr. Gaffson under-
stands so well what problems you have to face now, all
alone with no help on this big, unmanageable old place."

Shandy and Tim exchanged nods and stepped forth,
also with their pitchforks at the ready. They were just
getting nicely settled for a staring match when Cronkite
Swope charged into the yard on his motorbike.

"Hi, everybody. Say, Mr. Gaffson, this is luck. I was going to interview you next. It is true you're about to be indicted for violations of the building code in your new condominium development? What about that sewage overflow? I understand the abutters are petitioning for a cease and desist order on—"

"No comment!" roared Gaffson, and stalked back to the car. "Mrs. Fescue, if you're quite through wasting my time on wildgoose chases—"

"But, Mr. Gaffson!" yelled Cronkite and Loretta simultaneously. The realtor started to say something else, then took a closer look at Henny's two new hired men, nodded with a meaningful smile, and drove her angry client away.

"What was she smirking about?" Tim asked.

"I think she twigged us," Shandy replied. "Nice try, Swope, but I'm afraid it will take more than a cease and desist order to get that pair off the Horsefalls' backs. One hears rumors that Mrs. Fescue is a hard woman to say no to."

"I'll say she is! You ought to hear my Aunt Betsy Lomax—she's not really my aunt, only some kind of cousin by marriage, but I always call her Aunt Betsy. Come to think of it, she helps out at your house, doesn't she? Last time I saw her she said you and Mrs. Shandy were—" Cronkite, who had after all only got to Lesson Eleven of the Great Journalists' Correspondence Course, blushed and floundered. "I mean, she sort of hinted there might be a little stranger in the Shandy household one of these days."

"Our little stranger has already arrived," Shandy told him gravely.

"Already? Gee, that was pretty fast work, wasn't it? I mean, you and Mrs. Shandy have only been married—" Cronkite realized the implication of what he was saying, turned bright cerise with crimson spots, and shut up.

"Since January," Shandy finished for him. "The little stranger was last seen trying to fall into Mrs. Lomax's scrub pail. You met her last night when she climbed up your pant leg and did her trapeze act on your necktie. Always check your data, Swope."

"Oh, hey, she meant Jane Austen. That's pretty funny." Swope would no doubt have laughed if he hadn't been in such a hurry. "Speaking of data, I've already been to see President Svenson, and I'm here to take a picture of the runestone if Mr. Horsefall doesn't mind. Gosh, this is the biggest story I've covered in my whole journalistic career! Except the time the sprinkler system went crazy in the soap factory."

Without waiting for Henny's formal permission, Cronkite checked to make sure his Polaroid camera hadn't bounced out of the carrier and gunned his motorbike over the swale beyond which lay the hottest scoop since that long-to-be remembered night when the massed barbershop quartets of all Balaclava County had sloshed down Lumpkin Avenue in hip boots singing, "I'm Forever Blowing Bubbles."

Henny didn't give two hoots whether Cronkite photographed the runestone or not. He was too busy fulminating about that dad-blagged Loretta Fescue and the equally dratted Gunder Gaffson.

"Is Swope right about Gaffson's being in trouble with the housing authority?" Shandy managed to ask when Henny stopped cussing long enough to get his breath back.

"If he ain't he dern well ought to be. Way he throws them shacks together's a damn disgrace. Ain't nothin' holdin' 'em together but the wallpaper, from what I hear. Ralph's son that married the Bronson girl was savin' up to buy one till he found out from a friend of his'n that had got stuck with one what a gyp they was. Gaffson's right there with 'is hand out when it comes to the money, but if it's a case o' fixin' somethin' that ought to work an' don't, you might as well forget about askin'. An' the prices is enough to curl your hair, if you had any."

Shandy, who was getting a bit thinner on top than he cared to be reminded of, winced. As Henny took off his old felt hat to polish his own bare skull with a bandanna, though, Shandy realized no offense was meant and therefore withdrew his umbrage. They worked along for another hour or so, then Fergy arrived with Miss Hilda's groceries. A short time later, though none too soon for Ames and Shandy, the old lady came out to beat on the contraption of strung-together horseshoes that served the Horsefalls for a dinner bell.

" 'Tain't much of a meal," Miss Horsefall apologized in accordance with time-honored farmwife etiquette as she sat them down to fried potatoes, fried ham, fried eggs, coleslaw, stewed rhubarb, pickles, and several kinds of pie.

"Darn sight better'n I'd get if I was by myself," said Fergy, shoveling in the food with enough enthusiasm to make any cook feel she had not labored in vain. "Mind passin' the pickles, Henny? An' the bread? An' the apple butter? Might as well stoke up the ol' furnace while I've got the chance."

"You paid for it, you might as well enjoy it," Henny grunted.

"Heck, all I bought was the ham, which was no more than what one neighbor ought to do for another. Anyway, I'll be takin' most of it back with me at the rate I'm goin' here. These sure are good pickles, Miss Hilda. Remind me of the kind my mother would o' made, maybe, if she'd ever got around to it. Ma did open a great can o' spaghetti, though."

"Nice way to talk about your own mother," Miss Hilda sniffed, slapping another slab of ham on his plate. "How long's she been gone?"

"Gosh, I can't quite remember. Funny how it slipped my mind. I guess there's some things you don't want to remember."

Shandy, eating fried potatoes, recognized all too easily what Fergy was really saying. The man probably hadn't the faintest idea whether his mother was living or dead and didn't give a damn either way, and no doubt he had good reason not to. Whoever she was, she certainly hadn't strained herself to teach him table manners. Shandy was using his own paper napkin to set a good example when one of the younger Horsefalls burst into the kitchen.

"Hi, Aunt Hilda. Am I too late for dinner?"

"Ralphie! Why ain't you in school?"

"This was our last day. I only went because we were burning the principal in effigy. After that there was nothing left to hang around for, so I thought I'd come and see if I could help Uncle Henny. I mean, like if he wanted me to drive the tractor or anything," Ralphie said innocently, helping himself to just about everything that was left on the table.

"How about like if you was to drive a manure fork for a while?" Henny grunted.

"Whatever you say, Unc. I cleaned out the hen house last Saturday, didn't I? At least cows don't have chicken lice."

"Neither would the hens if they was took care of proper."

Miss Hilda made the remark automatically, as if her heart wasn't in it. She had her hair elegantly crimped today, suggesting a night on kid curlers and a resolution that if Sven Svenson happened by to suggest another walk she wasn't going to be caught unprepared.

A vague uneasiness that had been at the back of Peter Shandy's mind all morning began to crystallize into full-fledged anxiety. Now that young Ralph was here to help Henny, it might be the part of prudence to get Tim back to the Crescent for a rest, as his daughter-in-law had ordered. Laurie had strong-armed her elderly father-in-law into getting his first medical checkup since he'd been rejected for the draft during World War II, and he'd been found to have an elevated blood pressure, which wasn't surprising considering the number of years he'd lived with his wife, Jemima, before her sudden, lurid demise.

They thanked Miss Hilda for the dinner, told her they'd be back later, maybe, and went out to the car. As Tim paused to impart a few words of wisdom on the proper composting of poultry manure, in which, oddly enough, the boy appeared to be passionately interested, Fergy caught up with Peter.

"Say, Professor, can I talk to you a second?"

"Of course."

The question seemed to be redundant since Fergy had already been talking to, at, or around him for upward of an hour, but Shandy was prepared to listen to whatever the junk dealer had on his mind. It proved to be the runestone.

"I dunno why, Professor, but I'm worried about it. I

wish to hell Miss Hilda hadn't got Cronk Swope started on them runes."

"What runes?"

"Why, the ones he found on—oh, I get it. I'm not supposed to know. Huh!" Fergy didn't look offended, only somewhat amused as far as Shandy could tell through the orange whiskers. "Try to keep anything secret around this burg."

"It was just that—er—Miss Horsefall didn't want all the youngsters running down there and tearing their good clothes on the briers," Shandy half apologized. "We realized, of course, that Swope's—er—journalistic instincts must inevitably lead to public disclosure."

"Huh. Name me one soul in Balaclava County who ain't got journalistic instincts, will you? Look, I haven't been shootin' my mouth off and I don't intend to. When Henny told me about them runes, I warned him not to talk too much. But I knew damn well Cronk would be writin' up a piece for his paper an' sendin' it around to half a dozen more, like as not. Can't blame the kid for tryin' to make a name for himself, can you? It's just that—I dunno. I got a funny feelin', that's all."

"Could you—er—describe this funny feeling?"

"Well, see, when I first heard about that runestone, I thought it was a pack o' foolishness, like they usually are. But then with Spurge dyin' that awful way just when Cronk an' Miss Hilda was headin' down to see it, well, hell. It was kind of like a warnin', if you get what I mean. Like as if there was somethin' in that oak grove that didn't want to be disturbed, if you get what I mean. Sounds crazy, don't it? Go ahead an' laugh if you want to."

"I shouldn't dream of laughing," Shandy assured him. "I'm worried myself, if it makes you feel any better. Setting aside any possible—er—mystical connection between Spurge's death and the runestone, there's no doubt that the publicity about the two coming so close together is bound to be hard on the Horsefalls. Being a friend of theirs, you naturally feel uneasy, even though you may not be quite sure why. It's simply because you know something's going to happen as a result of what already has occurred, and you're not sure what."

"Yeah, that could be it." Fergy didn't sound the least bit convinced. "It's just that every time I think o' that runestone . . ." His voice dwindled away.

"You never knew it was there?"

"Hell, no. How should I? I ain't from around here. I don't even know how I got here, to tell you the God's honest truth. I was always sort of a wanderer, I guess you'd say. I kind o' drifted into the area lookin' for somethin' to do an' met a man that run a flea market. He was doin' pretty good an' it didn't look like too hard of a job, so I worked with him awhile to learn the ropes, then struck out for myself. I stuck around here because the pickin's wasn't bad. Folks are more into antiques an' stuff. But I've only had the barn for maybe twelve or fourteen years."

"Swope gave me to understand you'd been around here a lot longer than that."

"Ah, he's just a kid. Twelve years is more'n half a lifetime to him. Anyway, by the time I come on the scene, I guess that runestone must o' been all grown over. The old folks had forgot about it an' the young ones didn't know. I never heard of it till Spurge got to ramblin' about it the other night, like I mentioned before, an' then I figured he didn't know what he was talkin' about. Goes to show, don't it? Maybe that's why I got this creepy feelin'. Spurge mentions the stone an' then he gets killed by limestone."

"Good Lord, so he did. I hadn't thought of that."

"Yeah, makes you sort o' wonder what's goin' to happen next, don't it? If I was Cronk Swope, I'd sure as hell get the brakes on my bike checked, him bein' the one who—cripes, Professor, you must think I'm soft as a grape, goin' on like this. A man can't help wonderin', that's all. I better quit gabbin' an' go unload my truck. Spurge always used to help me. Goin' to feel strange doin' it alone," Fergy muttered as he climbed aboard his fairly new and lavishly jazzed-up vehicle.

Shandy stood staring down at the hard-packed driveway for a while, then collected Tim and went back to the Crescent.

CHAPTER 10

"Just a tiny sliver," said Helen. "I shouldn't eat another bite, but it's so good I can't resist."

Peter could have resisted easily enough, but he reflected that Laurie's cooking was at least a damn sight better than Jemima's and she ought to be encouraged to keep it up, so he took another sliver, too. It was worth a belly-ache to watch Tim enjoying a pleasant evening in his own home.

The dining room suite Jemima had bought at the time of her marriage to Timothy Ames and proceeded to bury under a quarter-century's accumulation of clutter had been excavated and cleaned up. Roy and Laurie had painted the wainscot and dado in the dining room a soft antique red and papered the upper half of the wall with a marvelous allover pattern of exotic roosters. They'd switched their biological researches from penguins to poultry, and Laurie went in for relevance.

The main course, not unexpectedly, had been chicken prepared from a recipe Laurie had got in Peru, or maybe Patagonia. They'd had whiskeys by the fire and wine with dinner, and Peter was feeling blurred around the edges even though it was only about half-past seven. After working all morning at the Horsefalls' he'd taken a notion to build a rockery in his own yard as a surprise for Helen. Now he wished he'd taken a nap instead. Well, they wouldn't have to stay long. Tim always turned in early. So, for different reasons, did the newly-weds.

"Shall we go back to the fireplace for coffee?" Laurie suggested after they'd finished the rather strange dessert. "Oh, excuse me a second. There's the phone."

"I'll get it."

Roy, who'd never lifted a hand except under duress while Jemima was alive, leaped to oblige. He was a good-looking young chap, Shandy thought. He'd inherited his mother's build, which was a good thing since Jemima had been at least a foot taller than her husband, and her reddish hair. It had been so long since anybody had seen Tim's face that there was no telling how closely Roy resembled his father, but he didn't look like his mother and he did have the old man's feisty sense of humor, along with his shrewd brown eyes and his ability to become totally absorbed by the job in hand. Having been smart enough or lucky enough to marry a competent, sensible, good-tempered woman who not only shared his interests but clearly thought he was the cat's whiskers, Roy should be heading for a far happier life than his father ever had.

He didn't look happy when he returned to the dining room, however. "That was Henny Horsefall, Dad. There's been something in the paper about a stone getting ruined on his property—I didn't understand it, but anyway he's having trouble with trespassers. He called the police but they wouldn't come, so he wants you and Professor Shandy."

"Stone getting ruined?" said Shandy. "Are you sure he didn't say runestone?"

"Probably he did. Why?"

"There's a runestone on his property. Young Cronkite Swope from the *Fane and Pennon* rediscovered it yesterday, and President Svenson's uncle went out there last night. They think it may be a real one. Swope has undoubtedly written something about it for the paper, but that doesn't come out till tomorrow."

"No, it came today," said Laurie. "Just before you people arrived. Some boy came whizzing around on a bicycle. I went out because I heard the thump when he threw the paper up on the porch, and thought it might be you. I didn't take time to look at it."

"Where is it, quick?"

"In the woodbox." She fished it out. "I almost used it to start the fire."

"Good God! They've put out an extra."

Shandy stared aghast at what was usually a placid enough little weekly. DID VIKING CURSE KILL LAST OF LUMPKINS? was plastered across the front page. QUICKLIME CLAIMS HEIR TO FORTUNE ON HORSEFALL FARM. There was more of the same, but he didn't stop to read it.

"Come on, Tim. We'd better get out there. You too, Roy."

"How about us?" Laurie demanded. "Helen and I demand equal rights."

"Forget it. That's the New Hampshire road and they're probably getting a bunch of drunks from God knows where."

"Then Daddy Ames can't—"

"Daddy Ames can still hold a pitchfork," snapped her father-in-law.

"Then we can boil oil," said Helen. "Isn't that the traditional woman's role during invasions? Come on, Laurie, at least we can drive them over and move the car away where it won't get a rock through the windshield."

This was no time to argue. They piled into the Ameses' new car and headed for Lumpkin Corners. Before they got to Fergy's Bargain Barn, it was clear they were heading into a massive traffic jam.

"Let us out here," Shandy commanded. "Don't get trapped in this mess, Laurie. Turn around and go back, fast. Get hold of President Svenson and any able-bodied males you can find around campus. Bring them over here and send them in through that old logging road—it's by the big boulder on the right, about a quarter of a mile back. Tell them to guard the runestone or people will be hacking it to pieces for souvenirs. And if you happen to come across that bastard Swope, shove him head-first into the cow pond with my kindest personal regards."

Shandy did Swope a grave injustice. When he reached the Horsefall farm with Roy a close second and Tim a very poor third, he found Cronkite already manning the barricades, aghast at the monster he'd unleashed.

"Hey, you can't come—oh, Professor Shandy! Gosh, I never thought—"

"Obviously. Know anybody within running distance who owns a mean bulldog?"

"Would a couple of dobermans—?"

"Go get 'em. *Schnell!*"

Cronkite vanished at a little under the speed of light. Shandy took a rapid survey. Sightseers were milling around regardless of the young plants Henny and the late Spurge had toiled to get started, knocking down the wire around the hen run, disturbing the cows, chipping off bits of the spreader where Spurge had met his doom, demanding, "Where's the runestone?" as if they had a right to know.

Eddie, Ralph, and an assortment of sons and neighbors were trying to cope, doing a lot of shoving and yelling but not accomplishing much. Up at the house, though, all was in hand. Miss Hilda had borrowed the Lewises' geese. She and some other women were keeping them herded close to the house. Anybody who got too near was confronted by a hissing gander with great wings beating savagely and neck outstretched to attack. Henny was standing in the barn door with a loaded shotgun, daring anybody to come in. The buildings were safe. The grounds were the problem. Cars and tramping feet could ruin the place if something wasn't done to keep them out.

Luckily it was still daylight. "Here," Shandy said, handing out all the pitchforks he could find. "Four of you get down by the end of the driveway. Surround any car that tries to turn in and tell 'em to stay the hell out if they don't want their tires punctured. Tim, take my notebook and pen. Write down the numbers of any cars already parked on the property. We'll make damn sure they get tickets for trespassing and you can tell 'em so if they ask. Ralphie, take this shovel and go with Professor Ames. If anybody tries to interfere with him, let them know you're not there for fun. The rest of you guard the plowed fields. Head people over toward the oak grove. They won't get far when they strike the squirrel briers. Now clear off. I'm going to start the tractor."

He drove the noisy old clatterbox straight down to the mouth of the driveway, scattering trespassers right and left. "Listen to me," he bellowed. "This is private property. You have no right to trespass and it's damned indecent to create a disturbance the night before a funeral."

"Boo! We want to see the runestone," yelled one young smart-mouth, and others took up the chant.

"It's not here," Shandy roared. "Go back down the old logging road. Half a mile past Fergy's Bargain Barn. You'll have to walk in because it's overgrown. Somebody will be there to show you the way."

He hoped.

Cronkite's arrival with two huge, lean black dobermans straining at their leashes helped to convince some of them. His gasping "Help me! I can't hold 'em" convinced a few more.

Ralph took one of the dogs, gave his pitchfork to a willing young neighbor, and went to guard the path Swope had cleared yesterday to the runestone. Eddie took the other up to the barn, to give Henny some relief. Shandy started patrolling back and forth with the tractor. Gradually something like order began to take shape on the farm, though what was happening down along the logging road he didn't care to think. He could only pray Helen and Laurie had managed to bring Thorkjeld over there in time to guard the runestone.

Some determined invaders had braved the squirrel briers, but by now enough of them were trapped among the viciously clinging vines to serve as direful warnings to the rest. Swope was up on the tractor with Shandy, going wherever the crowds were thickest and most unruly, snapping pictures as fast as his Polaroid would allow.

"Boy, what a story this will make," he chortled, conveniently forgetting who'd started the brouhaha with his previous story. "WHERE WERE POLICE WHEN RIOT RAGED? WHY WON'T CHIEF PROTECT PROPERTY SISTER WANTS TO SELL DEVELOPER?"

"Don't ask me," snarled Shandy, who was pretty well fed up by now. "Ask him. Could you get through that traffic jam with your motorbike? Take some of these pictures to show him what's happening out here. Leave the best ones with me, in case he takes a notion to confiscate them for evidence or some damn thing and keep them out of the paper. If we don't get police protection there'll be hell to pay once it gets dark. Ah, I see we're getting reinforcements from the college."

He'd spotted a few Balaclava Busters football helmets

among the mob. Helen and Laurie must have managed to rally the troops. "But there aren't many men around campus right now, and they're not trained for this sort of thing anyway. Oh, Christ, why didn't I think to have them bring in Bashan of Balaclava?"

"Huh?"

"Our prize bull. He's roughly the size of a tyrannosaurus rex and ought to scare the pants off anybody who comes lurking around the barn, though in fact he's fairly amiable as bulls go. We'll get him over here tomorrow. Horsefall will have to put chastity belts on the cows, I suppose. Bashan takes his profession seriously. Get going, will you?"

Cronkite got. Shandy turned over the tractor to Roy and went on foot to reconnoiter. Traffic on the twisty two-lane road was backed up God alone knew how far by now. He hoped Helen and Laurie had managed to get clear after they'd delivered their passengers. How he and the Ameses would get home, if they ever did, would have to be figured out later.

He made the mistake of trying to use sweet reason with a couple of louts who were trying to uproot one of the Horsefall gateposts and found himself embroiled in a fistfight that was only resolved by some of the stalwart lads of Balaclava, using the old flying wedge formation. As he was dusting himself off and wishing he'd had time to change out of his good suit, he heard a thunder of hooves and a hearty "Hi-yo, Horsefall!" The Lolloping Lumberjacks of Lumpkin Corners had arrived, spearheaded by a disheveled but triumphant reporter on a motorbike.

"The cops gave me the runaround," Cronkite panted, "so I called out the cavalry. Okay, Professor?"

"Good thinking, Swope."

"It was your idea really," the youth replied modestly. "When you mentioned about the bull, I thought of horses. Want me to try the Headless Horsemen of Hoddersville?"

"Let's—er—hold them in reserve for the moment. Get a few of the mounted men out in the road directing traffic, will you? If we can break up this jam, maybe some of these oafs will go home."

"Sure thing, Professor."

Cronkite began deploying his new recruits. Shandy decided it was safe enough now for him to leave the scene of major turmoil and find out what was happening down by the runestone. He walked along the narrow road, anxiously scanning the tangle of cars for any sight of his wife and Laurie. To his relief, he didn't find them. With any luck they were safely back at the Crescent now, drinking the coffee he could so well have done with a cup of himself and talking over their experiences as women have such a profound need to do.

Fergy's parking lot was choked with vehicles. The Bargain Barn appeared to be doing a land-office business thanks, no doubt, to the spate of traffic. Fergy had a couple of helpers, Shandy noticed. There was a woman presiding over the cashbox wearing three or four sweaters although the evening was still balmy. Perhaps she was the current Mrs. Fergy, or a reasonable facsimile thereof.

He also noticed how dark it was getting. The college owned some portable searchlights. If the Lumberjacks could get the road passable, maybe they could be got over here. He'd have to ask the president, if Svenson was in fact among those present.

The logging road toward which Shandy had been so glibly directing sightseers all evening even though he himself had never gone up it proved easier to find than he'd expected. A huge boulder did in fact mark its opening and a cordon of Balaclava students in a remarkable assortment of protective coverings had it well policed.

"You'll have to go to the end of the line, sir, and wait your turn," said an individual wearing a black velvet riding cap, a fencing visor, hockey shin guards, and a baseball catcher's chest pad.

"I'm Professor Shandy."

"Oh, sorry, sir." The student lifted her steel-mesh mask for a better look. "We're trying to keep them from all jamming in at once."

"And you're making an admirable job of it. Keep up the good work. I have to see President Svenson about searchlights. Is he in there?"

The visored vigilante so far forgot herself as to giggle. "Can't you hear him?"

"Now that you mention it, I do catch a distant rumble. I thought it must be an oncoming thunderstorm. I gather he also has the situation well in hand."

"With nickel-plated knobs on, Professor. Walk straight in and don't trip over the blackberry vines. Nobody remembered to bring any Band-Aids. Move along there, please."

The latter remark was addressed not to Shandy but to the lines of people who were entering the road shoving and snickering, and coming back awestruck and silent. Shandy joined the ingoers and found out why.

By now it was getting quite dark there under the oak leaves. The runestone stood in a little pool of yellow light provided by a battery lantern the president in his infinite wisdom had thought to fetch along. Over and behind it loomed a shape such as nightmares are made of.

Thorkjeld Svenson was wearing gray work pants and a dark gray flannel shirt with the sleeves turned back halfway to the elbows. Lost in the gathering murk, the gray clothing turned his body to an amorphous mass. The great hands and forearms, the noble yet ferocious head loomed impossibly large, incredibly threatening, as though the spirit imprisoned in the stone had sprung forth as a living menace. The fact that Svenson was leaning negligently on his own personal forged-to-order double-bitted ax with a handle five feet long did not tend to dispel the illusion. Anybody blind enough or mad enough to stretch forth a hand toward the runes caused him to emit a rumbling "Arrgh" that could reduce even the boldest to a palpitating jelly.

"God, President," Shandy gasped, "you scared the hell out of me."

"Good." Svenson shifted his position slightly, striking a dull glitter from the sharpened ax edge in the lantern's rays. "What's happening?"

"Riot, rapine, and general pandemonium, but I think we're getting it under control. The students are doing a great job."

"Damn well better."

"What's worrying me now is the light situation. Could we get those portable floodlights over here from the college?"

"Why the hell not? Call Buildings and Grounds. No, don't. Yackasses all goofing off this time of night. Security. Lomax boys. Tell 'em I said get a move on. Arrgh," he added as some near sighted maniac got too close to the runestone.

"How long do you plan to stay here, President?" Shandy asked.

"As long as Orm needs me," replied the great man simply.

"In that case, *requiescat in pace*. Mosquitoes bothering you much?"

"They wouldn't dare."

He should have known better than to ask. Shandy slapped at a whining pestilence that was trying to feast off his own less august person and took his departure, remembering to look suitably grave, as indeed he felt.

Out on the road, things were looking up. At least the traffic was beginning to move, though at a crawl, as the Lumberjacks lolloped up and down the lines urging drivers on. Nobody cared to argue with them. Their steeds were no slim-ankled equine playthings but mighty Belgians, Clydesdales, and Suffolk Punches that could tow an automobile or demolish one with a few well-placed kicks. So far the horses hadn't been required to do so and probably wouldn't have to. Like Thorkjeld Svenson, they were intimidating enough just to look at.

Nor were the riders puny racetrack jockeys with schoolboy figures and secret yearnings to write like Dick Francis, but burly farmers raised on home-pressed cider and home-fried doughnuts whose rhetoric was unpolished but whose views on damn fools who didn't know enough to get their cussed carcasses out of where they didn't belong were loud and efficacious. In short, when a Lumberjack told you to git, you got.

Spectators were still entering the barnyard to view the by now perfectly clean spreader where Spurge Lumpkin had met his ghastly doom, but they weren't getting any farther and word was beginning to spread that there really wasn't much of anything to see. Shandy saw that Roy was letting young Ralphie drive the tractor now, and moseyed on up to the house.

He was familiar enough with geese to be no more than

reasonably intimidated by their hissing and flapping. He dodged his way through the flock with only minor attacks on his pant legs and put in his SOS to the college. After considerable bickering and a liberal use of President Svenson's name, not to mention some of the president's favorite expletives, he got a promise to have the battery-operated floodlights shipped over to Lumpkin Corners as forthwith as traffic conditions would permit. Then he called home, got no answer, dialed the Ameses', and found, as he'd hoped, that Helen and Laurie were there drinking his coffee.

"What's happening, Peter?" Helen asked. "Do you need more helpers? We've already scared up as many of the students as we could, but we might try scouting around down in the town."

"No need. The Mounties are on the job." He explained about Swope's alerting the Lolloping Lumberjacks. "And I believe the Headless Horsemen are planning to take over the late shift. I've just arranged with Security to send us some portable floodlights. All in all, it looks as if the tide of battle has turned."

"Is Daddy Ames all right?" Laurie piped into the phone.

"Having a whale of a time. When last seen, he was cleaning Henny Horsefall's old over-and-under."

"Good heavens, he isn't shooting at people! He's blind as a bat."

"Oh no. I believe Henny let off a few blasts of rock salt earlier on. He's pretty sore about all this, as you can imagine. He was all set to give young Swope a pantload for writing that article, but the young idiot's been knocking himself out to make amends, so it appears that Horsefall's decided to forgive and forget. So long as Swope stays out of range, anyhow."

"And Roy? What's he doing?"

"Commanding the heavy armored division. That reminds me, would you call Security right away and ask them to bring along a few spare cans of gasoline for the tractor? I don't know whether Horsefall has any or not."

"Sieglinde phoned a while back to see if we'd heard from anyone." That was Helen again. "She says Thorkjeld's uncle is having fits about having been left at home. Apparently he had a date with Miss Horsefall."

"He wants to rune her reputation, if you ask me. Tell Sieglinde the president has the situation under control, as she might expect. God knows when we'll be home. Don't forget about that gas. We need the tractor."

Peter hung up, grabbed a cup of the coffee Miss Horsefall and her goosegirls had prepared, and went back to the fray. It was really dark now and, as he'd anticipated, the new crowd that were bulling their way through the cordon made the earlier lot seem in retrospect like a bunch of Sunday school picnickers. What they needed was light.

He collected Roy Ames and Cronkite Swope. The three of them spent an interesting quarter-hour fiddling wires on the illegally parked cars. No doubt their owners would be surprised to find their headlights on at high beam, and no doubt a good many of them would have run-down batteries to contend with, and no doubt there'd be a few more fistfights and a lot more profanity, but Shandy went right on fiddling. In his considered opinion, it served the bastards right.

CHAPTER 11

Peter Shandy was not sure when or how he got to bed. He had some faint recollection that a bus came over from the college to collect the president and his cortege. He had a dim notion that Roy Ames boosted both him and Tim aboard, and that one of the Lomax brothers who worked for Security was driving, though it might have been their sister-in-law herself for all he knew. He was out on his feet by then.

Long after the traffic had been set in motion and dispersed, the invasion of trespassers quelled, and the last tussle over who turned on whose headlights quieted down, a Lumpkinton police car had at last appeared. Shandy vaguely recalled that the two officers in the car had threatened to run Henny Horsefall in for disturbing the police and that the Lolloping Lumberjacks, respectable citizens and taxpayers though they were, had backed their mounts up in a circle around the cruiser and prepared to have their trusty steeds kick the living hell out of it if the cops didn't lay off their old friend and comrade Henny; and furthermore where the hell had the cops been when they were needed, and if they thought Town Meeting was going to vote them the raise they'd been bitching for on the strength of tonight's performance, they'd better think again. The Lumberjacks had thereupon dispatched a posse to gallop to the police chief's house and wake him up and ask him who the hell he thought he was anyway, and the minions of the law had decided to adopt a more conciliatory attitude.

As to what arrangements had been made for the morrow's onslaught, Shandy neither knew nor cared. He lay rapt in slumber until half-past eleven the next, or maybe the same, morning, and woke to find Helen bending over him with an expression of wifely concern.

"Peter darling, are you all right?"

"I don't know yet," he mumbled. "Kiss me and see if I respond."

"You're all whiskery."

But she kissed him anyway. "I couldn't bear to wake you. I expect Tim isn't up yet either. You've missed the funeral."

"Mine or his?"

"That poor Lumpkin man's, of course. Roy went because he thought his father would want him to. He really is a darling boy. Oh, speaking of boys, Cronkite Swope is in the hospital."

"Huh?" Shandy hurled himself out of bed. "Why?"

"He had an accident on his motorbike. Or off it, I suppose."

"Good God! When?"

"Sometime in the small hours, I believe. They found him in the road."

"Who found him?"

"Peter, I don't know. Grace Porble got the news third-hand from somebody who got it from Mrs. Lomax. At least, I assumed it was from Mrs. Lomax. It generally is."

"When did you talk to Grace Porble?"

"Around a quarter to nine. I called to let Dr. Porble know I wouldn't be at the library this morning because you'd been out all night being a hero. He's frothing because you didn't send for him."

"What could Porble have done with that mob? Bop them over the head with Webster's Unabridged? Drive them off with hard words? Fine them a nickel a trespass?"

"He could have glared. He glares beautifully. Any man who can reduce a library full of students to absolute silence with one haughty glance is not to be taken lightly. Now go shave off those dreadfully unbecoming whiskers while I make your breakfast. Or lunch, or whatever. How about pancakes and sausage and fried apples and things?"

"Sounds pretty good for starters. What hospital is Swope in?"

"How many hospitals do we have around here? He's over at the Hoddersville General, of course."

"Good. Swope can't have much wrong with him, then. Anything worse than an infected hangnail would overtax their facilities."

"You're in one of your moods, I see. I'll go start the pancakes."

Helen went off to the kitchen. Peter stood in the bathroom scraping off his overnight accumulation of hispidity and pondering. Was it a strange coincidence that Swope had been injured so soon after he'd called attention to the runestone? Was it a natural result of Swope's having torn all over hell and gone on that flimsy bike for so many hours that he was no doubt as punchy as the rest of them?

Or was it something that Shandy, if he'd had half a brain, could have prevented? To how many people had Fergy repeated his superstitious blether about the curse of the runestone? How many others had thought up curses of their own? Shandy cussed himself a little and stood in shorts and undershirt wondering what to put on. Time was when he'd only have had to choose between a good gray suit and the corduroys he wore in the turnip fields. Now that he had a wife, his wardrobe was growing more complicated. He settled for a short-sleeved blue shirt and a pair of darker blue slacks, and presented himself at the table.

"Helen, do you believe in Viking curses?"

"Of course. How many sausages?"

"Pay attention, drat it. This is serious business. Six. Eight. Well, maybe three or four to start with. These are excellent pancakes, by the way. My compliments to the cook. Aren't you having any?"

"Oh, is the cook allowed to eat with the master of the house? I may just toy with a sausage, now that you mention it."

Helen fixed a plate for herself and sat down across from Peter. "In the matter of curses, by which I assume you refer to the fact that Cronkite Swope, whom I deduce from the comparative nattiness of your attire—I do like blue on you, Peter—that you're about to visit, is supposed by half the people in Balaclava County to have fal-

len prey to it—where on earth was I? Oh, you asked me
if I believe in curses. Certainly they work, if you believe
they do. I mean, if you'd managed to convince yourself
that Orm Tokesson really had it in for you because you
messed around with his runestone, you might very well
steer your motorbike into a fallen branch or whatever
without consciously meaning to, and lay the blame on
poor old Orm instead of admitting that your conscience
was bothering you for having almost wiped out Henny
Horsefall's farm. Mightn't you?"

"So you think Swope was punishing himself for incit-
ing to riot."

"Why not? If one were the vindictive type, one might
say he had it coming."

"One might indeed. But how would you square these
alleged guilt feelings with the fact that Swope was
charging around in high glee all evening, taking pictures
and burbling about what a story that brouhaha was going to make? I submit, madam, that while Swope, who
appears to be a decent enough youngster, no doubt had
some qualms about what was happening at the Horsefalls' and was doing his best to make amends, he had no
reason to feel guilty over having hauled off a competent
piece of journalism, which is what he gets paid for doing,
and in fact felt none."

"A hit man might haul off a competent murder for
hire and feel some guilt about it," Helen argued, helping
Peter to another sausage. "Subconsciously, anyway."

"If he had that kind of subconscious, he'd choose a different profession," Peter replied with his mouth full.
"Anyway, I'd be happy to know it was Swope's subconscious mind and not somebody horsing around with his
motorbike that landed him in the hospital. Did Grace
Porble happen to mention whether he's allowed visitors?"

"No, but I could phone the hospital and find out."

"So you could and so you shall since you're on this
helpful helpmeet kick today, but you might as well finish
your breakfast first. The odds are they won't tell you
anything anyway. They never do."

"This is not my breakfast but my lunch and I've had
all I want, thank you. Naturally I shan't bother to ask

anything but his room number. Then you can go straight on up instead of having to stop at the desk and be told you can't. That's what I always do."

"God, women are unscrupulous."

"Yes, dear. More coffee?"

"Just half a cup. I ought to get going. Er—were you about to call about that room number?"

"With never a scruple, my love."

Helen went to the telephone and was back in a minute with a note in her neat librarian's handwriting. "There you are. I wrote it down so you won't forget. Give him my regards. Does he have family to run errands for him and whatnot?"

"Madam, you speak in jest. His mother is Mrs. Lomax's late husband's own cousin, who is related to Henny Horsefall's great-niece by marriage. Her name, if I recall correctly, is Bertha. He also has two brothers who work in the soap factory, so if you were entertaining any notions of rushing over there to soothe his poor orphan brow, you might as well shelve them. I expect the relatives are lined up in rows over there, flipping coins to see who get first whack at soothing."

"Oh, shucks! Then I may as well flounce off in a huff to the Buggins Collection. Will you be home to dinner?"

"As of now I see no reason why I shouldn't. At that time you may soothe my poor orphan brow, if you so desire."

"You overwhelm me with kindness, sir."

Helen gave him a kiss on the forehead for practice. Then they rinsed the dishes, shoved them into the dishwasher, and left the house together. Helen walked up the hill to the library and Shandy stepped across the street to see how Tim was getting on. He found his old comrade still eating breakfast and being lovingly fussed over by his young daughter-in-law for having stayed out so late.

"It's all your fault, Professor Shandy," Laurie pouted. "You led him astray, and I expect you're here to do it again. I don't know what I'm going to do with the pair of you."

"You'll think of something, no doubt," Shandy replied. "I just wanted to tell—Tim hook up, will you?"

He tapped his friend's shoulder and motioned to the switch on Tim's hearing aid.

"Oh, sorry, Pete."

"Daddy Ames," cried Laurie, "do you mean you've been turned off and I've wasted all my nagging?"

"It's a waste of time anyway, honey. You haven't the temperament. Too bad you never got the chance to take lessons from your late mother-in-law. Now, there was a woman who understood the fine art of driving a man up the wall. What's happening, Pete?"

"Young Swope's taken a spill off his motorbike. Apparently it happened shortly after we left the Horsefalls' last night. Anyway, he's at Hoddersville General. I thought I'd take a run over there and try to find out how it happened. Do you want to come along?"

"Not specially. I was thinking I ought to see Henny."

"Roy and I will take you," said Laurie. "Roy told me he'd be back to pick us up after the funeral, so he ought to be along any time now. I still haven't got to see that runestone, you know. By now I must be the only person in the county who hasn't. You had quite a night of it, didn't you?"

"I shouldn't be surprised if they're also having quite a day," Shandy replied. "No doubt there's another mob using the funeral as an excuse to gate-crash. Then I'll meet you over at the Horsefalls' after I've been to Hoddersville."

He went down and got his own car, and drove over to the hospital. Thanks to Helen's cunning, he was in Swope's room before he could be barred from going there. He found the patient swaddled in plaster and bandages, with two black eyes and Merthiolate-daubed scratches where the skin was allowed to show, but awake and reasonably cheerful.

"Hi, Professor. It sure is nice to see somebody who doesn't want to jab a needle into me."

"What's the score, Swope?"

"I'm supposed to have a concussion, along with lacerations, contusions, a busted collarbone, a pulled tendon in the off hind hock, and the *Fane and Pennon*'s brand-new Polaroid camera smashed all to heck and gone, for which I'll probably be docked a week's pay. Not much left of my bike either, they tell me."

"From the look of things, you're lucky there's that much left of you. What happened?"

"Search me. The last I knew, I was bumbling along, not going very fast because I was beginning to feel sort of bushed by then. Besides, I didn't have my helmet on."

"Why not?"

Shandy had a clear mental picture of Swope coming back at the head of the Lolloping Lumberjacks, his head encased in a beetle shell of turquoise-blue plastic complete with chin guard and safety goggles.

"I couldn't find it. I know I had it earlier, but when I went to leave, it wasn't hitched to the bike where I usually hang it when I take it off. I don't know if I laid the helmet down someplace and forgot where I put it, or if some jerk swiped it for a keepsake. Anyway I looked around for a while but didn't have any luck, so I thought what the heck and started off without it. Which reminds me, if you happen to know a girl from the college who wears hockey shin guards, a chest protector, and a fencing mask and has eyes sort of like limpid pools of night, if you get what I mean, would you mind kissing her for me?"

"Er—any special reason why?"

"Because she probably saved my life, if that's good enough for you. See, she also had one of those velvet riding caps with the hard inner linings. When she saw me bareheaded she said anybody who rides a bike without a helmet is nuts, and stuck her cap on my head. I didn't even have time to say thanks because the bus was leaving and she had to run for it. The doctor thinks I must have gone straight over the handlebars, and if I hadn't been wearing that cap they'd have had to put my skull back together with Elmer's glue."

"Good God! I shall certainly find out the young woman's name for you and—er—pass on your thanks in a suitable manner, if my wife doesn't object too strenuously. But getting back to your accident, if you don't mind talking about it, you say you were bumbling along feeling—er—bushed. Could you have dozed off?"

"I doubt it. I wasn't the least bit sleepy, just beat. I

mean, gosh, that had been the most exciting night I'd
ever put in, better than the flood at the soap factory,
even. I was still keyed up mentally, thinking about how
I was going to write up the story and trying to remember
all the different things that had happened because there
hadn't been any time to make notes. Besides, I had to
stay alert because I was having a little trouble with my
headlight. I don't know what was the matter, but every
so often it would kind of flicker."

"A loose connection?"

"I suppose so. I should have stopped to make sure the
bulb was in tight, but it was so darn late and the road
was pitch dark and I was afraid if I started to monkey
with it, it might go out altogether. Besides, I hadn't far
to go. I live with my folks, just over in Lumpkin Upper
Corner. So I figured I'd push along with my fingers
crossed and catch a little sack time, and check it out in
the morning when I could see what I was doing. But then
I—"

Cronkite shook his head. The movement must have
caused pain, for he winced and shut his eyes. "I don't
know what happened. The bike just went crazy."

"And you haven't the slightest idea why?"

"Orm. That's all I can—"

"I'm sorry, sir." An irate nurse had appeared. "You'll
have to leave. This patient is supposed to have absolute
rest."

"Then why didn't you put a 'No Visitors' sign on the
door?"

"We left instructions at the reception desk. Naturally
we assumed people would have sense enough to stop and
ask before they came up."

So much for Helen's foolproof system. Shandy slunk off
in ignominious retreat.

CHAPTER 12

Except for the minor wound to his dignity, Shandy didn't mind being kicked out of the hospital. He'd got the information he'd come for and Swope didn't appear to be in any grave danger. Bless that child with the riding cap, whoever she might be. Thorkjeld Svenson would know.

As to how Swope had come to take that header off his bike, the president wouldn't be able to tell, but Shandy could take an educated guess. The time, the place, the circumstances, the malfunctioning headlight, and the missing helmet were at least one coincidence too many.

To be sure, there'd been plenty of vandalism last night. Shandy himself was not altogether guiltless in that regard, considering how many headlights he personally had tampered with. However, Swope's bike wouldn't have been a particularly vulnerable target, one might think. In the first place, the reporter had hardly been off it except for the time he'd spent riding around on the tractor taking pictures. That had been some time before dark. Long afterward he'd been scooting back and forth from hither to thither, rallying the Lumberjacks, trying to find strategic placements for them and their horses, chasing off trespassers who were making particular nuisances of themselves, rushing down to see how things were progressing at the runestone, rushing back to the scene of action at the farm, rushing up to the house to phone late developments to his editor, since the *Fane and Pennon* was evidently preparing an unheard-of double extra for that week. He couldn't have taken the bike into the house, of course, but it would have been left inside the protective circle of geese.

And that gave one something else to chew on. Among

the gooseherders were not only Marie and Jolene but
also the Lewis woman whose son Henny had originally
accused of doing damage around the farm and an assortment of other Horsefall youngsters and oldsters, including the incredibly well preserved and maybe slightly
crazy Miss Hilda. They'd have had a better chance than
anybody else to get at the bike.

That didn't mean one of them had done the dirty work.
Anyone at all might conceivably have managed to reach
out and give the headlight a little twist in passing, just
enough to loosen the bulb or wire and cause that blink-
ing Swope had found so bothersome. As to the helmet,
that could have been taken only very late in the evening.
Otherwise, Swope would have missed it before he set out
for home. By then, no doubt, he'd have been as punchy as
the rest of the defense squad even though he insisted he
wasn't. Those helmets were cumbersome things to be
wearing on a warm night. Maybe the young reporter had
taken the thing off to cool his head or swat a mosquito
that had worked its way inside, or simply because he
couldn't stand its weight any longer. Stealing the helmet
and twisting the lamp could have been a sudden chance
somebody saw and grabbed. Engineering the accident
would have meant simply getting down the road Swope
was about to take a little bit before him, and having
something handy to grease the road with.

As Shandy drove slowly up the road toward the Horsefalls', he had no trouble finding the exact spot where the
crash had occurred. Bits of glass and metal still glittered
at the sides of the road where they'd been swept after the
wreck. He parked and got out.

By bending over and squinting along the macadam, he
could see the remains of an oil slick. One might naturally assume it had come from the smashed bike, and no
doubt that was what whoever poured the oil there had
counted on. Shandy had ridden a wide enough assortment of vehicles himself over the years to know what
hitting a slippery patch unexpectedly could do to a two-
wheeler. The place chosen was ideal: a tricky wiggle at
the bottom of a gentle incline. Swope would have picked
up a little more speed going down than he realized. He'd
have swung his handlebars, expecting to take the curve,

and been over them headfirst, just as he'd said, the instant his front tire hit that oiled surface.

Dozens of cars, maybe a hundred or more, must have passed over this spot since the accident happened. There couldn't be enough left of the oil on the road to test for evidence that two different kinds might have been spilled here last night. Even if such a finding were made, how would it be possible to prove the brand that wasn't Swope's hadn't simply dripped out of somebody's crankcase during that mammoth traffic jam earlier? Swope himself probably wouldn't believe he'd been the victim of a deliberate attempt to murder or maim him. If the young fellow hadn't survived to mention the headlight and the helmet, Shandy might not have believed it, either.

He got back into his car and drove slowly on. As he neared the logging road, he was not at all surprised to see the verge crowded with parked cars and the police chief himself maintaining law and order with all the diplomatic charm of a Prussian general whose boots were pinching his corns. Shandy pulled in behind a collection of rusted metal so shamefully derelict that it could only belong to President Svenson, managed after some argument to persuade the strong arm of the law that he was indeed Professor Peter Shandy and a member of the archaeological party, which in fact he was not, and was allowed to enter the road.

As he expected, he found the president there with his Uncle Sven, a bodyguard of students, and a couple of excited strangers who must be bona fide archaeologists.

"What the hell are you doing here?" was Svenson's cordial greeting.

"I came seeking information."

"Urrgh?"

"Who was the young lady clad in shin guards, a fencing mask, and a catcher's whatsit who was a member of your goon squad last night?"

"Why?"

"She saved Cronkite Swope's life."

"How?"

"By making him wear her riding cap after somebody swiped his helmet prior to wrecking his motorbike."

"Who?"

"He appears to be under the delusion it was Orm Tokesson."

"Arrgh!"

"No doubt."

Shandy waited, knowing how unsafe it was to try to hustle the president. At last Svenson uttered again.

"Where?"

"About half a mile back, where the road turns off toward Lumpkin Upper—"

"Not there where," snapped Svenson. "Where's Swope?"

"Oh. In Hoddersville General with a fractured clavicle, a pulled tendon, and a damned sore head. He'd have fractured his skull if that young woman hadn't shown such excellent sense. To repeat my earlier question, who is she? He wants me to kiss her for him."

"Send her over. Kiss her himself. Do it better. Jennie, Julie, some damn thing. Jessie. Jessica Tate. Pretty. Mrs. Mouzouka. Go."

Shandy went. He'd learned all he needed to know. Jessica Tate was taking special instruction in either Restaurant Management or Farm Food Processing. Mrs. Mouzouka, high priestess of the Dietetic Department, would track her down for him on request. As to the kissing, Svenson's suggestion that he take Miss Tate over to the hospital and let Swope handle that detail himself was undoubtedly the wiser, although Helen was kind enough to maintain Peter kissed rather nicely. Miss Tate must be a real eyeball-popper if Svenson was willing to call her pretty. Having Sieglinde for a wife and seven daughters who took after their mother naturally gave him elevated standards of feminine pulchritude.

Having accomplished his first two objectives, Shandy went on up to the Horsefalls' and paid his respects to Miss Hilda and Henny. As he'd expected, the place was mobbed with Horsefalls unto the third, fourth, and fifth generation once, twice, and thrice removed, along with friends, neighbors, and members of the Ladies' Aid anxious to make sure Miss Hilda didn't overtax herself and louse up the Grand Birthday Party by having a heart attack.

Fergy was there with his hair slicked down and his beard combed into a pretty good imitation of the second Smith Brother's. He had on a tan suit with a bright yellow tattersall check and looked altogether less like the stage hick in a television country music show and more like the sort of real estate agent who sold choice building lots in the middle of mangrove swamps. Perhaps he was feeling out of place among this welter of Horsefalls; at any rate he greeted Shandy like a long-lost brother.

"Say, Professor, you're a sight for sore eyes. What's happenin'?"

"I've just come from visiting young Swope at the hospital."

"Who, Cronk? What's he doin' there?"

"Recovering, I hope. Didn't you hear about his accident last night?"

"No! When did it happen?"

"Sometime after midnight is the best I can tell you. Shortly after I myself left on the bus with the—er—Balaclava contingent. He cracked up his motorbike down the road from you a way."

"Well I'll be damned. First I've heard of it."

"You didn't hear the disturbance? I expect they must have had an ambulance and so forth."

"They could o' had the Angel Gabriel with a brass band an' I'd o' still slept through the racket after what went on around here last night. I don' know if you noticed, but I had kind of a busy time myself. They was pilin' into the barn like there was no tomorrow. That's how come I never got over here to lend a hand. I didn't dare turn my back on 'em for a second an' by the time they cleared out I was too pooped to pop. Besides, I got company stayin' with me." Fergy winked. "Real nice little lady I met down in Florida."

That would be the woman with the three sweaters Shandy had noticed making change last night. "Is your friend here now?"

"Naw, she's back there mindin' the shop. She ain't one to butt in among strangers, specially when it's a family gatherin' like this here. Oh, Jesus! Talk about buttin' in."

A purple car driven by a large woman in a purple

dress and a purple hat had just whizzed past them and screeched to a halt in the driveway. Mrs. Fescue got out, all teeth and gush, and wormed her way through the multitudes.

"Now what's she got up her sleeve?" Fergy muttered. "Say, I meant to ask you, is Cronk hurt bad?"

"Fairly well banged up. He has a broken collarbone and a mild concussion, among other things."

"Concussion, eh? Is he conscious? How come they're allowin' visitors?"

"They're not. I—er—sneaked past the receptionist and was thrown out as soon as they caught up with me. If you were thinking of going over to the hospital, I'd suggest you wait a day or so. He has a good many relatives, I believe, and no doubt they'll expect priority."

"Them an' his girl friends," Fergy said rather absentmindedly, with an eye on Loretta Fescue. "Cronk tell you how it happened?"

"He doesn't seem to know."

"Yeah? That don't surprise me none. Awful dangerous things, them flimsy little bikes. Wouldn't catch me on one even if they made the seats broad enough to hold me. Come on, let's mosey over an' see what she's up to. I don't trust that woman as far as I could throw 'er, which between you an' me I wouldn't mind doin'. Don't take no college education to figure out why Jim Fescue drank hisself to death."

They sauntered toward the porch, where Mrs. Fescue by now had Henny Horsefall backed into a corner. Her loud, nasal voice was easy to pick out over the rest of the babble.

"So you see it's only a matter of time before they declare this whole area a historic monument. You'll be smart to sell out now, before the government snatches the place right out from under your nose for ten dollars an acre if you're lucky enough to get it."

Henny looked scared as well as trapped. By now Mrs. Fescue had caught the attention of many besides himself, Shandy, and Fergy. There was much clearing of throats and shuffling of feet among the Horsefalls, then an outbreak of mutters.

"Knew that damn runestone would—"

"Never can tell what the government's goin' to—"

"Get it while the gettin's good."

"Too much for him to handle anyway, now that Spurge is—"

"At the price she claims she can—"

"No!"

Above Mrs. Fescue's strident whine, above all the adult rumblings, rose the voice of young Ralphie Horsefall. "Don't listen to her, Uncle Henny. She's puttin' you on about that historic monument stuff."

"Look here, Ralphie," some grown-up began. "You stay out—"

"Why the hell should I? I'm as much a member of this family as you are, ain't I? You're all ready enough when it comes to the big bucks, but how many of you are ever willin' to come over on a Saturday mornin' an' tail onto a manure fork? I never see anybody here workin' but Uncle Eddie and his kids and my own dad and my brothers and my sister Hilly once in a while when she can spare the time from hangin' around the telephone in case some guy decides to give her a break for a change. An' Mum an' Aunt Jolene," he added as an afterthought. Mothers, after all, were expected to work.

A teenaged girl whom even Thorkjeld Svenson would have deemed passable threw her brother a dirty look but stuck up for him nonetheless.

"Ralphie's right, Uncle Henny. I don't believe for one second the government could walk in here and take over the farm just on account of that runestone. And what if they did take that one tiny corner it's standing on? Then they'd have the pain in the neck of having to look after it, wouldn't they? And it would bring people past the farm and you could put up your vegetable stand like you used to. And maybe I could get a scholarship to Balaclava and take that course in Farm Restaurant Management. Aunt Hilda and I might start a lunchroom. We could sell sandwiches and hot coffee—"

"And have all the drunks reeling in here on their way back from New Hampshire," sneered a vinegar-faced second cousin once removed who knew he stood no chance of being cut in on the pie no matter what happened but figured he might as well put in his two cents' worth on general principles.

"What if we did?" cried Hilly. "Their money's as good as yours, isn't it?"

"And they part with it a dern sight easier," snickered somebody who never had liked the second cousin once removed much anyhow.

"I must say it's nice to see wise heads on young shoulders for a change," said a portly aunt by marriage, fanning herself with last Sunday's church calendar that she'd picked up during the funeral, for she minded the heat. "You listen to those children, Henny. Don't let anybody rush you into anything. I never do. Hilly dear, since you're so keen to be a waitress, how'd you like to bring your poor tired old auntie a drink of water?"

"There's lemonade for them as wants it," said Miss Hilda, coming out with a frosty pitcher and a tray of glasses, "which don't include nobody with no more common decency than to come weaselin' in on a family gatherin' at a time o' mournin'," she added with a glare that not even Loretta Fescue had brass enough to ignore.

"Of course not, Miss Horsefall," the realtor replied sweetly. "I must be running along anyway. I just wanted to do you the favor of letting you know which way the wind's blowing before it's too late for you to do something about it. You have my office telephone number, Mr. Horsefall, if you need to get hold of me in a hurry."

CHAPTER 13

"Considerin' what happened to the last poor geezer that got hold of Loretta, you better think twice before you pick up that phone, Henny," Fergy chuckled as he accepted a glass of lemonade. "Thank you kindly, Miss Hilda, though I didn't mean to butt in on the family."

"Hell, you ain't comp'ny. You're just folks," Miss Horsefall reassured him. "Hilly, bring Fergy a piece o' that there layer cake. Jolene made it, but it ain't bad. Professor, you want some, too?"

"Thank you, but my wife gave me a large meal just before I left the house," Shandy replied.

"He only got married in January an' it ain't wore off yet," Miss Hilda explained in a loud aside to the aunt who suffered from the heat. "Now who's that comin'? Oh, the mailman. Bunch o' sympathy cards from folks that's too lazy to write a decent letter, I s'pose. Go get 'em, Ralphie."

Ralphie obliged. The old woman flipped through the handful of mail, her glasses far down on her nose and the envelopes held out at arm's length.

"Here's one for you, Henny. Prob'ly your draft notice from Gen'ral Pershing. Way the gov'ment operates the post office these days is a cryin' shame. We used to pay two cents for a letter an' a penny for a postcard an' get two deliveries a day. Now you have to sign your life away to afford a stamp an' the Lord knows whether your mail will ever get delivered or not. Well, open it, can't you for the land's sake? What's it say?"

"Don't spring your corset stays, Aunt Hilda. Give a man time to—well, I'll be damned!"

"Like as not, but you don't have to brag about it out loud in a house o' mournin'. Speak up, can't you?"

"Hold on a minute, can't you? Here." Henny handed the message to Shandy. "You read it, Professor. I want to make sure I understand what it says. I'm hopin' it's him an' not me that's gone crazy."

Shandy scanned the page, feeling more apoplectic at every line. "Why, that low-down son of a b— I beg your pardon, Miss Horsefall, but of all the unmitigated—Horsefall, he can't do this!"

"Looks like he's already done it, ain't he?"

"Done what?" screamed Miss Hilda.

"Canute Lumpkin appears to have filed suit against Hilda and Hengist Horsefall, court-appointed guardians of his cousin Spurgeon, for gross negligence resulting in said Spurgeon's death from exposure to a corrosive substance without due warning or precaution. Lumpkin's claiming a million dollars in damages."

"A million dollars?" she gasped. "Where the flamin' perdition does Nutie think we could ever get our hands on that kind o' money?"

"A million dollars?" From all sides the banshee wail rose. "He must be out of his mind."

Nutie the Cutie was thereafter alleged to be a number of other things, some repeatable and some not. Drawing, quartering, boiling in oil, and stomping his lousy, rotten guts out with a pair of hobnailed boots were brought forth as appropriate methods of dealing with Lumpkin's incredible demand. The feeling that he might as well cut their throats and be done with it was expressed with heat by many voices. Only the vinegar-faced second cousin once removed appeared to find anything to smile at in the lawyer's epistle.

"Only one thing you can do now, Henny. Get that Fescue woman back here pronto, strike the best deal you can get for hard cash on the line, stuff the money inside your socks, and head for Paraguay."

"Paraguay? What the hell for?"

"Because Lumpkin's cooked your goose good and proper, far as I can see. Of course he doesn't expect to get a cool million. He'll settle for whatever he can get out of your property, which ought to be a tidy amount if

Gunder Gaffson's as hot to get his mitts on it as that Mrs. Fescue claims he is. You'd be crazy not to get out while the getting's good, Uncle Henny. Be a couple of years, most likely, before the court gets around to trying the case. By that time you and Aunt Hilda will both be six feet under anyway, like as—"

"How'd you like a punch in the mouth, Adelbert?" inquired Great-nephew Ralph and Great-nephew Eddie in one voice.

"What are you two lighting on me for? I'm only trying to talk a little sense into this old—"

Miss Hilda wasted no time on words. She simply handed the lemonade pitcher to Jolene and the glasses to Marie, then whanged down the heavy metal tray on Adelbert's head.

"Any name-callin's to be done with my nephew, I'll handle it myself, thank you kindly. You always was a nasty, whinin', sneaky-handed little brat, Adelbert. Why your folks ever bothered to raise you was more'n I could ever figure out, an' I still say you wasn't worth the effort. If you wasn't my own flesh an' blood, though a dern poor specimen of it, I'd make Henny run you off this place with a pitchfork. We got enough trouble around here already without you shootin' your mouth off about Paraguay. An' furthermore I ain't your aunt, praise the Lord. Your grandfather was my cousin an' that's as close to you as I ever want to get, so don't start claimin' what you ain't entitled to."

"I beg your humble pardon, I'm sure," Adelbert replied with what shreds of dignity he could scramble together. "Since I don't appear to be wanted here, I'll take myself off. Just don't say I never warned you when you find yourselves out on the street with no roof over your heads."

"It'll be a cold day in hell before we ever try to set foot under any roof o' yours," Henny retorted. "Me an' Aunt Hilda's managed to hang 'er tough this long. I guess we can make it the rest o' the way, since accordin' to you we ain't got far to go."

Young Hilly flung her arms around the old man's scrawny neck. "Don't pay any attention to silly old Bertie, Uncle Henny. You'll live to tell awful lies to my

grandchildren, and Aunt Hilda will bake them ginger-
bread boys the same as she did for us. I'm counting on
you both."

"I declare, Marie," Jolene surprised everybody by ob-
serving, "I couldn't be prouder of your Hilly if she were
one o' my own. And Ralphie, too, the way he spoke up for
his family."

"And his uncle and aunt and cousins, which is no more
than you deserve. I hope your young'uns appreciate what
they've got for parents," Marie replied.

"Lord a'mighty," Miss Hilda marveled. "If that's what
it takes to get them two talkin' civil, we better get Adelbert back here so's I can thump 'im again."

Henny laughed and Shandy was glad to see him do it.
He had a hunch that might be the last laugh old Horsefall was likely to enjoy for some time to come.

Shandy had managed to locate the Ameses by now.
Laurie and Roy were over by the hen run with some
small children researching the borrowed geese. Tim appeared to be showing some of the adolescent Eddies and
Ralphs how to do soil tests. A good time was evidently
being had by all, so Shandy merely waved to let them
know he was around, and wandered off by himself to
mull over this latest nasty development.

Anybody who could pull off a stunt like this at such a
time would stick at absolutely nothing. Shandy was not
only willing but eager to believe Nutie the Cutie had
murdered his cousin and missed assassinating Cronkite
Swope only by the fluke of a young woman's kindly im-
pulse. But how had he managed his tricks? Had he been
here last night? Among that unruly mob, getting in
would be no problem. He could have worn a false beard
or a woman's wig or something, and stalked young
Swope until he'd seen his chance for another quick kill.

But why Swope particularly? Maybe Lumpkin had a
grudge against the young reporter. Maybe it was just
that a fellow whizzing around on a light motorbike presented a likely chance for some dirty work. Maybe getting somebody rubbed out last night was part of a campaign to keep the pot boiling on the Horsefall farm.
Maybe the idea was to downgrade Spurge's death by
making it look like part of a major harassment or even

the Viking curse at work, so that the police wouldn't start getting too nosy about why the one barrier to Nute's collaring the Lumpkin fortune had been so conveniently removed. Maybe, furthermore, Nute had found the alleged fortune to be far smaller than he'd expected, and was hoping to make up the shortfall by pressing this infamous lawsuit against the Horsefalls.

The hell of it was, Nute did have a case of sorts. He was officially on record as having tried to remove his cousin from the Horsefalls' custody on the grounds that they weren't able to take proper care of Spurge. He could take an "I told you so" attitude of indignation against an unjust verdict and probably get a fair amount of public opinion on his side, for whatever that might be worth.

Mrs. Lomax claimed Miss Horsefall had managed to make a good many enemies during her long and evidently scandal-ridden life. Henny was not what one could term a colorful personality, and there might not be any great number of people who'd be willing to stand up for him. No doubt plenty of his neighbors thought Henny was taking a ridiculous attitude about parting with the land he was too old to farm, especially those who'd succumbed to the lure of quick money and were sore because he'd had the fortitude not to.

Timothy Ames and maybe a few others could fully appreciate what a triumph Henny had made of his life. For most, it was Nutie the Cutie, with his knack of getting rich people to give him large sums of money for things they could perfectly well have done without, who'd be tagged successful. Somehow, popular favor often did tend to fall on the side that looked to be winning.

Shandy recalled that he'd meant to check on the amount of the Lumpkin inheritance and hadn't yet done so. He might go over to Town Hall and spend the rest of the day wading through probate records. On the other hand, he might ask Mrs. Lomax.

He stood a moment in thought. Mrs. Lomax had been to the Shandys' yesterday, to the Ameses the day before, and maybe to the Enderbles' on Monday if it wasn't her club day. Normally she'd be at the Stotts' today, but Professor Daniel Stott, Solon of Swine, was still off escorting his bride of two weeks, the former Iduna Bjorklund, on

visits to one and another of her eight new stepchildren
and their families. Therefore it was well within the
bounds of possibility that Mrs. Lomax might even now be
in her flat up over the dry goods store communing with
her cat and turning out her closets, pastimes to which
she was much addicted. He would telephone.

Where from? It would not be prudent to do it from
here, with so many relatives and Ladies' Aiders hanging
around with their ears flapping. Nor would it be very polite to leave yet, as he'd just arrived and there were still
things he wanted to do. Fergy must have a phone at the
Bargain Barn, though. Now that they'd become such
buddies all of a sudden, surely Fergy wouldn't mind his
strolling down there and introducing himself to the real
nice little lady from Florida.

The lady herself couldn't have been more pleased.
Shandy found her alone among the chipped porcelain
doorknobs and graniteware chamber pots, puttering
around with a dustcloth when what she'd have needed to
cope with the dust was an obliging tornado. Shandy was
perhaps a less handsome and dashing figure than Helen
thought he was, but he must still look pretty good in con-
trast to Fergy. The lady quickly hid her duster, put on
her company face, and advanced to meet him.

"My name is Shandy." he told her. "Fergy sent me
down to make sure you're managing all right down
here," he added mendaciously. "He's rather stuck at the
Horsefalls' for the moment. You know how those things
are."

She replied that her own name was Millicent Peavey
and she did indeed know how those things were. "It's always like pulling teeth to get away once you've got yourself stuck someplace. Fergy's been after me for ages to
drop up and pay him a little visit, but you know how
these things are. First it's one thing, then it's another.
Finally I found somebody to feed the canary and managed to get away, and now look what I've landed myself
in the midst of. Not that I'm in the midst of it myself, I
mean, because I'm not one to butt in on strangers, as
Fergy may have told you."

"Yes, Fergy did—er—mention that you're not one to
butt in. The Horsefalls are hoping, of course, that they'll

—er—get to meet you after the—er—excitement has died down."

The Horsefalls were perhaps hoping exactly the opposite, but one could hardly say so. Millicent Peavey looked to Shandy like the sort who cried easily.

"When did you arrive, Mrs. Peavey? Or is it Miss?"

"Oh, it's Mrs., all right. Actually Joe Peavey was only my second. I've had two more since him, but I've always been sort of partial to Peavey so I go back to it between-times. Get a good name and stick to it is what I always say. You married, Mr. Shandy?"

"Yes—er—very much so," he replied rather nervously. "I—er—hope my wife shares your view about getting a good name and sticking to it," he added just in case Mrs. Peavey was beginning to have notions about a fifth Mr. Peavey. "Did you have a good flight up?"

"Flight? I wouldn't get on an airplane if you paid me. Fergy sent me a bus ticket. I don't mind riding on buses. The drivers are real friendly, some of them, and they even have little bathrooms now."

"So you got here just in time for the big doings," Shandy persisted, wondering why the woman couldn't have answered a simple question instead of dragging in all her former husbands and the bus driver. "Were you here when Spurge Lumpkin was killed?" ·

"Wasn't that the awfulest thing you ever heard of? I cried and cried when Fergy told me."

"Then you'd met Spurge?"

"Well, no I hadn't, but I'm awfully tenderhearted. I bet Fergy told you how tenderhearted I am."

"He—er—didn't happen to mention it, but I'm sure you are," Shandy replied, backing away because he'd seen that same tenderhearted look on women's faces a few times during his years of bachelorhood. "Do you happen to recall which bus you came on, Mrs. Peavey? I'm interested because a—er—friend of mine just came up from Florida on the bus, too. Tall, dark, good-looking chap with a little mustache," he improvised, desperate for some way to capture Mrs. Peavey's undivided attention. "My wife says he reminds her of—er—what was the name of that movie actor chap?"

"Clark Gable? He's dead now, of course, but I always—"

"Er—yes, that's the one. Was he on the bus with you?"

Mrs. Peavey shook her more or less blond head sadly. "I don't think so. Which bus did he come on?"

"Which bus did you come on?" said Shandy, getting back to the root of the matter. "Yesterday or the day before?"

"Yesterday," Mrs. Peavey admitted at last.

"Morning or afternoon?"

"Noontime, because Fergy met me with the truck and took me for a hamburger before we came on here. I was sort of hoping for something besides a hamburger, to tell you the truth, only don't mention it to Fergy because I'd hate him to think I wasn't grateful and I knew we had to hurry because he couldn't leave the barn for long. Running your own business means you've got to be right on top of it every second, doesn't it? That's a lovely truck Fergy's got. He does all right here, doesn't he? Last night they were swarming in so fast I could hardly keep up and it isn't as if I hadn't had plenty of experience. I worked in a supermarket as a checker for almost fifteen years and now I'm cashier at a real nice diner in Vero Beach, which is how I happened to meet Fergy. He comes in to eat all the time when he's down there. On account of me, he says, but don't think I haven't heard that one before." Mrs. Peavey giggled and cocked her head. "It's been slow today, I must say. I suppose he averages out pretty well at the end of the week, though?"

Shandy tried to look knowing. "There—er—seems to be a general feeling around here that he—er—averages out pretty well at the end of the week. After all, not everyone can afford to—er—take the whole winter off as he does."

"That's what I thought. And at least you wouldn't have to fill the ketchup squirters when things were quiet at the register."

Aha! So Millicent Peavey was here on business. Somewhere among the feathers inside her head there must, after all, be a vestigial brain. Shandy continued his uphill fight for information.

"Fergy didn't seem to have heard about the accident last night."

"What accident? I'm not surprised, the way they were bumper to bumper all up and down this poky little road, but—"

"It happened later on, after the traffic had more or less cleared out. A young chap on a motorbike."

"Was he killed?"

"No, just maimed a little. Broken bones and so forth."

"Oh." Millicent sounded disappointed at missing another chance to demonstrate her tenderheartedness. "No, we never knew a thing about it. By the time Fergy and I got to bed—I mean, by the time we—well, you know what I mean. Anyway, I was so worn out by then I'd have slept through anything. I suppose they had ambulances and fire engines and everything."

"I daresay they did."

"And we missed it all. Well, that's how it is. Anyway, Fergy and I had had a little drink to celebrate. You know how it is. I mean, we'd been so busy all evening we hadn't had time. We were going to have a nice dinner —Fergy had TV dinners all ready in the freezer and I was going to make us turkey Tetrazzini, but we wound up thawing out some pizzas instead because you can eat them while you work. So what with one thing and another I really didn't have much in my stomach and then he insisted we ought to have a highball or two because it was my first night, though in Florida we mostly just go for burgers and beer. So we had a few balls even though he knows the strong stuff just puts me right to sleep. You know how it is."

Shandy said he knew how it was and would Mrs. Peavey mind if he used the telephone?

Luckily a customer came along while Mrs. Peavey was showing him the phone inside a sort of office Fergy had made for himself by walling off a former horse stall with Homasote, so he got to make his call without an audience. Mrs. Lomax was indeed at home, much exercised over the fact that her cat had been found to have fleas. Shandy said he knew how it was and moved to the subject of the Lumpkin inheritance before she could get rolling about the pros and cons of flea collars. He was in any event familiar with her views in this regard, since her cat always did get fleas around the end of June.

Mrs. Lomax had a good head for figures. She knew to the last cent how much had been spent upon which separate piece of litigation, what had been its effect on the principal, the interest, and the litigants. Her summation took time, but Shandy could have no doubt of its accuracy. The upshot was that as of today's market conditions and interest rates, less legal fees and inheritance taxes, Canute Lumpkin stood to collect somewhere between $727,341.16 and $727,341.29. Mrs. Lomax was sorry she couldn't be more exact.

Shandy said that was close enough for practical purposes, thanked her profusely, sent his condolences to the cat, said he mustn't tie up the line any longer because he was using somebody else's phone, that being a reason at which Mrs. Lomax could not decently take offense, and severed the connection.

So Nute Lumpkin wasn't going to wind up a millionaire, but he'd be a lot richer than most people in Balaclava County, even if he never fleeced another customer. Henny Horsefall, on the other hand, had maybe forty-five acres, a big farm by local standards, but parts of it neither buildable nor arable. The going rate for such land in this area would be somewhere around five hundred dollars an acre.

Mrs. Fescue claimed Gunder Gaffson was willing to go as high as eleven hundred. If she was telling the truth, that would set a new record for Lumpkin Corners property. It would be peanuts in a fashionable suburb, though, and it was still peanuts to a man about to collect the Lumpkin inheritance.

Suppose Nutie the Cutie did win his case and forced Henny to sell out in order to settle the claim as best he could? By the time court fees and the realtor's commission were paid, Nute would wind up with maybe thirty-five thousand dollars, if he was lucky. What was that to him now, and what in Sam Hill was the point of this scurrilous lawsuit against the Horsefalls?

CHAPTER 14

"Gold! They've struck gold!"

"Who? Where?" Shandy and Mrs. Peavey cried in unison as Fergy hurled his bulk into the Bargain Barn, rolls of avoirdupois quivering like St. Nick's bowlful of jelly.

"Orm's place," he gasped, sinking down on a roll of rusty chicken wire. "Get me a beer, Millie. I'm plumb—whoo!"

Mrs. Peavey ran to fetch the restorative. Fergy took a few reviving swigs from the can, panted awhile, then got his voice back.

"Cripes, a man my size ain't built for runnin'. Couldn't wait to tell Millie. You two make yourselves acquainted?"

"Oh, Mr. Shandy and I are old friends by now," Mrs. Peavey giggled. "Who's Orm, Fergy? Funny name. I've known an Oscar and an Orville, but I've never run across an Orm before. Where's he live?"

And is he married? Shandy supplied the rest of Mrs. Peavey's question mentally. Millie would of course want to know.

"He's dead," said Fergy, taking another gulp of beer. "Leastways I should think he must be by now. Eh, Professor?"

"I—er—shouldn't doubt it," Shandy replied. "Do you mean some—er—golden relic has been found in the vicinity of the runestone?"

"Right smack dab in front of it, buried less'n a foot deep. An' to think I been right here practic'ly across the road from it all these years!"

Fergy bowed his head over his beer can in what was no doubt deep mourning, and heaved a mighty sigh.

"How the hell was I to know?" he demanded of nobody in particular. "Nobody never said nothin' to me about no runestone."

"I wish you'd tell me what a runestone is," Millicent Peavey exclaimed pettishly. "What kind of gold? How much did they find?"

"The runestone's that rock in the woods they was makin' such a time about last night. An' the gold's a little bitty coin 'bout as big around as a nickel with the edges chewed off. You wouldn't think it would be worth botherin' with, but them professors was glommin' on to it an' gloatin' over it like it was the Hope Diamond or somethin'. O' course, at today's prices—"

"I expect the historic and numismatic value would incalculably outweigh any actual monetary worth," said Shandy. "Was it in fact a Viking coin?"

"Them professors seemed to think so. They wouldn't let me close enough to look at. I was out o' there before I was in, darn near. Say, Professor, not to be personal nor nothin', but is that president o' yours by any chance a little bit nutty?"

"Many people have made the mistake of thinking so. I expect he may have been somewhat—er—elated over the find. Dr. Svenson is not one to repress his feelings."

"You can say that again. Jeez, I ain't seen nothin' like that since King Kong."

"The resemblance has been—er—remarked."

In fact, around campus, President Svenson was seldom called anything else. Except, needless to say, in his hearing. "How did you happen to get close to the runestone in the first place? I thought the police were keeping spectators away."

"Oh, I cut down through the path made behind the Horsefall place an' snuck up on 'em from behind, just in time for the big hoo-ray. Say, the gov'ment don't waste no time, does it? They got men out there surveyin' already."

"Surveying? I can't believe it."

"Well, if they ain't they're puttin' up a pretty good imitation. They got transits an' charts an' all. I guess that Fescue woman was right about Henny's land bein' declared a national monument, much as I hate to give 'er the credit. Henny better do like she said an' grab what he can while the gettin's good. Not that it's any of my business an' I wouldn't say so to his face. Won't have to."

Fergy crumpled the beer can with a wide, fat paw and threw the remains more or less in the direction of a trash basket. "You heard the way them relatives was growlin' an' mutterin' back there. Just because one or two lit on that guy Adoniram or Athelstane or whatever his name was don't mean he didn't get 'em thinkin' just the same. An' now that they've already started the surveyin'. . ."

Shandy shook his head. "It can't be the government. They'd never get around to moving this fast, especially when the runestone hasn't even been authenticated yet. Maybe the water department has got the bright idea of digging up the pipes to discourage traffic along the road, which would be an excellent idea in view of the situation as it stands."

"Excellent for who, Professor?"

"Er—yes, of course. Sorry, it wouldn't be so hot for you, would it? Er—as a matter of curiosity, where does Horsefall's boundary line lie, and who owns the property next to his?"

"Cussed if I know. How about another beer, Millie? You want one, Professor?"

"Thank you, no. I must be getting on. By the way, I made a call on your phone."

Fergy's piggy eyes became slits. "Where to?"

"Just to my housekeeper in Balaclava Junction. That's not a toll call for you, I believe?"

"Oh no, that's all right. Housekeeper, eh? I thought you said you was married."

"I am. Mrs. Lomax comes in—er—to help out."

"Uh. Wife workin' steady?"

"As a matter of fact, yes."

"Hey, not bad. One to do the work an' one to foot the bills. How come I never thought o' that?"

"I'll leave you to mull it over," said Shandy, who was feeling he'd had about enough of Fergy and his nice lady friend. "By the way, it might be wiser not to mention that gold piece to anybody else. You know what's going to happen if the word gets around."

"Yeah, I know. Don't worry, Professor. I wasn't born Tuesday. See you around."

"No doubt. Enjoy your visit, Mrs. Peavey."

Shandy left the Bargain Barn, deep in cogitation. He paused to look back toward the logging road, and sure enough, there were two men wearing the hard hats and fluorescent orange safety vests of surveyors. They must have been back in the woods somewhere when he'd come by before. Now they were on the pavement, one sighting through the transit, the other doing something with a plumb bob.

He thought of going down to ask them what was up, but he'd learn soon enough, no doubt. Fergy's other news concerned him far more. If a piece of genuine Viking plundered treasure had in fact been unearthed, all hell was going to break loose once the word got around. He had little faith in Fergy's ability to keep his mouth shut, and none at all in Millicent Peavey's. If the Horsefalls didn't already know, he'd better go right now and alert them to batten down the hatches and call all hands to the pumps.

At least the company had left by now. Only the Ameses' new car was in the yard, and Shandy found Miss Hilda sitting at the kitchen table, having a quiet cup of tea with Roy and Laurie. With them was Sven Svenson, his head swathed in gauze bandage.

"Good God, what happened to you, Dr. Svenson?" Shandy asked.

"Orm got 'im," Miss Hilda answered for the shaken Swede. "I tell 'im that's what he gets for messin' around with sacred places."

"But the runestone's not a sacred place, is it?" said Roy Ames. "I'd got the impression it was anything but."

"H'mph, dunno where you got that notion." Miss Hilda tossed her head in assumed dudgeon, but her twitching lips rather spoiled the effect.

"Well, the inscription's all about rotten liquor and mean women," Roy insisted. "What's so elevated about that? And Orm's not buried under the stone, I assume. If he'd died there, he'd have been in no condition to complain, would he?" Roy did have the scientific approach.

"What is the nature of your injury, Dr. Svenson?"

Shandy repeated. He was having an awful time getting straight answers today.

This time it was Laurie who took it upon herself to reply. "He got conked on the head falling out of a tree."

"What was he doing in a tree?"

"Climbing it, I suppose."

The old man shook his bandaged head. "Not climb. Up."

"You mean you'd already climbed the tree and you were up in it and a branch broke or something?"

"No. Not climb. Up."

"I'm afraid I don't understand," Laurie said.

"Well, don't go pesterin' the man now," Miss Hilda told her. "Here, old-timer, I'm goin' to put some more sugar in your tea an' you dern well better drink it. Sugar's good for what ails you."

"Unless you happen to be ailing from diabetes," Roy murmured.

Laurie had already learned the wifely art of silencing her spouse with a look. "Miss Horsefall means sugar is good for shock, and she's absolutely right. Dr. Svenson must have got a dreadful jar from that fall. It's a mercy he didn't break his neck."

"I'd still like to know why he was in the tree," Shandy fretted.

"Nobody seems to know. The president lugged him in here a little while ago and told us to take care of him. Maybe we ought to take him to the hospital, but on the other hand, maybe it's better not to joggle him around too much. He doesn't seem to have any bones broken. He did cut his head, but it isn't bad, really. Miss Horsefall bandaged it to stop the bleeding."

"So I see."

"I suppose, being so little and light, he didn't fall very hard. But one would have thought, at his age, his bones would be so brittle that he'd have really done a number on himself."

"One would indeed," Shandy replied. "I'd be inclined to leave him alone for the time being. He appears to be responding to treatment."

In point of fact, Sven Svenson was now making what might, for want of a coarser term, be called advances to

Miss Hilda. She was not discouraging him very hard, perhaps out of pity for his recent injury.

"Where's your father, Roy?" Shandy asked to cover his embarrassment at the goings-on. "And Mr. Horsefall?"

"Henny's upstairs resting. The funeral sort of did him in. Dad's out communing with Bashan of Balaclava. The Animal Husbandry boys brought old Bash over this morning in a horse trailer, and left him up there on the rise in case anybody takes a notion to cut through the swale to the runestone."

"Do tell," Shandy replied. "What time this morning?"

"Sometime during the funeral, I suppose. The bull was here by the time I brought Laurie over because we went up to say hello to him."

"What did they do, just stake him out?"

"No, they set in some posts and strung electrified wire to make him a large enclosure, which was a darn good idea. The wire looks flimsy enough to discourage anybody from trying to get near, especially when Bashan gets to stamping and snorting, putting on his act."

Roy, having grown up on campus, spoke as if he found the bovine behemoth's histrionics rather cute. "But you know Dad. He always did get along with bulls. After living with Mother so long, I think he finds them restful company."

"Huh! Nice way to talk about your own mother," snorted Miss Horsefall, moving a little closer to Dr. Svenson, Sr. "Come on, you old he-devil, you better go lay down awhile."

"Sure, tootsie. Ve take little rast, hah?"

"I didn't mean me, drat you, an' keep your grabby hands to yourself. Come on, I'll bed you down on the sofa."

As she was leading him away, they heard a thump at the knocker on the front door.

"Now who in tarnation's that?" said the old woman fretfully. "More trouble, I s'pose. Laurie, get this hellion laid down an' cover 'im up with the afghan while I see who 'tis. An' you behave yourself for a change, Sven Svenson. She's a married woman even if she don't look it."

"How should a married woman look?" Laurie asked in

a rather pettish tone since she was, after all, straining every nerve to leave her Antarctic adventures behind her until she'd learned to be a model wife.

"Like she's sorry she ever bothered. Quit that bangin', whoever you are. I'm comin' as fast as I can. Oh, it's you." Miss Horsefall sounded sorry she'd ever bothered. "What are you after now? Our back teeth? If you are it's too late 'cause I ain't got none left an' neither has Henny."

"I came for my late cousin's personal effects."

That mincing voice could belong to none other than Canute Lumpkin. Shandy thought he'd better go join Miss Horsefall.

At the moment, the old lady was managing nicely on her own. "What effects? If you mean Spurge's other pair o' socks, why can't you come straight out an' say so? You always was an aggravatin' little bugger an' you ain't improved none by gettin' older an' fatter."

"Slander won't help your case, Miss Horsefall," Nute replied sweetly. "Would you kindly show me to my late cousin's room?"

"You try to step over that threshold an' I'll lay you out flat as a pancake with this here umbrella stand. You could never be bothered to set foot inside this house while Spurge was alive an' you ain't never goin' to do it now, not while I've got a breath left in this ol' carcass o' mine. Stay out there where you won't stink up the air an' I'll fetch 'em out to you, such as they are. Too bad corpses' eyes don't get weighted down with copper cent pieces no more. You might o' filed a claim for them, too."

Lumpkin only glanced over her shoulder and drawled, "Ah, Professor Shandy, how do you do? I'm so glad you overheard that remark. Now you can testify at the hearing that I was subjected to verbal abuse and threats of physical violence when I attempted to carry out my proper function as next of kin to the deceased."

"Certainly, Lumpkin. If you don't feel sufficiently abused, perhaps I could help you there, too. It is a shame about the two cents. However, if you'll wait here as Miss Horsefall suggests, I'll help her fetch out whatever—er—effects your cousin may have left."

Canute Lumpkin spread a mauve silk handkerchief

over the seat of the least-battered rocking chair, hitched
the creases of his pinky-beige trousers ever so carefully
over his knees, and planted his pudgy bottom on the
handkerchief.

"How kind of you, Professor Shandy. I shall be quite
content to entrust the mission to a person of your stature
and probity. It won't take too long, will it? I should so
hate to cause a scene by violating the sanctity of Miss
Horsefall's threshold if I were kept waiting."

There was no cause for delay. Spurge Lumpkin's personal effects consisted of two worn but clean and mended
suits of long underwear, some much-darned socks, a couple of flannel shirts with turned collars and patched elbows, a pair of work pants, a plaid mackinaw much like
the one Shandy himself had worn until Helen had
threatened him with bodily violence if he didn't buy himself something fit to be seen in, a pair of heavy boots
with run-down heels, and a cap and mittens knitted from
odds and ends of bright worsted.

These last brought tears to Miss Horsefall's eyes as
she laid them on top of the pitiful heap. "I knitted these
for Spurge one Christmas before my hands got so bad.
Never seen a man more tickled. We had a good Christmas that year. Times was better then. Ayup. Well, I'll be
in a better place myself before long, the Lord willin'."

"Nonsense, you mustn't talk that way," Shandy replied brusquely. "Is this all? No—er—pajamas or slippers
or whatever?"

"Hell, no. Spurge always slep' in 'is socks an' union
suit. It was as much as I could do to make 'im take a
bath an' change 'em once a week. Spurge did have a good
suit an' a white shirt that used to belong to Henny when
he was bigger, but we buried 'im in those. Ain't nothin'
else but the tobacco boxes."

"Good Lord," said Shandy, eyeing the stack of cartons
that filled one corner of the sparsely furnished little
room. "What did he keep in them?"

"Nothin'. He just liked to save 'em."

There must have been hundreds of the small tin and
cardboard containers, carefully stowed away in those
dusty grocery cartons. Shandy would have liked to make
sure the containers were in fact empty, but it would take

ages to open them all and he knew Nutie the Cutie was quite capable of staging the promised scene if they didn't get this stuff out to him right away. Anyway, the film of dust over them would be proof that they hadn't been tampered with, assuming there could possibly be anything of worth inside. There probably wasn't, judging from the lightness of the boxes, unless Spurge had gone in for collecting chicken feathers. Shandy picked up a tottering armload and juggled them out to the porch.

"You'd better start putting these in your car, Lumpkin. There are lots more."

"Oh dear. Perhaps I might just sort over the boxes ands leave what I don't—"

"Not on your life. You came for your cousin's possessions and you're damn well going to take them away."

Lumpkin shrugged and began loading the worthless boxes into his shiny new car. At last he sighed, "Is this all?"

"This is damn well all, an' no thanks to you for what little there is," Miss Horsefall snapped back. "Never seen you offer Spurge so much as a stick o' chewin' gum while he was alive. He'd o' been sent to the county home with nothin' but the shirt on 'is back if me an' Henny hadn't o' took 'im in. An' a hell of a lot o' thanks we ever got for it from your folks, not that we cared. Spurge was our—" She cleared her nose with a mighty sniff, wiped her sleeve across her rheumy eyes, and finished savagely, "Now you got what you come for. Take it an' git."

Nute Lumpkin picked his mauve silk handkerchief off the broken rocker seat, folded it carefully, tucked it into his breast pocket so that a precise inch of the edge stuck out, made Miss Horsefall a low bow, and got.

CHAPTER 15

"What in time do you s'pose he done that for?" the old woman muttered as Lumpkin drove off with his carload of junk. "Them things ain't no good to him."

"Just another of his little nastinesses, I expect," Shandy replied.

"Huh. Bein' nasty's 'bout all he's good for. Goin' to seem queer not having nothin' o' Spurge's around the place. Henny'll mind it worse'n me. Him an' Spurge always got on real good."

"Hey, tootsie!" From the parlor was coming a mighty roar. "Vere you bane?"

"Button up, you ol' rip," Miss Hilda yelled back. "I'm comin' fast as these worn-out pins o' mine will carry me. If it ain't one dratted man wantin' somethin' he ain't entitled to, it's another."

"I think this is where we tiptoe gently away," Shandy murmured to the two young Ameses, who'd been trying to keep the ancient Swede under control. "Let's go see what your father's up to."

As they left the house he remarked, "I'm surprised none of you has mentioned the gold."

"What gold?" Laurie asked.

"Fergy told me the archaeological party has turned up a gold coin right about where Cronkite Swope found that piece of helmet and started this whole shemozzle."

"You're kidding!"

"Fergy may have been, though I hardly think so. According to him, a coin of some appropriate date and description was found buried at the stone. Fergy claims there was general pandemonium among the savants, though he himself couldn't see why. I suppose it's possible, though most improbable, that Dr. Svenson swarmed up a tree in his elation and thus sustained his injury. In any case, one might have expected he'd allude in one way or another to the find, but obviously he hasn't. He seems to have his mind on—er—other matters."

"Maybe that whack on the head gave him amnesia," Laurie suggested.

"Or maybe the archaeologists agreed to keep still about the gold so they wouldn't start another stampede," said Roy. "How come Fergy knew? When we came by, they had cops out there keeping everybody away."

"They still have," Shandy replied. "I had a hard time convincing the guards that I was part of the archaeological team. Understandably, I suppose, since of course I'm not. President Svenson gave me the bum's rush as soon as I got to the stone, so I might as well have saved myself the trouble. Anyway, Fergy claims he sneaked down that path Swope made through the brambles, which you tell me is being guarded by Bashan."

"Yeah?" Roy scratched his ear much as Tim would have done. "Dad and Bashan must have been arguing about politics or something and didn't notice him."

"Fergy's that fat man with the orange beard and the neon suit, isn't he?" said Laurie. "He'd be a hard man not to notice, I should think."

"Dad could have kept Bashan under control long enough to let Fergy through without being gored if he wanted to. Does he like the guy, Professor?"

"He knows Fergy's been a good neighbor to the Horsefalls, at any rate."

"And Dad's a little miffed with the president right now for spending so much time on this Orm business when they were supposed to be working on a speech for the National Fertilizer Symposium on 'Phosphates I Have Known.' Dad was asked to give it, but of course he can't handle public speaking, so he asked the president to stand in for him. Dr. Svenson said he'd give the speech if Dad would help him write it. You know how great he is on a platform. So Dad's spent hours and hours writing up notes and now he can't get the president even to look at them, which he'd promised to do right after the wedding because the symposium's next weekend."

"Oh well, I daresay the president will come through with flying phosphates, but I can understand your father's annoyance," said Shandy, who'd been put in similar fixes once or twice himself. "Maybe you can get Tim to go home and sack in for a while. He did put in an awfully long and trying day yesterday. Spurge's death took a jolt out of him, too. By the way, since nobody else seems to be talking about that gold piece, I suggest you—er—follow precedent. I've already asked Fergy and his lady friend to keep quiet, though I'm afraid that may be a case of locking the stable after the bull is thrown. Let me go on ahead and chat with your father for a minute, if you don't mind. After that, I suppose I may as well go and beard the berserker in his lair. I still want to know what in Sam Hill Dr. Svenson was doing up in that tree."

He walked up the rise to where shiny new wire had been strung between hastily planted fence posts. It did indeed seem a paltry barrier, yet the immense beast penned inside had been conditioned to know he'd get a disconcerting buzz if he touched the wire. Bashan was standing placidly enough in the middle of the enclosure. Beside him, on an outcropping boulder with his feet drawn up and his beard propped on his knees, sat a kobold straight out of Arthur Rackham. Tim and Bashan appeared perfectly content with each other's company. Shandy was reluctant to intrude on their contemplations, but the day was wearing on and he did want to get back to Helen.

Knowing Bashan pretty well himself, Shandy had no qualms about slipping under the wire. Bashan emitted a roar that would have scared the heart out of any bona fide trespasser, and charged at him. Shandy stepped aside, knowing Bashan didn't really intend to trample him to death, and patted the bull's vast flank.

The roar must have registered on Tim's defective eardrums, for he switched on his hearing aid and looked around. "Hi, Pete. What's up?"

"The president's Uncle Sven was, briefly. He's fallen out of a tree."

"What the hell for?"

"Good question. Either his memory or his vocabulary

has failed him, and he can't say. I thought I'd go down
and ask the president."

"Stay here with Bashan. He's safer company, by a
damn sight."

"Granted, but duty calls. I don't know if it's struck
you, Tim, but there's one hell of a lot going on around
here."

"I'd begun to suspect something was up," his friend replied dryly. "Hell, Pete, I may be deaf but I'm not dumb.
So that old hellion was up a tree? Chasing a wood
nymph?"

"I shouldn't be at all surprised. Did you let Fergy in
through here a while back?"

"Fergy who?"

"Henny's neighbor, the chap who runs the Bargain
Barn."

"Oh, that tub of lard? I always thought his name was
Percy. Say, is there some new development down at the
runestone? Outside that old coot hurling himself out of
trees?"

"They've found a Viking gold piece, according to
Fergy."

"How the hell would he know? Probably a busted collar button." Ames hitched up his pant leg and scratched
his hairy shin. "Christ, Pete, if it actually was gold,
Henny's in for a worse time of it than he had last night.
He can't take much more of this punishment."

"You're not telling me anything I don't know, Tim.
They have been trying to keep quiet about the gold. Miss
Hilda hadn't heard, and she's been ministering to Dr.
Svenson."

"God help the poor bugger."

On this pious note the two friends parted. Shandy
picked his way down through the brambles to where
Thorkjeld Svenson was still working with the archaeologists. They were picking daintily at the ground in front
of the runestone, removing earth practically crumb by
crumb. Shandy couldn't imagine a more tedious job, yet
none of the three looked bored.

"President," he said.

"Arrgh," Svenson replied without taking his eyes from
the ground.

"What happened to your Uncle Sven?"

"Levitated."

"What?"

"Down, up, down. Landed on his head. Good thing. Man his age. Might have broken a hip."

"Let's run through that again if you don't mind. Your uncle was with you near the runestone, right?"

"Ur."

"What was he doing?"

"Dr. Svenson was examining a coin we'd found," said the younger and more enthusiastic of the archaeologists. "Marvelous thing. Norwegian, twelfth century."

"Possibly tenth," said the elder. "Maybe not even Norwegian."

"That was when he was still on the ground, right?" said Shandy, anxious to keep his facts straight.

"Right," said the president.

"Then what happened?"

"Then all of a sudden he was up in that tree there," said the younger archaeologist.

"Or possibly the tree next to it," said the elder archaeologist.

"Then what?" said Shandy.

"Then he was back on the ground, head first. Almost cracked his skull open on the runestone," answered the younger archaeologist.

"Missed it by at least eight inches," said the elder archaeologist.

"Are you saying this happened all in—er—one movement, so to speak?"

"Exactly," said the younger archaeologist.

"Or in a series of movements," said the elder archaeologist. "I should be inclined to separate the incident into three distinct phases."

"What I said," grunted Svenson. "Down, up, down."

"I see," said Shandy. "And how far up did he go?"

"Twelve or fifteen feet at least," said the younger archaeologist.

"Not more than eleven and a half," said the elder archaeologist.

"By either reckoning, an appreciable distance for a man his age to fall. You are agreed on that point?"

"Have we determined Dr. Sven Svenson's precise age?" asked the elder archaeologist.

"Hundred and two last November," grunted Thorkjeld Svenson. "Want a carbon dating?"

The elder archaeologist glanced at Thorkjeld suspiciously, as if he suspected an attempt at levity, but agreed to accept the data as given. "I think we can safely concur with Professor Shandy's theory that it was in fact an appreciable distance for a man Dr. Svenson's age to have fallen. More remarkable, it seems to me, is the fact that anyone well into his hundred and third year should have been able to achieve so considerable a height in so short a time."

"I couldn't agree with you more," said Shandy, prodding around the runestone. "Did you actually watch him ascending the tree?"

"Hell, no," growled Thorkjeld Svenson. "If I'd seen him, I'd have stopped him."

"Didn't he tell you anything about how it happened?"

"Said Orm threw him."

"Unscientific," snapped the elder archaeologist.

"He did give his head an awful whack," said the younger archaeologist.

Shandy cleared his throat. "Have any of you gentlemen read Robert Frost?"

"Urgh," said Thorkjeld Svenson.

"What for?" said the elder archaeologist.

"I started to," the younger archaeologist confessed. "But I got to the one about 'Something there is that doesn't love a wall,' and it seemed like a betrayal of my profession. I couldn't go on."

"M'yes, quite understandable. The point I wished to make is that in one of Frost's poems there's a reference to boys swinging on young birch trees. I've done it myself when I was younger and a good deal lighter. Birch saplings are extremely limber and springy. If you bend one down, then release it suddenly while holding fast to the trunk near the top, you can get whipped right up in the air. If you hang on, the weight of your body will pull you down again. If you don't, you go flying. In winter when there's snow on the ground to cushion your fall, it's fun to let go. At least, we used to think so. If the ground is bare, you keep your hold and shinny down the trunk."

The elder archaeologist sneered. "Thank you for the dissertation, Professor. So your theory is that Dr. Svenson had a sudden urge to return to the amusements of his youth?"

"There are lots of birch trees in Sweden, I believe," said the younger archaeologist.

"Ungh," said the president, wrapping his left forepaw around a withy young tree not far from the runestone. "Birch."

"My point exactly," said Shandy. "If you'll stand aside for a moment?"

He ferreted among the dead leaves and rabbit holes, and came up with a forked stick. "This explains Dr. Svenson's sudden flight, I think. Somebody bent this nice young birch over and held down the tip by pinning it to the ground with this forked stick. The soil is deep and humusy here, so that would be no great feat. You'll observe traces of leaf mold on both forks."

The elder archaeologist shrugged a very superior shrug. "Birch trees are not in my field."

"Naturally you wouldn't have noticed," said Shandy. "Your whole attention would have been quite properly focused on the runestone or, as it happened, on the coin you'd just found. As you see, this is not a white but a gray birch, so that would make it even less apt to attract your eyes. I submit that Dr. Svenson must have happened to lean against the bent sapling, perhaps to rest himself a bit. He may even have taken hold of the trunk. Was he actually holding the coin in his hand?"

"No, I was holding it," said the younger archaeologist. "He'd backed off a bit to get a better look. He's extremely farsighted, I believe."

"As presbyopia increases with age, he naturally would be," Shandy agreed. "Anyway, the weight of his body, or merely the jar of his touching the tree, could be enough to loosen the forked stick from this peaty soil, and he'd have been catapulted into the air just as you described. Not being prepared, he either wouldn't be holding the tree at all or wouldn't have a firm enough grip to keep from being thrown off. Since you can't seem to agree on which tree he fell out of, I suggest that he was never actually in either of them. He merely swished through their leaves, as it were, and came straight back down again. That's why we don't see any freshly broken branch."

"And he didn't even knock off any leaves," cried the younger archaeologist, "because they're still so young and sappy."

"Quite," said the elder archaeologist, giving his colleague an analytical once-over.

"Ur," said Thorkjeld Svenson. "Who?"

"Who's been in here, other than yourselves?"

"You."

"Did you notice me messing around with birch trees?"

"No."

"Then I daresay we can let me off the hook. Who else?"

"Fat slob. Orange."

"That would have been Fergy of Fergy's Bargain Barn. He told me he'd been here. I'm afraid he arrived just as you were all exclaiming over that gold coin you found. What did he do?"

"Got the hell out."

"I see. He didn't bend any birches en route?"

"He couldn't have," said the younger archaeologist. "He wasn't here that long. He just came into the clearing and President Svenson yelled—that is, requested him to leave—and he left."

"He would," said Shandy. "Anyone else?"

"Only the surveyors."

"Ah, yes, the surveyors. Did they happen to mention why they're surveying?"

"No, I don't think they said anything except 'Excuse us.' We did, of course. They weren't bothering us."

"Well, they're bothering me," Shandy snarled. "President, doesn't it strike you as odd that a surveying team should show up here the same day Nute Lumpkin slaps a lawsuit on Henny Horsefall?"

"No," said the president.

"Come to think of it, you're right. I must go have a chat with those chaps. Did they see you find the gold, by the way?"

"By gold, I presume you refer to the artifact," said the elder archaeologist.

"If you say so. Getting back to my question, were they here when it turned up?"

"Who knows?" said the younger archaeologist. "We were all in such a dither the Assyrian could have come down like the wolf on the fold and we'd never have noticed."

"To which Assyrian do you refer?" inquired the elder archaeologist.

"Arrgh," said Thorkjeld Svenson, settling the matter once and for all. "Go ask, Shandy."

"I shall, President. First let me ask how long you've been here. You didn't stay all night, I gather."

"Sieglinde wouldn't let me," the archon of academe confessed. "Left on the bus with you. Had to hoist you aboard. Out like a light. Bad example for the students. Thought you were sloshed."

"I was tired, drat it! Did anybody stay to guard the runestone?"

"Damn well better had. Headless Horsemen."

The elder archaeologist's upper lip drew back in a sneer. Before he could make whatever nasty remark he was formulating, Shandy explained.

"He means the Headless Horsemen of Hoddersville, a local workhorse association. They volunteered their services, as did the Lolloping Lumberjacks of Lumpkin Corners, and a good many other people."

"Get the Balaclava Blacks over here if we had anybody to ride 'em," said the President wistfully. "Hell of a time for a riot. Nobody on campus who knows a mane from a crupper."

"I used to ride a little," said the younger archaeologist.

"I'm afraid there's nothing little about the Balaclava Blacks," Shandy told him. "They were bred as draft horses, but they also have a remarkable amount of speed and—er—independence of spirit. We generally have some students who can handle them, but this year's cavalry contingent have all been graduated or gone off to summer jobs. Last night we—er—called out the militia, as it were, and I'm proud to say our people gave a good account of themselves. Doubtless they're girding their loins for another round right now. I hope so. The reporter who spilled the beans about the runestone is in the hospital, but no doubt news of the—er—artifact will get around one way or another. Tell me, weren't you surprised to find it so close to the surface?"

"Yes," the younger archaeologist replied. "Even more incredible is the fact that this young reporter simply picked up that helmet fragment off the ground yesterday. Even if the artifacts were simply dropped near the runestone by Orm Tokesson or his men, they ought to have been deeply buried by an accumulation of leaf mold and whatnot by now."

"Would you care to describe the chemical composition of whatnot?" said the elder archaeologist.

"Ask Ames," grunted Svenson, who must be as sick of the elder archaeologist by now as Shandy was. "Happens. Tree roots. Frost heaves. Animals digging. Kids playing treasure hunt. Done it myself."

The thought of Thorkjeld Svenson in merry childish play was unnerving. Shandy ascertained that the archaeological party had arrived at half-past seven that morning and found the Horsemen still on the job, then wished them good hunting and went on out to the road.

CHAPTER 16

One of the surveyors, the one who was doing things with a measuring tape and making marks on the road with chalk, looked vaguely familiar. A sunburned lad of nineteen or twenty, he straightened up and welcomed Shandy with a buck-toothed grin.

"Hi, Professor. Jeff Lewis, in case you don't remember. We sure had one wild time last night, didn't we? More of the same tonight, do you think?"

"I should keep the geese on the *qui vive*. They are your family's—er—gaggle, aren't they? I've seen you at school but hadn't realized you were one of the local Lewises."

"Sure. Born and drug up right here in Lumpkin Corners. I told Miss Hilda what you said in class last year about the geese saving Rome, and she happened to think of it yesterday. So it was your idea, really."

"How remarkable. I wonder what I ought to have been talking about at the time. Anyway, I hope the incident will inspire you to read a little history now and then. Shall I be having you as a regular student this year?"

"I hope so. I signed up for Advanced Agrology, but the course is so full I don't know if I'll make it."

"We'll have to—er—look into the matter. Tell me, Lewis, what's the object of this surveying caper you're up to?"

"It's my summer job. I have to earn my tuition."

"Of course. I should have phrased the question more succinctly. Why are you surveying this particular place at this particular time?"

"Because my boss told me to. Oh, I get you, Professor. You mean how come Nutie the Cutie has this much drag with the town surveyor's office? Hey, are you investigating, like you did when Belinda was kidnapped?"

"I've been asked to look into things a bit. Unofficially and on the q.t., Lewis. That, since you're so interested in ancient Roman lore, is Latin for button up."

"Oh, sure. But hey, Bill and I have been wondering ourselves. This is my buddy Bill Swope. Professor Shandy."

"A relative of Cronkite Swope, no doubt," Shandy observed as he shook hands with the other sunburned young man.

"Hey, you know Cronk?" said Bill. "Did anybody tell you he wiped out last night on his bike? He must be having a bird, stuck in the hospital with all this stuff going on."

"He may be by now. He was still a bit—er—out of it when I saw him a while back."

"They let you in? Boy, you must know the right people, Professor. My dad was going over on his lunch hour from the soap factory, but when he called up to see if it was okay, they said no visitors."

"Yes, they told me no visitors, too. When they caught me in his room, that is. I got what I believe is known as the bum's rush."

The fact of the great Professor Shandy's having been thrown out of Hoddersville General somehow made him one of the gang. The two young surveyors laughed their heads off and proceeded to chat at length on the town's time, asking for details of Cronk's accident and agreeing with Shandy that an oil slick on the road at night could definitely have caused the crack-up. He didn't tell them about the missing helmet and the defective headlight because, after all, one never knew.

"Now, getting back to this surveying job you're doing. What has Nute Lumpkin to do with it?"

"Why, this is his land now. I guess. Anyway, it's part of the Lumpkin property, all the way from Horsefall's line down to the bend in the road where Cronk took his header. What we're supposed to be doing is making sure Henny knows where his line is. Lumpkin claims that logging road where Cronk found the runestone belongs to him."

"Is he also claiming Horsefall's back teeth?" said Shandy. "Er—if it's not asking out of turn, Lewis, how does your family feel about Gunder Gaffson's offer to purchase the Horsefall property?"

"Lousy. We figure as soon as Gaffson got hold of Henny's place, he'd be trying to squeeze us out, too."

"And you don't care to be squeezed?"

"Why the heck do you think I'm out here with dust up my nose and blisters on my back, trying to put myself through Balaclava? Dad says he'll make me a full partner in the farm as soon as I graduate. You're not catching me in the soap factory like my brothers, punching a time clock and wishing the heck I were old enough to collect my retirement pension. I'm going to major in Orchard Management. I was sort of hoping to buy a few acres off Henny someday, but I know I'd never be able to meet Gaffson's price. We only have twenty acres now. But you said yourself that with proper rotation of crops you can get a high yield out of a small area. I don't know how you'd rotate an apple tree, though."

"You wouldn't. You'd select your varieties with care, plant so as to utilize your space as efficiently as possible, and keep your trees well pruned. Forget Advanced Agrology this year. Go straight into Arboriculture. Get in some work with Professor Ames on Soils and Fertilizers. Next spring you'll know enough to start planting, and by the time you're graduated you'll have the nucleus of an orchard."

"Hey, right on! That makes sense."

"Good. Now suppose you help me make sense. Is it possible this sudden insistence of Nute Lumpkin's on establishing accurate boundaries means he's planning to strike a deal with Gunder Gaffson?"

Young Lewis peeled a fragment of skin off his sunburned nose. "Sure, why not? Then he'd own the whole hill, as far as our place."

"And why should he want such a large tract to build on?"

"Because of the soap factory, maybe?"

"What?"

"My brother told me the soap factory's bought a com-

puter company and is planning to move it here to Lumpkinton."

"What would a soap factory want with so many com-
puters?"

"I dunno. It's what all the big firms are doing, buying
up other businesses that they don't know how to run. I
guess they call it progress or something. Anyway, that's
what they did. So a lot of engineers and executives and
vice-presidents and guys like that will be moving here
and they'll all want classy houses, so Gaffson's got this
jazzy development he wants to build. And I suppose Nutie the Cutie figures he'll sell them lots of antiques to
furnish their places with."

"Then Nutie the Cutie had better refigure. Anybody
who saddles himself with one of Gaffson's classy houses
at today's mortgage rates will be lucky to have money
enough left over for groceries, let alone Bow tea sets. I
think you've hit it, though, Lewis. That could explain
why Lumpkin is suing Horsefall. The Horsefall property,
being on the top instead of the slope of the hill, has a
better view and is less apt to be contaminated by sewage
runoff from all those other houses there won't be enough
good leaching beds for. Therefore it would be the more
desirable, and Lumpkin would have a better chance of
unloading the rest if he could tie it in as a package deal.
Thank you very much. Good to have met you, Swope.
Perhaps I'll see you later at the—er—barricades."

"I'll be here. We've already had to chase a bunch off.
Hey, should I bring my dog team over later?"

"You mean—er—hunger-maddened malemutes?"

"Yeah, only all they do is hang around and pig out
now that the dogsledding season is over. Maybe we can
kid people into thinking they're wild timber wolves."

"What a splendid suggestion. As a special favor to me,
would you mind driving them past the elder of those two
archaeologists who are in there with Dr. Svenson? I don't
suppose you'd care to disguise yourself as an Assyrian?"

"Huh?"

"Forget it. Just a passing fancy. Carry on, gentlemen."

Humming "With cat-like tread, upon our prey we
steal," Shandy again bent his steps toward Fergy's Bargain Barn. He found the proprietor in the act of selling a

rusted-out wheelbarrow to a lady who wanted something cute to plant geraniums in. That reminded him of Loretta Fescue, of whom he preferred not to be reminded.

Millicent was ever so glad to see him. Poor woman, she must be having a boring time of it here. He must be careful not to let Helen know or they'd wind up having Millicent over to the house for dinner. Helen's milk of human kindness tended to overflow sometimes. Anyway, the amount of money Fergy pocketed as he presented the deluded geranium lover with a hunk of otherwise useless wire mesh to line the wheelbarrow with so the dirt wouldn't fall through the hole in the bottom must be a comfort to Millicent if she was indeed contemplating becoming a permanency in the establishment. No doubt they had their moments of tedium among the ketchup squirters, too.

After the wheelbarrow had been loaded into the woman's car and the trunk lid tied down with some frayed rope Fergy donated as further testimony to his beneficence, Shandy asked what he'd come to find out.

"Fergy, while you were over there at the runestone, did you happen to notice a sapling bent over into a sort of arch?"

"Huh?" Fergy scratched his beard, now back to its accustomed state of dishevelment. "Seems to me—yeah, I did. It reminded me of McDonald's hamburgers, see, an' that made me think I ought to be gettin' back to Millie, so I hurried over here to let 'er know what was up. Say, she'd sure like to get a squint at that gold they found. Any chance?"

"I'm afraid not. They have the area cordoned off and police out at the road. By the way, how did you get past Bashan?"

"Oh, I just bulled my way through."

Guffawing at his own wit, Fergy went to get himself another beer.

CHAPTER 17

That would have made a fine exit line, and Shandy was more than ready to exit. However, there was still one point he hadn't dealt with, and Fergy, who probably took that insatiable thirst of his to the neighborhood beer joints, was as apt as not to have some information for him. He waited till the next slug of malt was halfway down the fat man's gullet, then asked, "Would you happen to know that son of Mrs. Fescue who works for Gunder Gaffson?"

"You mean Fesky? Skinny guy with black hair an' a front tooth busted off?"

"If you say so. I've never seen him myself. I thought perhaps you might have—er—hung out with him sometime or other."

"Yeah, we hoist one together now an' then over at Billy's Brewery. You ever go there?"

"No, I can't say that I have."

"I s'pose guys like you have to be kind o' careful," said Fergy with an offhand contempt that Shandy found rather amusing. "Well, anyway, him an' me sort o' got together 'cause our names is so much alike only we look so different, if you get what I mean. For such a skinny guy, he sure can put it away," he added with a tinge of envy.

"Has he any other talents, would you say?"

"I dunno. He fixed the jukebox one night when a Johnny Cash record got stuck. I guess he's one o' them guys that's naturally handy with their hands. He's mentioned doin' odd jobs for his mother sometimes, like if she's tryin' to sell a house with a big leak in the ceilin', for instance. He can fake it up so's it looks okay till she finds some sucker to unload it on. Course as soon as the next rainstorm comes along, forget it. We was kiddin' about it that night at Billy's, after he got the jukebox goin'. Fam'ly moves in, somebody happens to sneeze, an' Fesky's repairs all falls apart. They're left sittin' there in a heap o' lath an' plaster."

Fergy thought this was a great joke. So did Millicent. Shandy was not amused.

"How did—er—Fesky take your teasing?"

"Oh, he laughed. He's an easygoin' guy. Kids about it himself. He says that's how come he gets along okay with Gaffson. They're both good at fakin' things up to look like what they ain't. I guess that's what Fesky does mostly, patches up cracks in walls an' fixes the doors so's they'll open an' shut three or four times before they fall off. Or so he claims. Anyways, I guess he does all right for himself. Always has plenty o' the old do-re-mi. An' never mind askin' for an intro, Millie. Fesky's too young for you. Anyways, he ain't much for the women. All that gink cares about is beer an' goin' to the dogs."

"Do you mean figuratively or literally?"

"Huh? Oh, I get you, Professor. You talk so damn educated sometimes it takes me a while to figure out what you're tryin' to say. I mean like goin' out to the track. That's where he spends most of his nights, I guess, when he ain't at Billy's. I don't get over there too often myself so I couldn't say for sure, but whenever I do happen to see Fesky, he's always braggin' about how he won forty to one on some meathound or other."

"They say they train those greyhounds with real, live bunny rabbits." Millicent shuddered fetchingly.

"So what? Gotta get 'em to run somehow, ain't they? You wouldn't act so squeamish if you'd just won a few bucks on one yourself, I bet. You gonna fix us that turkey Tetrazzini for supper?"

"Don't let me keep you, Mrs. Peavey. I must be getting home," said Shandy, glad to take the hint. He didn't care to hear any more about live bunny rabbits and he'd found out as much as Fergy would be able to tell him about Fesky Fescue. If Loretta's son the odd-job specialist had been exercising his talents around the Horsefall place, Fesky would have been particularly careful to stay out of Fergy's sight. He turned to leave, then stopped.

"By the way, Fergy, did you hear that President Sven-son's uncle was injured down by the runestone shortly after you were there?"

"No! What happened?"

"He fell and cut his head."

"How bad?"

"I don't think it amounts to much. Miss Hilda is ad-ministering first aid and—er—tender, loving care."

"Hilda? That dame's about as tender as a rubber boot. Hey, don't go tellin' her I said that. I mean, she's a great old gal, but, jeez! I'd hate like hell to have her soothin' my fevered brow."

"You'd rather have me, wouldn't you, Fergy?" coaxed Millicent, who must have been feeling left out.

"Yeah, sure, anytime. Hey, I thought you was cookin' supper. Gotta soothe the ol' pauncho too, you know."

"Isn't he cute?" Millicent shook her frowsy curls and made a gallant attempt to wiggle her behind as she went off to the makeshift kitchen. Fergy watched her out of sight, then turned to Shandy.

"Hey, no kiddin', Professor," he asked in a sort of con-spiratorial hiss, "how did the old guy get hurt?"

Shandy looked at him in some surprise. "I can't tell you precisely."

"I knew it! It was the runestone, wasn't it? Go ahead an' laugh if you want to, but I ain't as dumb as I look. You can't tell me precisely how Spurge Lumpkin died ei-ther, can you? S'posed to be an accident. Huh! The stone's on what used to be his land, isn't it?"

"You've been talking to Nute Lumpkin, have you?"

"Me? Not today, but a guy was in here a while ago sayin' all that land you asked me about earlier turns out to be Lumpkin land, so that means it was Spruge's as much as Nute's, don't it? Cripes, I wisht Spurge was still alive. If I'd o' known he was a long-lost heir, I'd o' hit 'im up for a few bucks."

Fergy tried to grin, but it was a feeble effort. "Poor bugger. I felt like hell at that funeral, I don't mind tellin' you. An' I don't feel so hot right now, in case you're in-terested. Think it over, Professor. Here's Spurge gone an' Cronk ought to be, after that awful spill he took. An' now the old geezer who read them runes about the curse is laid out with a busted head an' Henny's in hot water up to his eyeballs an' then some. An' here's me smack in the path o' the—the whatever it is. Okay, I'm tryin' to kid myself I ain't scared, but I wouldn't be human if I wasn't, would I?"

Shandy scratched his chin. "Then it was remarkably brave of you to enter that enclosure with Bashan in order to get down the path to the stone."

"Oh, you know how it is. A guy doesn't like to admit he's a coward, so he does somethin' foolish to prove he ain't. Hey, you don't think it's more apt to rub off, like, if you get too close? Is that what the big guy was yellin' at me about? He said to get the hell out of there fast."

"By the big guy, I assume you mean President Svenson. I'd say the curse you ought to dread is his if you try gate-crashing again, which I gather you're—er—becoming less inclined to do."

"Yeah, I knew you'd think it was a big joke. But you brainy birds been wrong before, don't forget. Didn't I tell you Cronk better watch out? An' who's layin' over there in Hoddersville Hospital right this minute? Answer me that."

"I'm afraid I can't."

Shandy had just spied a television camera truck beetling up toward the Horsefall farm. In it were the driver, an announcer, a technician, and a bruised, battered, bandaged, but still reasonably comely young man with a now-familiar face. Cronkite Swope had made the big time.

"You'd better go eat your turkey Tetrazzini, Fergy," he said. "Something tells me this is going to be another of those nights."

He felt a desperate need for sustenance and wifely consolation himself. The hitch was that he'd left his car in Horsefall's barnyard. By going to get it, he risked being nailed by young Swope for an interview. Well, the hell with it. He was too beat to walk eight miles home, and damned if he'd hitchhike. He went back to the farm and, as he'd fully expected, Cronkite pounced.

"Hey, Professor Shandy! Wait, we want to—"

"Her name is Jessica Tate," he roared back, and stamped on the gas pedal with all his might.

Helen was standing looking out the window when he got home. From the relief on her face as she flung the door open and ran down the steps to greet him, he could see how worried she'd been.

"What's the matter?" he growled into her hair, knowing full well that their next-door neighbor Mirelle Feldster was lurking behind her living room curtains watching him embrace his wife right out in the open, and not giving a damn what Mirelle thought about this display of wanton conjugality. "Did you think Orm had got me?"

"Well, after what I've been hearing about that poor Swope boy—arms and legs all over the road and practically at death's door, they say—"

"Who's they?"

"People who came into the library."

"Well, you can tell them that when last seen, to be exact about fifteen minutes ago, that poor Swope boy was infesting Henny Horsefall's hen coop with a television crew."

"My stars! Hurry, let's put on the news."

"I'm not sure I want to."

Peter's protest availed him nothing. Helen had him into the den, settled in his armchair with his feet up and a gin and tonic in his hand, and the set turned on in front of him, all more or less in one movement.

They'd missed the first part of the report, but were in time to see Henny Horsefall and Miss Hilda standing there like strays from a Grant Wood painting while the announcer panted, "So does the curse of the runestone actually exist? Was the bizarre death of Spurgeon Lumpkin due to some malignant force emanating from that eerie oak grove on the old logging road? Why did the young reporter who braved the Viking's wrath have such a narrow escape from sudden death? Is the eminent Swedish archaeologist Dr. Sven Svenson yet another of the runestone's victims? Stay tuned for the next thrilling—I mean, Channel 2½ will be following this story very carefully. Mr. Swope, do you have any final word for our viewers?"

Cronkite, who was looking as white as his bandage and probably had sneaked out of the hospital while the doctor wasn't looking, grabbed the microphone. "Yes. I

want to beg everybody to stay the heck away from here.
The Horsefalls have been through enough already and it
was my fault for breaking the story and look where it got
me. I don't know what's happening here, but all I can say
is—"

Whatever it was, Swope never got to say it. He folded
neatly to the ground. As Miss Hilda bent over him, her
words were carried distinctly to the vast listening public.

"Vikin' curse, my backside! I been livin' next to that
runestone for a hundred an' five years an' it never brung
me nothin' I didn't go lookin' for, did it? Haul 'is carcass
in on the kitchen cot an' I'll ladle a swig o' my homemade gin into 'im. If that don't perk 'im up, he's a goner
for sure."

"Good God, you don't give alcohol to a concussion victim!"

Shandy leaped for the phone, but the Horsefalls' line
was already busy. Either Cronkite's mother had beaten
him to the draw or young Swope was in the hands of the
Norse gods. He hoped Odin, Freya, and the rest of the
Valhalla crowd were a match for Miss Hilda.

"Sit down, Peter," said Helen. "That boy looks like a
pretty sturdy specimen to me. How went the battle today?"

"Uncle Sven got levitated and Fergy has a real nice
little lady from Florida cooking his turkey Tetrazzini."

"Do tell."

"I'm telling, drat it. Give me time to sort out my
thoughts."

"Yes, dear."

Helen sipped her own drink. After a while, Peter began his narrative. At last he said, "So that's where we
stand as of this moment, to the best of my knowledge.
Does any of this make sense to you?"

"No, dear. I'd say the surveyor did it."

"You mean a *Balaclava* student? That nice young Lewis chap who wants to grow apples?"

"Why not? He's the unlikeliest suspect, isn't he?"

"You forget the geese."

"So I do. Perhaps you should take a gander at them."

"Thank you for those words of sage counsel, my love.
And how are things among the bookworms?"

"Peter, you can't imagine how exciting it is! I made another—no, Jane. Mustn't sharpen those little claws on Mummy's legs. Go to Daddy. As I was trying to say, I made another tremendous find today."

"A mint copy of Poe's *Tamerlane?*"

"Nothing so paltry. I was prowling through a boxful of old postcards and valentines, which could be worth a good deal to collectors, by the way, and came across Belial Buggins's private diaries."

"Belial? You mean the Buggins who donated the library? I thought his name was Bedivere."

"It was. Belial was Bedivere's brother the poet."

"Didn't know he had one. Helen, this creature is eating the buttons off my shirt."

"Then stop her. They'll make her sick. Come on, Jane, let's have some milk and cookies."

She scooped the ball of striped fluff off her husband's chest and carried it out to the kitchen. "That's why this find is so important. To me, anyway. Wait a second. Jane dear, do take your paws out of the saucer. Nobody knows what a mother goes through."

Helen came back with a plate of cheese and crackers. "It's only salad and cold meat tonight, so eat hearty. Peter, Belial was the most amazing man! He taught himself Finnish so that he could read the *Kalevala* in the original. Can you believe it? Right here in Balaclava County."

"And why not in Balaclava Conty? Every country schoolmaster spoke Greek and Latin in those days."

"That's pure academic chauvinism and you know it. Half of them probably couldn't have got through McGuffey's fifth reader. Finnish is an incredibly difficult language. That's why Finns tend to stand around looking handsome and not saying anything. I knew the most divinely stunning Finnish boy once. His name was Paali. I'd have followed him to the ends of the earth."

"Why didn't you?" snarled Peter.

"My mother wouldn't have let me. Besides, I don't recall his ever making the suggestion. All he ever uttered were things like 'Shut up and go back to bed.' "

"Good God! What for?"

"Because my brothers were making a racket, no doubt.

They usually did. He was our baby-sitter. I was about eight at the time."

"That, madam, is the anticlimax of the day. Unless of course you were about to tell me what Belial did after he'd read the *Kalevala* in the original Finnish."

"I was but I shan't if you're going to be nasty."

"It's just my insane jealousy," Peter replied through a mouthful of cracker. "Continue your narrative. Did he spend the rest of his life looking handsome and not saying anything?"

"No, he wrote a saga, like Longfellow only not the same."

"How not the same?"

"Well, I'm afraid a great deal less poetically, for one thing. He swiped from Hiawatha like mad and injected a sort of pseudo-mysticism that Grace and I couldn't make much sense of."

"Such as what?" Peter had a passion for doggerel.

"I knew you'd ask, so I copied down the first bit." Helen fished a crumpled sheet of paper out of her skirt pocket. "He begins:

> "By the brook of Balaclava,
> By the spirit-stirring waters
> Stands the bearded bard Belial,
> Man of mettle, man of moonshine.
> Still he stands, yet still he runneth—

"Peter, surely you don't want to hear any more of this nonsense?"

"Ah, but I do, my little lotus blossom." Shandy rose to kiss his wife chastely on the forehead. "Belial was no mystic, just a bit of a card. Try connecting the words 'spirit,' 'moonshine,' and 'still,' and what do you get?"

"A dreadful hangover, I suppose," Helen replied, flushing a most becoming pink. "Is it Grace's and my fault that we have such pure, innocent minds? He even spelled it 'metal,' referring, I suppose, to all those old washtubs and copper tubing or whatever that he made his distillery out of. I thought he meant bravery and was just mentally confused from reading all that Finnish."

"No Buggins was ever confused unless he chose to be.

There's been a legend around campus for eons, give or take a few decades, that it was a Buggins who invented the Balaclava Boomerang.* Your find may promote the Boomerang from myth to history. We must research this matter in depth, my love."

"You research it. I have to go research the dinner. You needn't think you're going to sit there swilling gin all evening."

"And who gave me the gin to swill, prithee? Did I ask for it, even?"

"No, but you would have. Darling, you don't have to go back to the Horsefall place again tonight, do you?"

"I hope not. After that broadcast, I expect the state police will be out patrolling the area, since the Lumpkinton police don't seem to be doing anything but—what's that?"

They hadn't turned off the television set. A moment ago it had been emitting those commercials for laxatives and clogged sink drains that advertisers deem so eminently suitable for mealtime viewing. Halfway down a drain, a scared-looking announcer was suddenly back in front of the camera.

"We interrupt this commercial to report that there's been an alarming new development at the Horsefall farm. An explosion of undetermined origin has blown a huge crater behind the barn where Spurgeon Lumpkin's recent horrible death occurred, killing several geese and injuring our television cameraman as well as an eminent scientist who was in the act of taking soil samples for—"

"My God! It's Tim." Shandy leaped for the door.

Helen tried to hold him back. "Peter, wait. At least eat something."

He grabbed another slice of cheese. "I did. Helen, I've got to go."

"Then I'm going with you."

---

*The Balaclava Boomerang is a potion composed of locally hardened cider and locally produced cherry brandy. Please do not request the recipe, because you would not be able to obtain the proper ingredients outside Balaclava County and it wouldn't come out right no matter how hard you tried.

"No you're not. One of us has to stay alive, for Jane's sake. Keep the home fires burning."

It was no use. He could run a great deal faster than she. Sighing, Helen went back to the kitchen wondering why men had to be heroes and why women loved those adorable knuckleheads so. She ate a little of the salad and cold meat, let Jane climb up into her lap, and sat pondering. As she stroked the kitten's satin ears, an idea stirred. She moved Jane to a cushion, found her private set of keys to the college library, and went to do some more research.

CHAPTER 18

"But I'm Professor Shandy."

"I don't care if you're the King of Norway. You can't go in there."

For once the Lumpkinton chief of police was on the job and giving it all he had. The whole area from the logging road up to the Horsefalls' was roped off and men were patrolling it in full riot gear, probably borrowed from the National Guard. Perhaps they were the National Guard. In any event, they formed what appeared to be an impregnable barrier until Laurie Ames happened to run down from the house.

"Professor Shandy, we've been looking everywhere for you. Daddy Ames is frantic. He thinks you were killed in the explosion. Can you come quickly, before he frets himself into a heart attack?"

Not even taking time to throw the vigilantes a triumphant look, Shandy broke through the barricade. "How bad is he?" he panted.

"I can't tell if he's in shock or simply drunk as a skunk," Laurie told him. "Miss Hilda's been dosing him with that homemade white lightning of hers."

"Great Scott! Has he seen a doctor?"

"They sent an ambulance unit with a couple of paramedics over from Hoddersville General to pick up the bodies, but they're sitting around the kitchen table right now, eating Jolene's layer cake and playing high-low-jack. The hospital keeps calling to see where they are, but they're having too much fun to leave."

Shandy said "Great Scott!" again and ran into the house.

Timothy Ames was, at any rate, not dead. He was bellowing like Bashan in a slightly slurred voice. "Where's Pete? For Christ's sake, haven't they found him yet?"

Following the roars, Shandy found his old friend stretched out on a bed upstairs, being held down by his son, Roy.

"Dad, you've got to—oh, Professor Shandy! Thank God you're here. Can you get him to quiet down?"

Shandy grabbed his comrade's horny, soil-dyed hand. "Tim," he bellowed, "I'm fine. Are you hooked up?"

Ames managed a grin. "I can hear you, Pete. I'm hooked up and stove up. Twisted my lumbago trying to get away. Whole damn manure pile whizzing at me. Hell of a way to go. Least Henny won't have to spread any fertilizer for a while. Must be knee-deep all over hell and gone. Miss Hilda gave me a bath. I think she put one of her nightgowns on me. I'm afraid to look."

"I gave you a bath, Dad," Roy said, looking as if he might have been crying a little. "And that's Henny's spare nightshirt you're wearing. Miss Hilda only supervised. She wasn't much impressed, I'm afraid. She says you young squirts don't have enough of what it takes."

"Thank God for small favors. Speaking of squirts, what happened to the kid? Is he all right? Saved my life, I think. Reflexes faster than mine. Got between me and the flak."

"He's okay, Dad. The last I saw of him, he was out under the hose and his mother was having fits."

"Don't wonder. Knows a lot more about organic fertilizing now than he wishes he did, I'll bet. Pete, we've got to wangle that kid a scholarship. I'll foot the bills and you fix it with Svenson."

"You're talking about young Ralphie Horsefall?"

"Great-nephew's kid. Skinny runt who comes to muck out for Henny. Got the makings of a farmer, Pete. Where the hell were you?"

"I'm ashamed to say that I'd gone home without telling you. Helen and I were watching the news on television. That whelp Swope had a camera crew over here, as you no doubt know, and they broke in with a report on the explosion. When I heard you'd been . . ." Shandy's voice, for some reason, deserted him. He cleared his throat and tried again. "What actually did happen?"

"Told you. Manure pile blew up. I was showing the kid how the soil in that area was overrich because of the leaching of trace elements. Next thing we knew there was this sort of gurgling whoosh and the horse buns started flying. First time I've ever seen that happen and I've been around a hell of a lot of dung piles. Orm's got a crude sense of humor, if you ask me."

"Good God! Are they laying this on the Viking curse, too?"

"Why not? Think I'll shut my eyes a minute if you don't mind."

"Sure, Tim."

Shandy gave the shoulder under Henny's spare nightshirt a clumsy pat and tiptoed out of the room. Roy followed him and shut the door.

"He's going to be okay, Professor Shandy. It's mostly shock. I'm a little shook up myself. Dad doesn't realize what a narrow squeak he and Ralphie had. If they'd been a few feet nearer and Ralphie hadn't kept his head, I—I guess I don't want to think about it."

"Neither do I, Roy. What's your opinion of the Orm theory?"

"Orm, hell! We had to do a little blasting in the Antarctic when we got stuck in ice packs, and of course it had to be done carefully on account of the ecological balance, not to mention blowing a hole in our hull. I think I know the effect of a well-placed charge when I see it. Come around and have a look for yourself. I don't know whether the state police bomb squad is there yet, but if they're not they damn well ought to be. I've been raising a worse stink than the explosion did, and that's going some, I can tell you."

Shandy didn't have to be told. Even up at the house, the aroma of ancient cow dung hung on the air stronger than that of sweat socks in the men's gym after a track meet. As they moved down toward the barn it became, though Shandy would not have thought this possible, even more pronounced.

"Watch where you step, Professor."

Roy's caution was a waste of breath. The bare patches were too far between to be of any use. Veteran of the rutabaga fields though he was, Shandy found himself treading gingerly as a cat on a wet lawn.

Now he could see the barn, looking oddly incomplete without that immense greasy brown sloping mass at the rear. A dark stain over most of the back wall provided visual evidence that the manure heap had in fact been there when he'd last looked, and Shandy was interested to notice that not one of the barnboards was so much as cracked or splintered by the explosion.

The news report had grossly exaggerated the extent of the crater, but there was a depression a couple of feet deep and roughly fifteen feet in diameter. There were also a good many gray and white feathers around, testifying to the demise of the Lewises' geese. Henny Horsefall was standing beside the hole looking like a gone gander himself.

Of the bomb squad there was as yet no sign. Roy uttered an imprecation. Shandy stepped forward, his nostrils now so numb that he could take a breath without too much effort of will, and peered into the crater. There wasn't actually anything to see except torn-up, nutrient-saturated earth and a few blown feathers. He turned his attention to the surrounding area.

On the whole there appeared to be more mess than serious damage. Flying manure had more or less buried the hen house and knocked down some fence posts, but that situation could be remedied easily enough. He walked over to one of the tilted posts and tripped over a trailing wire that was all but buried in ordure. A disagreeable tingly sensation shot up his leg.

"Horsefall," he yelped, "did you know you have a charged wire here?"

The old farmer took a long time to answer. At last he muttered, "Like as not."

"But why?"

"I built a little pen for Bessie out here last winter when I had my game leg. Thought she'd be warmer next to the manure pile. Had to get 'er out somehow. Bessie likes 'er fresh air. Gets moody if I keep 'er in the barn all day."

"And you made this pen by setting some posts and stringing electrified wire?"

"Spurge an' me. He set the posts, I strung the wire. All we could manage. Had to do somethin'. Bessie's a wanderer."

"How recently have you used the pen?"

"Eh? Oh, not lately. Take 'er up to the pasture now. Bessie likes the pasture better."

"Then why is current running through the wire?"

"Damned if I know." Henny didn't sound as though he cared, either.

"You'd normally keep it shut off when Bessie wasn't out here?"

"Yep. No sense wastin' the juice. Dang light bills are bad enough already."

"Where's the shutoff switch?"

"In the barn."

"Show me."

Old Horsefall obeyed, apparently only because he had no will left to resist. He led Shandy and Roy Ames inside the vast, cool, empty structure and pointed to a jury-rigged connection that would have given a fire inspector fits. Shandy tested it gingerly and found the switch had been thrown to the on position. He then went back out to the yard, managed with a good deal of unpleasant poking and prodding to locate the other fence wires, and found that all except the one he'd happened to trip over had been torn loose from their connections. That was exactly what he'd hoped to find.

"I think we have our answer, Roy," he said. "Start looking for a piece of metal."

"What kind of metal?"

"Any kind. It might be a horseshoe, an old iron spike, a hoe head, something that might naturally be lying around a place like this. There should also be a gadget made from two different kinds of metal and a spring, probably attached to a piece of wood. This may be very small and it would quite likely have been demolished by the explosion, but we can try. Come on, Horsefall, help us hunt."

The farmer didn't even bother to shake his head. He just stood there, turning over and over in his twiglike hands one of the long gray wing feathers off a dead goose. Shandy gave him a worried look, then picked up a spading fork and went to work.

It was quite a while before Roy turned up a short metal rod, squared off on the sides and threaded at both ends. "Could this be what you're looking for, Professor?"

"It could indeed, and probably is. Ah yes, see that?"

"You mean that piece of thin wire wrapped between the threads? What's that supposed to mean? Hey, don't tell me this is a bomb!"

"No, merely part of a detonator. The manure pile itself was the bomb."

"Are you serious?"

"Certainly. What powers the college generators, Roy?"

"Methane gas."

"And where does the methane come from?"

"Decomposition of animal wastes, mostly."

"And what have we been wading through for the past hour or so? On the strength of the evidence, I'd say somebody rigged a little doodad out of two pieces of dissimilar metals such as zinc and copper, hitched one side to the charged wire and the other side to this hunk of whatever it is. He, or she, planted the device inside the manure pile and disconnected the remaining fence wires so that if anybody should happen to touch one they wouldn't feel the juice.

"After that, it was only a matter of flipping the switch and going home to take a bath. Heat generated by natural fermentation inside the manure pile would gradually warm the metals in the detonator. The spring would get sprung and contact made, causing a spark that would set off the methane gas contained in the pile. The size of the explosion couldn't be calculated in advance because you wouldn't know how great a concentration of methane you were working with, but the odds were that it wouldn't do anything worse than make a spectacular mess, which in fact it did."

"You can say that again, Professor. How long would it take for the detonator to heat up?"

"I have no idea. The metal wouldn't have to get red-hot or anything like that. Essentially you're dealing with the same principle on which the earlier home heating thermostats used to work."

"It would take a while, though? You'd have a chance to clear out before the thing let go?"

"Oh yes, I should think so. Plenty of time, probably. The detonator might even have been set last night during that big mob scene, or more probably after the crowd had gone home. You'd have to dig down into the pile, unless you could bore through from the side in one way or another."

"Like with one of Dad's soil augers or some such tool. Maybe one of those electric snake things plumbers use, since you'd have juice to work it with."

"M'yes." Shandy wondered whether Loretta Fescue's son included plumbing among his repertoire of odd jobs. "Or you might use a posthole digger, or even a long crowbar, if you got enough beef on the end of it. You'd only have to make a small hole, then push in that rod with the ignition device wired to it and the fence wire trailing behind. I daresay that's why this particular object was chosen to be the ground. The threads would keep the wire from slipping off, and it's the right shape to go in easily. Let's see the thing again."

Roy handed over his find again, and again Shandy studied it carefully.

"I know damn well what this is a piece of, I just can't think offhand. It will come to me, sooner or later. Probably isn't important anyway. Shall we try to find the rest of the detonator? It will be like looking for a needle in a haystack, of course."

"I'd take the haystack, with pleasure." Yet Roy tried manfully to grin as he bent once more to his manure fork.

CHAPTER 19

They were still grubbing among the muck when the bomb squad from the state police finally arrived. Shandy displayed their finds, expounded his theory, and said he was sure the police would have made the same discoveries if they'd happened to get to the scene before him. The bomb squad experts said they were sure they would, too, but thanked him and Roy for saving them the trouble. They then reluctantly accepted the honor of continuing the hunt for the detonator, which they at last located in the shape of a few splinters from an old shingle and a glob of fused metals about the size of a walnut.

Meanwhile Shandy went back to the house to clean himself up and muse. What Roy had pointed out was perfectly true: nobody could know exactly when the device was set except the one who put it there, so neither could anybody be written off as innocent. For all he knew, young Ralphie might have had the contraption ready in his overalls pocket, wired it up, and pinched Tim's soil auger long enough to plant his booby trap while he'd been allegedly showing so much interest in soil testing out there.

The detonator might have heated up faster than he'd thought it would, and hoist him with his own petard before he could think of an excuse to clear out. Or he might have hung around the manure pile out of kiddish bravado, not realizing how potent the explosion might be and thinking only about giving himself an excuse to reek of manure, though a whiff of the stable on a boy who did farm chores shouldn't be anything for him to worry about.

On the whole, a pretty good case could be made out for

Ralphie, but what could be his motive unless the kid was a bit crazy? And how could the boy be crazy when Timothy Ames believed Ralphie had the makings of a farmer? Shandy thought he'd almost rather believe in Orm's curse than in his old friend's fallibility on that score.

And while he was thinking of Orm, what about those two young surveyors out there, allegedly trying to determine whose land the runestone was on? Young Lewis, the Horsefalls' next-door neighbor, was already doing a job for Nute Lumpkin, in a sense. Mightn't he be doing two?

It was all very well to give Professor Shandy a song and dance about apple orchards. If Lewis had brains, and he must have since he'd managed to pass the college entrance examinations, he'd know Professor Shandy would automatically warm up to a young man who talked of planting an apple orchard. He'd know Professor Shandy's reputation for sniffing out malefactors, and he'd be very anxious indeed to present himself to Professor Shandy as a model of rectitude.

Those were the Lewises' own geese that had perished in the explosion, but what of that? Wasn't it the oldest trick in the book to put yourself, or something of your own, in jeopardy as a way of demonstrating your innocence? The geese could be replaced at little expense. Lewis surely wouldn't be fool enough to take on a dirty-tricks campaign for Lumpkin without being well paid for it. Moreover, a college man with enough wits to be a surveyor would be far more apt to know how to rig up that clever detonating device to explode the manure pile than would a teenager who appeared to be barely squeaking through high school.

Miss Horsefall had wondered why Nutie the Cutie had made such a production of coming to collect his dead cousin's useless possessions. Shandy had brushed it off as petty harassment, but might the visit not also have afforded Lumpkin an excuse to meet with young Lewis? Or with the other chap, for that matter? Or with both?

But why should Nutie need Lewis at all? Why couldn't he have blown up the dung pile himself? Might not that byplay with the mauve silk handkerchief been a subtle way of showing what a fastidious dandy he was, so that

Shandy wouldn't think to connect him with so vulgarly bucolic an explosion?

In practice, Lumpkin couldn't possibly be so dainty as he'd made himself out to be. The antiques business had to involve a good deal of grubbing about with objects out of dusty attics and moldy cellars, not to mention hen coops and haylofts. Besides, whatever he might fancy himself to have become now, Nute must have been born and raised either on or near a farm. There hadn't been much except farms out this way until the soap factory and the Gunder Gaffson types moved in. Lumpkin no doubt knew his way around a barnyard as well as most of his neighbors.

Shandy couldn't see Lumpkin managing to rig that detonator during his visit to the house, though. For one thing, there was that pale beige outfit he'd been wearing. It had been spotless until he'd been forced to tote those cartons of tobacco boxes down to his car, and he'd thrown a fit about getting it smudged.

Might that be why he'd taken Spurge's old clothes, to protect his own? But how could he have put them on, sneaked back here, done his dirty work, and got away without being caught? The Horsefall farm hadn't been exactly a private place today. Even after the multitudes of relatives and assistant mourners had left, there'd been the Ameses and young Ralphie and Sven Svenson hurtling through the trees and God knows who else around the place. Lumpkin couldn't have used the back way through the logging road and the bramble patch because Bashan was at one end and Thorkjeld Svenson at the other. Moreover, he'd driven in and out through that police cordon already, so they'd be sure to know who he was if he tried coming twice.

Ah, but what if Lumpkin had already worn the clothes? Suppose he'd managed to sneak into the house and dress himself in Spurge's outfit last night under cover of the general hullabaloo. He could have set his odoriferous time bomb then easily enough.

He'd have had to put the clothes back afterward so they wouldn't be missed and commented on, but that wouldn't be hard. Spurge had slept in the little downstairs bedroom next to the woodshed that was always al-

lotted to the hired man or the hired girl in these parts. If
Lumpkin had been recognized as himself either going or
coming, he could have spouted some garbage about his
duty to his dead cousin, but the odds were he wouldn't
have been if he was reasonably careful. Lumpkin had
one of those bland, forgettable faces that tended to make
you think the person you saw was really somebody else.

Then the purpose of his performance today could have
been to remove the clothes in case he'd got his own hair
oil or something on them. That seemed like a piece of un-
necessary conniving, but Shandy had a hunch Nute
Lumpkin would rather connive than not. Furthermore,
maybe he'd wanted more than Spurge's clothes. Suppose
Nute had reason to think his cousin possessed a small
but valuable family heirloom, for instance, or some docu-
ment that might either bolster or weaken his claim to
the long-litigated Lumpkin estate? There weren't many
places to hide such a thing in that sparse little room except among that vast collection of tobacco boxes.

Nute wouldn't have dared stay long enough to search
through all those cartons, and why should he? He'd have
done exactly what he did today, call in broad daylight
and make himself so obnoxious that nobody would take
time to look them over before he carried them away. Perhaps he'd hoped the explosion would oblige him by occur-
ring while he shone in cleanly innocence up above. Perhaps he'd thought the diversion might give him time
enough to find what he wanted without having to carry
away all that junk. Who the hell knew?

Nobody could be let off the hook, not even Tim or Roy
or Laurie. Or Eddie or Ralph or Jolene or Marie or any of
their respective broods. Or Miss Hilda or Henny Horsefall, who was acting strange enough to make a person
wonder whether he was safe out alone now. Fergy the
junkman could have waddled across during the night, assuming he could have torn himself from the loving embrace of Millicent Peavey and wasn't too drunk to find
the manure pile, both of which assumptions would appear untenable on the strength of available testimony.

Fergy certainly couldn't have been messing around
the barnyard in that racetrack tout's outfit he'd worn to
the funeral, and he hadn't stunk noticeably of anything

except beer when Shandy had called on him later. Of the two, Millicent was no doubt the likelier suspect, were it not for the fact that she hadn't been around Lumpkin Corners long enough to know where Horsefall's barn was, much less find a motive to harass him, unless she turned out to be Gunder Gaffson's long-lost aunt. Shandy wouldn't be at all surprised if she was.

Would Gaffson himself risk coming here? The contractor was a big man. Shandy remembered how he'd towered over Loretta Fescue, who was no lightweight either, the one time he'd seen the pair together. And Gaffson was a short-tempered man, judging from the way he'd snapped at Mrs. Fescue and hustled her off the property. And he was used to getting what he wanted and doing what he chose regardless of the consequences to anybody but himself.

Gaffson must know at least the rudiments of electrical wiring, since he was in the construction business. He'd surely know how to make a simple thermostat. He'd have the strength and no doubt the right tool for burrowing into the manure pile. If he didn't care to take on the nasty job himself, he could have sent Fesky.

Or Loretta could have sent Fesky. Or Fesky could have got the bright idea of exercising his own initiative, and why in Sam Hill hadn't Shandy gone out and tracked down Fesky Fescue this afternoon instead of listening to Millicent Peavey dither about heating up the turkey Tetrazzini?

Was it too late to go now? What the hell time was it, anyway? It suddenly occurred to Shandy that the sun had gone down, and this on the longest day of the year, which hadn't occurred to him before. The summer solstice. A prickle much like the jolt he'd experienced when he tripped over the live fence wire jigged up his back. The old Norse had been rather big on solstices, hadn't they? Could this sudden epidemic of bizarre happenings centered around the runestone have anything to do with the summer solstice? Oh, Christ! Was he back to Orm Tokesson again?

CHAPTER 20

As he wound up his cogitations, Shandy realized he'd absentmindedly seated himself at Miss Hilda's kitchen table and consumed the tail end of Jolene's layer cake. He wiped the crumbs off his mouth and went out into the yard, switching on the porch light as he went, for night was gathering fast.

Through the ensuing charge of moths and June bugs, he discerned a purple automobile in the yard. A large woman in a purple dress and hat stood beside it, talking down at a bent old man in ragged overalls. Loretta Fescue, thanks no doubt to her brother the police chief, had got through the cordon. She was pouring the old snake oil over Henny Horsefall for all she was worth. And Henny was caving in.

Shandy leaped across the yard and took a firm grip on Henny's shoulder. He was not a moment too soon. The real estate agent was already taking a sales agreement out of her oversized purple handbag.

"So you see it's really a remarkably generous offer, Mr. Horsefall. But I'm afraid Mr. Gaffson won't wait any longer. He already holds an option on a piece of property over in Hoddersville that would suit his purpose almost as well as this. And with all the dreadful troubles you've been having here the past couple of days, and no telling what's going to come next now that they're digging up the runestone—not that I'm a superstitious person myself, but I don't mind telling you I almost fainted when I heard on the news about the explosion killing Professor Ames."

"Then you'll be relieved to know that Professor Ames was not killed or even seriously injured, and that the explosion had nothing to do with the runestone," Shandy told her. "That was merely another piece of vandalism, such as the Horsefalls have been subjected to ever since, by a curious coincidence, you first started trying to persuade them to sell their land."

"What? Are you insinuating that I—"

"I'm not insinuating anything, Mrs. Fescue. I'm merely pointing out a curious coincidence."

"Eh?"

For the first time since the explosion, Henny Horsefall looked more alive than dead. "What's that about vandalism?"

"Horsefall, you were with me when I discovered that fence wire with current running through it, and Roy found the piece of metal that had been used to ground the detonator. Didn't you realize how that manure pile was deliberately rigged to blow up?"

"Guess I didn't quite take it in," the old man mumbled. "Too many things happenin'. One right after another. That Swope boy—"

"Hit an oil slick somebody had conveniently arranged down at the bend in the road and took a header off his bike. Nothing supernatural about that either."

"But 'twas Orm that flang the Swedish feller into the tree," Henny argued. "He said so hisself."

"Dr. Svenson's a lot older than you are, Horsefall, and his English is none too good. He either didn't grasp what had happened to him or didn't know the right words to explain it."

Shandy described the crude but effective catapult that had been made from the limber birch sapling. "It was a stroke of luck, good or bad depending on your point of view, that a light little chap like him instead of someone big and heavy like his nephew happened to lean against the birch and get tossed when it sprang back upright."

"I'll be danged!"

Henny was looking a great deal brighter now, and Mrs. Fescue showed clenched teeth as her smile became more and more forced.

"So it was just more o' them cussed—great balls o' fire, what's that?"

From out of the night came a galloping of hooves. Into

the yard burst a coal-black horse, greater than any living beast. On its back loomed the majestic figure of a woman more beautiful than any woman could be, her long, golden hair streaming out behind her like an outrun aureole. And right on her steed's spurting heels came another rider, tiny atop another coal-black immensity, blond also but with hair cut into a curly nimbus. It was the Ride of the Valkyrie!

No, by George, it was Sieglinde Svenson aboard Odin, largest and swiftest of the mighty Balaclava Blacks. And the attendant page pounding toward them on Odin's consort Freya was none other than—

"Helen! Good God, are you trying to kill yourself?" roared her distraught husband.

"Don't be silly, Peter. Whoa, Freya. She's gentle as a lamb. A baby could ride her. Anyway, Sieglinde and I couldn't get hold of a car because Thorkjeld's got theirs and you've got ours and we didn't dare ask Dr. Porble and you simply had to know right away."

"This will be a blow the most shattering to Thorkjeld," sighed Mrs. Svenson, reining in Odin as if he were a child's hobby horse. "Be still, my noble steed. Peter, it is you who must tell him. I have not the heart."

"Tell him what? Great Scott, what's happened now? Is somebody dead?"

"Worse. Far worse. He has never lived."

"Who? You don't mean Birgit's had a miscarriage already?"

"Peter, don't be absurd," said Helen primly. "She's barely off on her honeymoon. It's Orm, of course. He's a fake."

"What?"

"Orm was another of Belial Buggins's little funnies, that's all. After you'd pointed out that joke about the moonshine I got to thinking about what a person with an odd sense of humor and a hang-up on the *Kalevala* might do, so I went to the library and did some more research on those diaries. He had it all written down. See, I've even brought the right book with me, in case Thorkjeld won't believe us."

She pulled a small paper-bound volume out of her pocket and waved it under his nose. "It's right here. Belial had also taught himself a little Old Norse, and boned up on runes. He thought it would be a barrel of laughs to carve that stone, get some archaeologists out here from Harvard, and make a big to-do, then reveal the hoax. This was about the time of the Cardiff Giant and all that, you know. They rather went in for intellectual whimsies in those days."

"My love, will you quit flaunting your erudition and get down off that elephant?" Peter entreated.

"You can't get down off an elephant. It grows on birds. I learned that old chestnut in second grade," Helen replied lightly. "Anyway, Belial was going to do it up in grand style. He managed to acquire a couple of genuine Viking relics from some old collector he'd met somewhere. One was that piece of helmet Cronkite Swope found, of course. The other was a coin. Apparently they were both of a late period and in bad condition, so the other man didn't mind parting with them. Anyway, Belial was going to bury them both under the stone. After they'd found them, the archaeologists were supposed to dig down a little farther and find a saga—or would it be an edda—that Orm had allegedly written. It was all about his voyage to this undiscovered land, only it had some pretty juicy local scandal worked into it and Belial was thinking of burying it inside a Lydia E. Pinkham's bottle. The diary stops right after that, so I don't know what happened next."

"Most likely somebody shot the bastard," said her husband with a good deal of feeling. "Belial must have been a public menace. Know anything about Belial Buggins, Horsefall?"

"Made the best white lightnin' in Balaclava County is all I know. My ol' grandpop used to go on about Belial's booze when Granny wasn't around. Aunt Hilda would likely remember some of 'is folks. Cripes, if we're bein' haunted by Belial's ghost, we're in a worse mess o' trouble than I thought we was."

But Henny chuckled as he said it and Mrs. Fescue quit trying to smile.

"Mr. Horsefall," she wailed, "you as much as promised."

"Like hell I did. Excuse me, ladies, I don't gen'rally

cuss in front o' females I ain't related to, but this woman's been pesterin' the daylights out o' me so long she's druv me to it. You get on back to Gunder Gaffson, Miz Fescue, an' tell 'im he can build anywhere he dern well pleases long as it ain't on my land. This is the Horsefall Farm, which it's been for the past two hundred an' forty-three years, an' it's goin' to stay the Horsefall Farm while there's a Horsefall alive to till it. Now if you folks'll excuse me, I think I'll step inside an' have a little nip myself. I kind o' feel the need."

"Go ahead, Horsefall," said Shandy, repressing an urge to kiss him. "Good for what ails you. We'll go too, if you don't mind. I'd like a few words with your aunt before we tackle the president."

"Come right ahead. She was in the parlor with Dr. Svenson last I seen of 'er." Henny led the way, then turned to apologize. "She'll raise ol' Ned with me for takin' you ladies in through the kitchen. Ain't been time to keep it picked up, what with all the goin's-on."

The room was in a certain amount of disarray. The cake plate Shandy had been eating from stood on the square pine table, a crudely painted, garishly colored bird against a dull red spatterwork background showing through a smear of frosting and crumbs. The pierced tin door of the dark pine pie cupboard hung open, revealing shelves cluttered with odds and ends of pastry that hadn't got eaten up during the onslaught after the funeral. About five generations of plates and teacups lay around the soapstone sink. Sieglinde and Helen exchanged looks.

Shandy caught them and scowled. "I think Miss Horsefall manages very well, all things considered."

"She has managed perhaps far better than she knows," said Sieglinde, carefully moving the worn comb-back rocker in order to get her large though elegant form through the narrow doorway into the hall. "We shall find her in here?"

They found her, all right. They could have chosen a worse moment to burst into the parlor, but it was obvious they hadn't missed that moment by much. Miss Hilda hadn't quite finished rearranging her garments and Uncle Sven's mustache was in a state of total dishevelment. As he tried to comb it out with his fingers Sieglinde said something sharp to him in Swedish and the ends drooped for a moment, but they snapped right back into a tight upward curl. Shandy thought he'd never seen a happier mustache.

"Er—don't disturb yourselves, folks," he said. "We'll be back a bit later. Mrs. Svenson just wanted to make sure the president's uncle was all right before we go down to the dig."

They backed out, all trying to pretend they hadn't seen what they'd indubitably seen, rounded up a few flashlights, and remounted Odin and Freya, Shandy riding pillion behind his wife. There was traffic on the hill road again tonight, but the police were being extremely severe with anybody who tried to loiter. The Balaclava Blacks, not to mention the spectacle of the president's wife with her hair down, awed them into easy submission, however. This time, Shandy had no trouble being let into the logging road.

The archaeologists were still at it. Shandy and his party could see them up ahead working under a couple of floodlights that must have come from the college. They'd completed what appeared to be a ridiculously small excavation considering the long day they'd put in. Thorkjeld Svenson looked fresh enough, but the other two were obviously ready to call it quits.

Sieglinde nodded at Helen. Helen winked back at Sieglinde. Both nudged their mounts into a gallop and swooped down upon the runestone with a Wagnerian "Ho-jo-to-ho!"

"My God, he's sent Brünnhilde after us!" shrieked the elder archaeologist, falling back in awe and terror.

"I—I'm not sure it's—"

The younger archaeologist's voice failed him as Thorkjeld Svenson plucked the Viking queen of battles from her saddle, kissed her mightily and at great length, then began to roar like Boreas through the pines of Norway on a night in January.

"You—you *know* this—this goddess?"

"Hell, I ought to," bellowed the president. "I've been sleeping with her for thirty-four years."

"In lawful wedlock," Sieglinde added primly. "I am the

wife of President Svenson and how do you do? It is only that I have lost my hairpins because Odin runs so fast."

"I hope you appreciate the honor that's being done you, gentlemen. My wife doesn't let her hair down for everybody."

Svenson was still laughing as he gathered up the radiant masses in his great hands. "Here's the purest Viking gold you'll ever see."

Sieglinde rescued her tresses and twisted them into a knot behind her neck. "Thorkjeld, could you not first have wiped the leaf mold off you hands? But what you say, alas, is true. Here is no Viking treasure, gentlemen, only Belial Buggins."

"What?" roared the president.

"I'm sorry, Thorkjeld," said Helen. "I found it in his diaries."

"Found what? I never knew Belial could write. Thought he was a moonshiner."

"He was, but he was also a number of other things, including a remarkably erudite practical jokester." Helen produced the foxed little book in which Buggins had recorded his secret japeries. "See, here's where he tells how he's carved the runestone, and where he bought the Viking relics he plans to bury."

The president studied the sputtery browned handwriting first with suspicion, then with fury. "Why, that son of a—"

"Thorkjeld!" chided his wife.

"But damn it, Sieglinde, I—I'm—Helen, you mean there never was an Orm Tokesson?"

"Not in Lumpkin Corners there wasn't. I'm sorry."

"Sorry? Is that all you can say? Sorry! Hell." He draped himself over the runestone like a stricken Titan. "I *liked* Orm."

Sieglinde went over and clasped his massive head to her equally massive but far more shapely bosom. "Be comforted, my own. You have still me, not to mention our seven beautiful daughters, our five handsome sons-in-law, our nine adorable grandchildren, our dear parents, our beloved sisters and brothers, our respected friends, and many aunts, uncles, nieces, nephews, and cousins to the fourth degree, though I see no need to invite them all to the engagement party."

"What engagement party? Good God, you don't mean Frideswiede?"

"I do not. I mean your Great-uncle Sven and Miss Horsefall, between whom affairs have progressed to a state where someone must step in and observe the proprieties. I say this in the presence of others because I am overwrought by your grief, my dear husband, and I trust to the discretion of all here not to repeat. To the discretion of Miss Horsefall and Uncle Sven I trust not at all, so we waste no time. At least this way we get to use up all that herring left over from Birgit's wedding reception."

As Thorkjeld strove manfully to overcome his pain at the loss of Orm Tokesson, Sieglinde turned to the two archaeologists. "Learned sirs, you have labored in vain. My husband will now take you to our home and our daughters will give you sustenance. I can only wish that the excellence of our herring may be some compensation for your fatigue and disappointment."

"I'm not a bit tired," the younger archaeologist lied gallantly. "It's been a privilege and an honor to work with President Svenson, and I'm crazy about herring."

"Herring disagrees with me," said the elder archaeologist, "and I've been convinced from the start that this would turn out to be another hoax. Therefore I have not labored in vain. I never do. I am writing a book about archaeological hoaxes. Mrs. Shandy, if you are in fact Mrs. Shandy," he added with a cold glance at the arms Peter had wrapped about her petite form so tightly that they'd have cost Sieglinde another round of herring, no doubt, had not the Shandys been duly united and therefore within the scope of her tolerance, "I trust you'll allow me access to the diaries of Belial Buggins."

"I shall have to consult with our library director, Dr. Porble," Helen replied demurely, "but I expect he'll be willing to let you see them. I'm only assistant for the Buggins Collection. And I am indeed Mrs. Shandy."

"Oh. Pity. Perhaps I might just give you my card in case you contemplate a divorce anytime in the reasonably near future."

"Thank you. I'll add it to my applicants file. Peter darling, must you do any more detecting tonight, or can I persuade you to come home to your wife and family for a change?"

"There's still that trifling matter of who killed Spurge Lumpkin, my love. I'm afraid I'd better go back and have that talk with Miss Horsefall if she can keep her mind off more—er—immediate concerns."

"Ah yes," said the president's wife. "I too must chat with Miss Horsefall."

"Then do let Peter put in his licks first if you don't mind, Sieglinde," Helen entreated. "You know how you get carried away on the subject of smorgasbord. What's happened to the Ameses, by the way?"

"Roy and Laurie thought they'd better drive Tim over to Dr. Melchett at the hospital for a once-over," Peter explained. "He did something to his back trying to keep from being buried alive by that explosion, which is another reason why I'm damned anxious to get this business cleared up."

"Of course, dear. Boost me back up on the nice horsie, then, and let's go do it."

CHAPTER 21

As they were riding back up the hill, Helen asked, "Peter, how much was that Gaffson man offering Mr. Horsefall for his farm?"

"I'm not sure. As a generous guess, I'd say somewhere around fifty thousand."

"For the whole place?"

"That was my impression."

"Good heavens! Sieglinde, did you hear that? Peter says Mr. Horsefall would have got fifty thousand dollars for his property. Can you imagine?"

Both women went into gales of somewhat hysterical laughter.

"What's so funny?" Peter demanded.

"What's so funny is that you don't think it's funny, you silly old learned gentleman, you. Sieglinde, is there a man alive who knows anything?"

"Men know everything except what matters. Thorkjeld would also not think it funny for Mr. Horsefall to turn down fifty thousand dollars. He would think it noble and heroic."

"Well, I suppose it is, really. But it's still funny."

They were off again. Shandy, riding behind Helen with his arms around her waist, gave her a warning squeeze.

"Madam, if you don't stop this unseemly tittering I may be forced to take a bite out of your neck. Precisely why is it so funny?"

"Oh, Peter, honestly! What have we been doing for amusement this past couple of weeks?"

"You know damn well what we've been doing. Do I

have to offend Sieglinde's sense of propriety by saying it
out loud?"

"I don't mean that. I was referring to the conch shell
for the whatnot."

"You mean running around to antique shops? I presume it amuses you. I myself have not been roused to
heights of hilarity. Why people choose to pay astronomical prices for other people's old junk—"

"Ah, but people do. That's what's so funny. Instead of
standing there snarling like a trapped wolverine whenever I wanted something, like that sweet glass paper-
weight I bought with the money Aunt Bessie sent us for
a wedding present, you might have spent the time to better advantage noticing what sort of old junk people are
paying those astronomical prices for. The Horsefalls
have probably close to fifty thousand dollars' worth of old
junk in their kitchen alone, and I'd swear their parlor set
is genuine Belter."

"You mean that woodcarver's nightmare with all the
bumps and squiggles on it? Helen, do you know what
you're talking about?"

"Helen knows what she is talking about, Peter," said
Sieglinde. "Thorkjeld would also not recognize genuine
Belter."

"Would Nute Lumpkin?"

"If he wouldn't, he's in the wrong business," said his
wife. "That incredibly ornate pierced carving is hard to
mistake and also hard to find. Belter never made much
of it in the first place because how in the world could he?
Furthermore, prices for Victorian antiques are getting
higher by the minute now that earlier pieces are almost
out of the market. But the Horsefalls have real Colonial
and Federal things, too. I'll bet you anything their kitch-
en table and that pierced tin pie chest are easily two
hundred years old."

"My God! Then the Horsefalls have been sitting on a
fortune all these years they've been scratching to make
ends meet."

"But it is only within recent years that great prices
are paid for such things," Sieglinde pointed out reasonably. "Had they not sat, there would now be no fortune.
Anyway, for the Horsefalls it would be not antiques but

Great-aunt Matilda's wedding china. They would think not in terms of money but of sentimental attachment."

"Maybe so," Shandy replied, "but I think I know what Henny Horsefall's going to say when you point that out to him."

He was right. A few minutes later, Odin and Freya were in the barn having a bait of oats and Henny was listening slack-jawed as Helen and Sieglinde gave a cautious estimate as to what his family relics might be worth at current prices.

"Of course," Helen concluded with some embarrassment, "their sentimental value to you and your family—"

"Hell," Henny interrupted, "you can't eat sentiment."

Shandy nodded. "Damn right, Horsefall. I knew you'd say that. Find somebody with more money than brains and unload a bunch of the stuff. Use the cash to build on a wing. Let Eddie and Ralph draw straws to see who gets which rooms, and Bob's your uncle. Sell a few more things and get yourselves a pair of good workhorses and some decent livestock, with no offense to Bessie. Clear the squirrel briers out of that lower field and put it to corn for the stock. Plant a big truck garden. By the time your antiques give out, this place will be entirely self-sufficient and the hell with everybody."

"Time the antiques give out I'll o' guv out myself, most likely." Henny didn't sound as if he meant it. All of a sudden he was twenty years younger and ready to outlive Aunt Hilda's mark. "Would you two ladies happen to know how a person might go about peddlin' antiques without gettin' skint?"

"Mrs. Shandy and I will be glad to take upon ourselves the task," Sieglinde promised, her fjord-blue eyes gleaming at the prospect as what right-thinking college president's wife's eyes wouldn't, and Helen agreeing for all she was worth as any right-thinking assistant for the Buggins Collection naturally would.

"I don't want to put you to a lot o' bother," the old man demurred. "It's just that I got a hunch Nutie the Cutie ain't—Christ on a crutch, Professor, you don't s'pose he *is?*"

"Out to get his pudgy mitts on your ancestral pie cupboard? Horsefall, I've already supposed so many things about that louse I'm quite prepared to suppose a few more. Do you think you could pry your aunt away from Dr. Svenson long enough for me to have a little talk with her?"

"Please do," said Sieglinde, "and while you talk with her, I shall have a few words with Uncle Sven. In the meantime, Mr. Horsefall, perhaps you would take Mrs. Shandy upstairs and let her get some idea of what is in the bedrooms?"

"What's in the bedrooms is prob'ly Aunt Hilda an' Uncle Sven," Henny snickered. "They seem to be takin' to each other real good."

He caught a frosty dart from Sieglinde's eye and muttered, "Maybe 'good' ain't the word you had in mind. I'll go find 'er. Aunt Hilda! Aunt Hilda, Professor Shandy wants to talk to you."

Sieglinde and Helen followed him down the hall. Shandy waited in the kitchen until Miss Horsefall came rattling her starched apron at him, every hair in place and every button done up. She was too old a bird to be caught twice.

"You lookin' for me, Professor?"

"Yes. I was wondering if you knew anything about Belial Buggins?"

She snorted. "I dern well ought to. He was my own gran'father, or so I always suspected. Anyways, I can remember settin' on 'is lap an' playin' with 'is gold watch an' chain when I was 'bout knee-high to a grasshopper. He'd be recitin' po'try an' tellin' stories an' laughin' fit to bust a gut when my mother fussed at 'im about me bein' too young to hear them kind o' things."

"What things were these, Miss Horsefall?"

"Hell, how'm I s'posed to remember? That was a hundred years ago. I just remember him settin' me up on 'is knee an' givin' me that watch to play with 'cause he said pretty girls was always partial to gold, which is true enough though dern little of it ever come my way, I can tell you."

"Er—perhaps your luck's due for a change."

"Then it better change damn soon."

There was no way to answer that. Shandy only said, "What happened to Belial's gold watch when he died?"

"I s'pose some o' the Bugginses got it. Not that there was many Bugginses left by then, leastways not around Balaclava County. Ol' Balaclava Buggins, he'd spent all 'is money startin' that college you work at, an' most of 'is kinfolks had took off one place or another 'cause they was so provoked with 'im for layin' it out on foolishness like education when he might o' left it to them instead. Belial was a son o' Balaclava's brother Bartleby, him an' his brother Bedivere. That branch o' the Bugginses always did have a queer streak in 'em about books and po'try an' suchlike. As I recall, Bedivere even married a schoolteacher. They never had no kids that I know of, leastways none that lived to grow up. S'pose she'd had enough o' brats by the time she managed to get 'erself hitched. An' the ones Belial fathered, their mothers wasn't admittin' to."

"Belial never married?"

"Never had to. Oh, he was a fine-lookin' man! Whiskers down to 'is middle an' a black broadcloth frock coat. Got killed in a train wreck the year I started grade school. Only time I ever seen my mother cry. I cried, too, 'cause I knew I'd never get to play with that gold watch again."

"M'well, these things are sent to test us, Miss Horsefall. Then you have no idea what became of Belial's—er—effects?"

"Cripes, we back to effects again? Why didn't you say so in the first place?"

Miss Hilda smoothed her apron and searched her memory. "I s'pose Bedivere would o' got 'is books an' stuff, an' the rest would o' went to that Mrs. Lomax who kept house for 'im. Did a few other things for 'im, too, from what I heard, but that's neither here nor there. She was some kind o' connection o' Jolene's father by marriage. Don't ask me what. I never could keep track o' them Lomaxes. Widow woman. Seems to me 'er first name was Effie."

"Thank you, Miss Horsefall. I can easily find out all I need to know about the Lomaxes. May I use your tele-

phone? I—er—believe Mrs. Svenson was wishing to have
a word with you when it's—er—convenient." ·

"Now's as convenient a time as any, I s'pose. Phone's
right at your elbow there on that little shelf."

She rattled her apron again and left him to it. As
Shandy was dialing a well-known number he heard a
joyous cry of "Tootsie!" With Sieglinde around to chaper-
one, Uncle Sven would have to curb his ardors. It was
unlikely, however, that she'd insist on a long engagement.

His authority on the Lomax history was at home and·
in good voice. She answered promptly.

"Good evening, Mrs. Lomax. I hope I haven't—oh, you
weren't. He isn't? Perhaps he's just not hungry. This
warm weather, you know. Puts them off their feed. Are
his pads damp? Ah, then he's sweating. No, perfectly
normal. Cats sweat through the soles of their feet. You
didn't? Yes, that's the advantage of higher education.
Fan him a bit and let him sleep. He'll be peckish enough
by morning, I shouldn't wonder. Actually what I called
about is to ask whether you happen to know what became of certain properties that were left by Belial Buggins to his housekeeper, a Mrs. Effie Lomax, sometime
before the turn of the century."

Shandy waited patiently, knowing it was useless to do
anything else, while Mrs. Lomax raced up and down the
many branches of the family tree. At last she located the
late Mrs. Effie.

"Born Effie Fescue, was she? You surprise me. I hadn't
realized the Fescues were such an old family in these
parts. Oh, they're not? Only since the Civil War? No, the
exact date isn't important. Don't bother looking it up. It
was really the Buggins property I—did she? That was—
oh, I see. Yes, bad practice not making a—I should imagine there—yes, of course an auction. Only thing to do under the—you were? What an interesting coincidence.
And what did you—really? Yes, one can always use another umbrella stand. And would you happen to remember who—"

Ridiculous question. Certainly Mrs. Lomax remembered who'd bought what at the auction held after the
niece to whom the late Effie Fescue Lomax had willed

her own Buggins Collection died intestate and unwed. Shandy nodded from time to time as she went down the list. All at once he stopped her.

"What? You're quite sure? Yes, of course you are. I—er—hadn't realized he was—er—among us at that time. Tell me, Mrs. Lomax, did the late Jim Fescue know the late Mrs. Effie Lomax at all? She'd have been an elderly lady when he was a kid, I suppose. Oh, did they? And she'd have told him stories about her life with Belial Buggins? No, I don't expect she would, but there must have been other—so I understand. Yes, quite a card. Chatty old lady, was she? No, you wouldn't, but no doubt your Aunt Aggie—ah, yes. Thank you, Mrs. Lomax, you're a veritable compendium of useful information. No, I shouldn't worry. I'm sure he'll be—yes, I'll give Jane his regards and I'm sure she—er—reciprocates. Good night."

It had been a long call, but well worth the time. Now he knew. His only problem was to prove it. He stuck his head in the parlor where the rest were now all gathered, and spoke to his wife.

"Helen, I'm going out for a while. Can you get home if I—"

"Of course, Peter. Shh!"

Sieglinde was talking of smorgasbord. Shandy tiptoed away. Who could compete with a herring?

The night was black and sticky as the inside of a tar pot now. No wonder Mrs. Lomax's overstuffed feline was sweating through the soles of his feet. Maybe Jane's tiny pink pads were moist, too. He wished passionately that he were back in the small brick house on the Crescent with Helen in his arms and Jane prowling across their backs wondering why kittens didn't get invited to join this interesting game. He wished to God he'd done what he should have done earlier, asked what he ought to have asked, seen what was under his nose, instead of risking lives to oblige a murdering devil who didn't mind maiming or slaughtering whoever came handiest.

He shouldn't be risking his own life, if it came to that, now that he had a wife and a cat to care for. But how was a person supposed to protect himself against someone who attacked with such crazy weapons in such unpredictable ways? Was it any more risky to be inside the lion's cage than out of it, once the bars were down?

He was dealing with a totally ruthless person here, somebody who evidently went beyond a lack of regard for human life, somebody who didn't even seem to know what humanity was. Somebody who could set the stage for a quick, expert murder by means of a stolen helmet, a damaged headlight, and a puddle of oil on a dark road, and never stop to realize that a sensible, quick-eyed young woman might lend the intended victim her hard hat. Somebody who knew how to rig an explosion in a manure pile that an old man might be working near but couldn't visualize a young boy using his own body as a protective shield.

Shandy thought of Spurge Lumpkin with his face burned off by the seething quicklime he hadn't had sense enough to stay away from, of old Henny Horsefall mourning his hired hand, of Miss Hilda's face as she'd watched Nute Lumpkin carry away Spurge's collection of old tobacco boxes. He thought of Fergy in his circus clown's getup of bushy orange hair and yellow-checked suit, taking the morning off from his work and his nice little lady from Florida to attend the funeral of the mentally retarded man who'd helped him unload his truck and drunk his beer and talked his ear off because what the hell, Spurge was human, too.

Fergy's was the place to start. Shandy just hoped to God he hadn't left it too late.

CHAPTER 22

Shandy was almost down to the end of Henny Horsefall's driveway when he met a stray menhir. At second glance, the huge, craggy object proved to be Thorkjeld Svenson, standing alone in the dark.

"The heart bowed down by weight of woe," Shandy remarked, not that he was feeling all that flippant. "What's the matter, President? You look like a leftover from Mount Rushmore."

"Shut up," said the great man. "I am suffering, damn it. Where are you off to now?"

"To get killed, I think."

Shandy explained why. Svenson brightened up as much as one who had just lost an Orm might reasonably be expected to, said, "Arrgh," and fell into step with him. They hadn't gone much farther before they encountered eight large dogs with their tongues hanging out.

"Are they rabid?" the president inquired politely of the young chap who had them in tow.

"No, just sweating." Shandy recognized the voice as that of Lewis's buddy Swope. These must be his sled dogs.

"I thought dogs sweated through the soles of their feet," Svenson replied, patting all eight at once.

"That's cats," said Shandy. "You brought your team, I see, Swope."

"Yeah, and now the police say they don't need 'em."

"Good, because we do. Can you get them turned around and headed the other way?"

"Sure. Come on, guys."

Young Swope made a few noises and the eight malemutes wheeled as one.

"I sort of like the tongues," said young Lewis, who proved to be among those present, also. "Makes 'em look ferocious."

"So it does." Shandy was feeling considerably less queasy about this expedition than he had a few minutes ago. "I feel like Peter and the Wolves. This way, gentlemen. And ladies, should there happen to be any on the team."

"Where are we going?" Lewis asked.

"We're going hunting for the person who blew up your geese and tried to kill your friend's cousin."

"Hey, right on!"

"You'd better understand, Lewis, that this is serious, dangerous business. Spurge Lumpkin was deliberately and cleverly murdered. Cronkite Swope would be dead now if it weren't for that young woman's lending him her hard hat after his helmet was stolen and his headlight tampered with."

"I didn't know that!" cried the cousin.

"You know it now, so keep your heads, both of you, and don't do anything stupid. Essentially what we're trying to do is stir up enough evidence to make a case with. What you may possibly see or overhear is more important than what you do. Swope, take four of your dogs and move around to the far side of the Bargain Barn as quietly as you can. Go in from the rear so you won't be spotted, and keep the dogs quiet if you can. Lewis, take the other four if you're sure you can handle them, and stay on this side. The dogs are to protect us all as much as anything else. If you see someone trying to escape and you can interfere successfully without getting hurt, do so. If I call for help, bring the dogs and come around to the front. If you're threatened with a weapon of any sort, get out of the way. We'll let the police handle any rough stuff."

Thorkjeld Svenson's only reply was an amused snort.

"Don't get your hopes up, President," Shandy told him. "Our bird may not be anywhere near here."

"What happens if we draw a blank?" Lewis wanted to know.

"We hunt some more. Got the dogs sorted out? Then start moving, you two. Come on, President, we go in from the front. Quit gritting your teeth and try to look amiable and nonchalant."

"What the hell for?"

"Because I say so, dammit."

Surprisingly, Svenson accepted Shandy's edict, though his version of amiable nonchalance would have been pretty ferocious by any standard but his own. The pair of them sauntered up to the open barn, passing a battered sedan that was parked out front. Its inside was crammed with paintpots, pieces of lumber, and tools of various descriptions. Its outside appeared to be an old shade of brown. Or was it something else? Shandy turned his flashlight on the car and decided it might well be purple, that trickiest of all colors under incandescent light. His heart catapulted into his throat. He muttered to Svenson, "We're in business," and went in.

It was past Fergy's closing time now. The man who'd driven up in Loretta Fescue's cast-off purple car was clearly no customer but a visitor. He was a thinnish, youngish fellow with black hair falling coarse and unwashed over a gaunt, high-cheekboned face that could have stood a shave. A couple of his teeth were broken. The lips that didn't hide them were rather too full and slack, though curved now in a smile of mild amusement, perhaps because his right hand was curved lovingly around a large economy-size can of beer. So this was Fesky, and what happened now?

Fergy wasn't in sight at the moment. His drinking buddy was being entertained by Millicent Peavey. She paused to greet Shandy with cries of delight and act properly flustered at getting to meet Thorkjeld Svenson. Then she took up her tale again.

"Isn't that the craziest thing you ever heard of? Oh, I was just telling Fesky here. Would you believe, Professor Shandy, somebody came in here and stole the little whatsit out of a pair of those porcelain doorknobs over there? I mean, Fergy would have sold the whole thing for a dollar, knobs and all, but this wise guy had to unscrew the knobs and leave them right there on the table, and walk off with the dingus that held them together. Honest, the things you run into!"

"You sure it was there in the first place?" Fesky

drawled. "How'd you ever remember one piece from another in this junk heap?"

"Listen, mister, if you'd done as much waitressing as I
have, you'd notice things all right. Try leaving a spoon
off the table, or like if you give somebody a water glass
with a crack in it, you get a squawk from the customer
and a look from the boss and an extra trip back and forth
with your corns killing you every step. Who needs the
aggravation? So you learn to notice, see? And I darn well
noticed there were six of those doorknob sets earlier because I dusted them, see. Professor Shandy saw me dusting around here. Didn't you, Professor?"

"I believe I did, now that you mention it. And you say
one is gone now?"

"I say nothing of the sort. I say the knobs are there
but the middle part isn't. There's five whole sets and one
pair of loose knobs. Go look for yourself, right over
there."

Millicent was a little bit drunk, Shandy could see, but
he had no inclination to doubt she knew whereof she
spoke. He walked over to the table she was pointing at,
picked up one of the knobs so enigmatically freed from
its shank, studied it for a second, then took out the short
piece of rod Roy had found after the explosion, and
screwed the knob to its threaded end. It was, as he'd expected, a perfect fit.

Millicent Peavey screamed. "Why, for Pete's sake! I
saw what you did. Don't think I don't notice things. You
took that thing right out of your own pocket. Aren't you
the little kidder, though. Trying to play a joke on li'l ol'
Millie."

"Not I, Mrs. Peavey. I obtained the shank from an—er
—outside source and, believe me, it wasn't taken from
here as a joke. Would you care to confirm that, Mr. Fescue?"

"Who, me? How the hell would I know?"

But Fescue's hand closed tight over the flimsy beer
can and foam spurted out the hole in the top, wetting the
front of his dark blue T-shirt. Thorkjeld Svenson closed
in behind him and the hand that held the beer began to
shake.

Trying to show them how cool he was, Fesky drained

off his drink, threw the can on the floor, and shoved his betraying hand into the pocket of his jeans. Then he dragged it out again, looking down in puzzlement at what his fingers held.

"My goodness, what a coincidence," chirped Millie, still trying to keep the party bright. "You take the same kind of allergy pills as me."

"The hell I do! I never take no pills."

Fesky flung the package away from him and it landed among the doorknobs. Shandy went over and picked it up. The pills were set into a die-cut sheet of cardboard, to be popped out one at a time. Four of the holes were empty.

"How often do you take your pills, Mrs. Peavey?" he asked.

"Aren't you sweet to take an interest. Most men don't want to hear about a woman's troubles. It's the rose fever with me. Every year about this time it drives me crazy, only this year it hasn't been so bad and since I got up here I swear I haven't so much as sniffled. I bought a new package of capsules before I came and I haven't even opened it yet. I tell Fergy it's because the air up here agrees with me. Don't I, Fergy," she called out to the fat man who'd just come in from the trailer with three cans of beer in his hands.

"Sure you do, Millie, whatever you said. Oh, hi, Professor Shandy. Say ain't you President Svenson, mister? I'd shake hands, only I'm kind of overloaded here. Take one, Millie. Here, right off the ice. An' this one's got your name on it, Fesky. Excuse me a second, folks. I'll slide on back an' get a couple more."

"Don't bother for me," said Shandy. "I'll take this one."

He reached over and plucked the can of beer from Fesky's still-shaking hand. It was a shockingly rude thing to do, and no wonder Fergy expostulated.

"Hey, no. Wait, I got some real good booze back there. You give that cheap stuff back to Fesky. He don't care what he drinks long as there's lots of it."

"I'm quite sure he wouldn't care to drink this one," said Shandy, still holding the can away from Fergy's grasp. "By the way, we found that doorknob shank you mislaid."

"Huh? You tryin' to be funny or somethin'?" Fergy edged toward the open doorway.

"On the contrary. I'm telling you the fun is over. Swope! Lewis!"

The dogs had Fergy on the ground before Shandy finished calling for help. Thorkjeld Svenson cursed a bit at having been beaten to the draw by a team of malemutes, then went out to bellow for a policeman.

CHAPTER 23

Cronkite Swope had visitors. The *Fane and Pennon*'s demon reporter was looking a great deal brighter than the pallid wreck who'd collapsed in front of the television cameras day before yesterday, possibly because Jessica Tate was among those present. Shandy couldn't see that the young woman's eyes particularly resembled limpid pools of night, but she was withal as comely a wench as ever crossed campus, though in his personal opinion Mrs. Mouzouka's pastry classes were doing more for her figure than needed doing.

Helen, the Svensons, the three Ameses, and Henny Horsefall were also crowded into the small hospital room. The nurse in charge would no doubt have been looking askance had she not been hovering nearby herself, agog to hear what was up. Shandy cleared his throat and began.

"Er—as you all know by now, the man who appears to be known to the police as Ferguson Black, among other things, is now under arrest for murder, conspiracy, and killing geese out of season. I don't know when he first developed the idea of hounding the Horsefalls out of their house so that he could get hold of their antiques. No doubt he's had his eye on the stuff ever since he first crossed their threshold. However, it apparently was not until he got back here from Florida this spring that he got his chance. The niece of the late Belial Buggins's housekeeper had died over the winter, and her possessions were being sold to settle her estate. At the auction, Fergy managed to get hold of a box of so-called junk that contained Belial's Viking relics.

"He knew the story, you see. His drinking buddy's father happened to have been a nephew of the niece, if you follow me. This Miss Fescue had been fond of the also deceased Jim Fescue as a lad. She'd told him many tales she'd heard from her own Aunt Effie, the housekeeper, about old Belial, including the runestone hoax he took so much trouble planning but never got a chance to complete. This nephew was, of course, husband to Loretta and father of the chap known as Fesky. He appears to have been a good-natured slob who took to drink in self-defense when he found out what sort of hornets' nest he'd married into, but that's not germane to our tale.

"The point is, he told the stories in turn to his son, who's rather a chip off the old block and probably the only one he could get to listen. Fesky repeated the Viking story to Fergy during one of their barside chats. Fergy listened, just as he'd listened to Spurge Lumpkin's ramblings and used them in his campaign of persecution at the Horsefalls'. When the Viking relics fell into his hands, he knew exactly what they were and decided to carry out Belial's plan."

"Knowing perfectly well what it would do to the Horsefalls," said Cronkite. "And I was dumb enough to help him out!"

"If you hadn't fortuitously stumbled on the story yourself, you may be sure he'd have found a way to rub your nose in it," Shandy reassured him. "Fergy's bright in his nasty way, you know. He fully intended to create utter chaos at the Horsefall place by churning up a story about a Viking curse, and thereby drive Henny and Miss Hilda to sell out from desperation. He would then play the hero's role, offering to take all their old junk off their hands at what would seem like an overly generous price."

"I was absolutely certain it was Nute Lumpkin who was working that angle," Helen sighed. "He's such an utterly ghastly man."

"He is indeed, and I had him down on my list as number one suspect until I learned that Lumpkin had never been allowed to set foot inside the house and therefore wouldn't know the Horsefalls had anything worth swindling them out of. I assume Lumpkin merely grabbed the chance to kick the Horsefalls while they were down, in order to get back at them for having made a fool of him in court."

"Arrogant bastard," growled Thorkjeld Svenson.

"He is indeed. As a matter of fact, that revolting personality of Lumpkin's did have some bearing on the plot. Last night after he realized he had no way out, Fergy spilled his guts. He admitted he'd always resented having to pass on any decent stuff he came across to Lumpkin. Nutie the Cutie never missed an opportunity to twist the knife a bit about the difference between a rag-and-bone man like Fergy and a high-class antique dealer like himself. Fergy put on a rather pathetic turn about wanting to ruin Lumpkin by setting up in straight competition. He couldn't pass up a golden opportunity to acquire all the stock he'd need for a comparative pittance, since the Horsefalls had no idea what their possessions are worth on today's market."

"What are they worth?" asked Cronkite eagerly. "It's okay, I won't print it. I'd just like to know."

"We are having an appraiser from Boston come out to set values," Sieglinde told him. "Miss Horsefall and her nephew will then have a better idea of what they wish to keep and what to sell. I do not suppose she will wish to take many things to Sweden when she becomes the wife of Uncle Sven. He has a fine house with many treasures. Of the wedding you may print all you like," she added kindly. "We have decided to eliminate the engagement party and proceed directly to the nuptials, so you must hurry and get well. Perhaps Miss Tate will care to come, also?"

"Oh, I'd love to!" gasped the young student, who so far hadn't dare utter a word in so august a company. "I'm hoping to become a food columnist and Cronkite says I can write an article for the *Fane and Pennon*. Maybe I could—" She blushed and faltered.

"You could write of smorgasbord," cried Sieglinde. "Later we shall talk, you and I. For the wedding I have planned already sixteen different kinds of herring."

"Cripes, I can't get used to the idea of Aunt Hilda makin' it legal after all these years," Henny muttered. "S'pose there's hope for me yet?"

"Once the news about your antiques gets around, half

the widows in Balaclava County will be lined up at your door," Laurie promised him.

"Damn right," Tim corroborated. "They were even after me, till the kids came home to protect me."

"Jolene was over last night to the farm while Peter and President Svenson were off catching that dreadful man," Helen murmured to Laurie. "After she'd heard about Miss Hilda and Uncle Sven, she told Henny she shoped he wasn't planning to get married and raise children now that the great-nephews and their families had decided to move in with him. Miss Hilda said, 'Hell, he ain't riz nothin' but garden sass for the past thirty-seven years.' I do adore that woman."

Professor Shandy, taking a leaf out of Dr. Porble's book, glared his wife into silence. "As I was attempting to tell Swope here, Fergy and Fesky agreed to work together on a campaign of terror. Fesky claims he had no idea of the scope of Fergy's ambition. He thought Fergy had a client for some barnboards and wanted Henny's because they were handy. His own noble motive, or so he would have us believe, was simply to help his mother. He knew she was desperately trying to secure the Horsefall property for Gunder Gaffson and decided he'd play the dutiful son for a change. As there would have been a fat commission for Mrs. Fescue and no doubt some sort of bonus for Fesky himself out of the deal, it's even possible he's telling the truth."

"Darn," said Helen. "I did want Mrs. Fescue to be one of the bad guys."

"I was convinced for a while that it was she and Fesky who constituted the demolition team," Peter admitted, "but apparently Mrs. Fescue is single-mindedly concentrated on selling real estate and knows no more about antiques than the Horsefalls. Anyway, Fergy and Fesky launched their dirty-tricks campaign, starting with minor pranks such as teenagers might play in the hope of starting a major feud between the Horsefalls and their good neighbors the Lewises. When that didn't work, they turned vicious.

"Fergy was the brains. Fesky did most of the tricks because he's a less noticeable type. At a distance, he could easily pass as one of Ralph's or Eddie's sons. I expect that's how he managed to plant that detonator in the manure pile yesterday morning while Fergy was at the funeral establishing himself an alibi. If Fesky had been challenged by any policeman who didn't know him, he could have passed himself off as one of the Horsefall tribe doing chores. And of course any cop who did know him would also know he's the chief's nephew."

"I bet he'll get off with probation," Cronkite Swope remarked cynically. "But he wouldn't have fooled the Horsefalls themselves. How did he get in and out all those times?"

"Spurge Lumpkin had a secret path he'd cut through the woods from behind the barn over to the old logging road. Rather a long and tortuous affair. Also quite well camouflaged, which I suspect was Fesky's doing. I gather its original object was to give Spurge an escape route over to Fergy's on the nights Miss Hilda was after him to take a bath and change his socks. Of course he'd bragged about it to his good buddy Fergy, and the cloak-and-dagger boys took it over."

"Must be how he got past Bashan yesterday," Svenson grunted.

"Undoubtedly. He only wanted to make sure you'd taken Belial's bait, and I suppose to find out whether his birch tree had been sprung yet. That was just another bit of stage dressing, I expect, to carry out the theme of eerie doings around the runestone. Fergy didn't mind getting the bum's rush once he'd seen things were going as planned."

"I just wisht I knew which one of 'em put that quicklime in my spreader," Henny sputtered. "I'd give 'im a dern sight more'n the bum's rush for what he done to Spurge."

"Fesky insists that was Fergy. He claims he put up a squawk when he learned what a rough game Fergy was playing, and tried to back off. That, presumably, is why Fergy loaded Fesky's beer with Mrs. Peavey's allergy pills last night. Those things don't mix well with alcohol. If Fesky had tried to drive home with that dose inside him, he'd have racked up his car and maybe wrecked somebody else's as well, and chalked up another for the Viking curse. I don't know whether Fergy aimed to kill

Fesky or just scare him into submission, and I have a ghastly hunch he didn't really care. I don't think he gave a hoot whether you died when you crashed without your helmet either, Swope; or if that quicklime killed Spurge Lumpkin or only maimed him for life."

"Cripes," said Henny Horsefall, "an' here was me thinkin' the world's prize bastard was Nute Lumpkin."

"Oh!" Helen jumped up from the foot of Cronkite's bed, where she'd been perched beside Laurie. "Here's a scoop for you, Mr. Swope. I forgot to tell my husband because he's been so busy this morning pinning the rap on Fergy, or whatever it was he had to do down at the police station. Mrs. Lomax told me why Nutie was in such a swivet to get his hands on Spurge's possessions. It seems he's looked everywhere under the sun for his parents' marriage certificate and can't find it. He had a last, lingering hope his cousin Spurge might have been hiding it from him."

"No doubt because that's what he'd have done himself," said Shandy. "But wasn't the marriage recorded somewhere?"

"Apparently not. There's nothing to prove Nute's parents ever bothered to formalize their relationship before the father went overseas and was killed in the war, leaving the mother pregnant. She claimed they'd been married before he left, naturally, and her family backed her up, naturally; but now it appears Nute's only a Lumpkin by hearsay, as it were. In the meantime, some long-lost Lumpkin from Arizona had just blown into town with all the right credentials. She's an ardent conservationist who wants to turn the Lumpkin property into a wildlife sanctuary and use the money for environmental defense."

"Hey," shouted Roy, "that's terrific! Hear that, Dad?"

"I heard. Dammit, you don't have to burn out my batteries." Timothy Ames leaned over and gave Henny Horsefall a mighty slap on the shoulder. "All's well that ends well. Eh, old friend?"

"It's straight out of Tolkien," cried Laurie, her dark eyes gleaming like limpid pools of night. "Fergy winds up in jail for a million years, I hope. Nutie the Cutie loses the big inheritance he schemed to get. Loretta Fescue loses the sale she had no business trying to make in the first place. Gunder Gaffson loses his chance to pull another shady deal. Fesky loses his job for being a fink, no doubt. And Miss Hilda's going to be married and Henny gets to keep his farm and all the Horsefalls will live happily every after. The Hobbits win and the Orcs get clobbered!"

Thorkjeld Svenson winced. "Did you have to say Orcs? Makes me think of Orm. I still can't believe—" His head fell on his chest.

Sieglinde rose and took him firmly by the arm. "Come home, dear husband. There is much to be done. In getting ready for Uncle Sven's wedding reception you will become so infuriated you will forget this cruel deception."

"Damned old rake." The president looked a shade less woebegone. "At least maybe she'll cure him of chasing widows."

"Dern right she will," Henny agreed. "Ain't no man alive could stand up to Aunt Hilda, an' you can bet your bottom dollar on that."

"Then our pretty Laurie is right and virtue has again triumphed," said Sieglinde. "Perhaps, Thorkjeld, we should stop at the fish store on our way home. Mr. Swope, this is not for publication but I am going to tell you all a little Norse secret you will not find on any runestone. To wed is good, but to live happily ever after you must always keep in the house plenty of herring."

CHARLOTTE MACLEOD
America's Reigning Whodunit Queen

PRESENTS

"Murder among the Eccentrics of Boston's
Upper Crust"* with

Art Investigator Max Bittersohn
and Sarah Kelling

THE FAMILY VAULT	49080-3/$2.95 US/$3.75 Can
THE PALACE GUARD	59857-4/$2.95 US/$3.50 Can
THE WITHDRAWING ROOM	56473-4/$2.95 US/$3.75 Can
THE BILBAO LOOKING GLASS	67454-8/$2.95 US/$3.50 Can
THE CONVIVIAL CODFISH	69865-x/$2.95 US/$3.75 Can

AND

"Mystery with Wit and Style and a Thoroughly Engaging
Amateur Sleuth"**
Professor Peter Shandy

REST YOU MERRY	47530-8/$2.95 US/$3.95 Can
THE LUCK RUNS OUT	54171-8/$2.95 US/$3.50 Can
WRACK AND RUNE	61911-3/$2.95 US/$3.50 Can
SOMETHING THE CAT DRAGGED IN	69096-9/$3.95 US

and coming soon

THE CURSE OF THE GIANT HOGWEED	
	70051-4/$2.95 US/$3.75 Can

*Mystery magazine
**The Washington Post